"Are we enemies?"

Rebecca ran her hands through her hair. She'd never had an enemy before. She wasn't sure she'd even had a real critic. All she'd ever done was what people expected of her.

"No, we aren't. Just stay...away. I'm not your project." Cole waved a hand. "I don't need your charity, and I sure don't need another cause to keep me awake at night."

Rebecca straightened. "Is that was this is about? Because I suggested you should do something to help those boys, we're fighting again?"

"No, we aren't fighting, but I haven't joined the Rebecca Lincoln fan club. It'll be okay. You don't have to make another unexpected visit. I made a promise to stay out of trouble. Easiest way to do that? Keep my nose to myself instead of sticking it where it doesn't belong."

Dear Reader,

After finding a stray dog, which led to volunteering at my local animal shelter, I was introduced to a special program where selected prison inmates provide weeks of obedience training to rescue dogs. At graduation, the lucky, well-trained dogs are adopted. I've been dog crazy since I could toddle after a beagle named Jake, so I appreciate programs that give animals a second chance and I understand the power of a dog's unconditional love.

Cole Ferguson is a man who needs these gifts—a second chance *and* man's best friend. His prison experience opens the door, but a do-gooder, her friends and some student volunteers will convince him that this new life is sweet. Please visit me at cherylharperbooks.com to find links to adoption programs like this one, to let me know what you think about *Keeping Cole's Promise*, to sign up for my newsletter or to find out what's coming next. Thanks for reading!

Cheryl

HEARTWARMING

Keeping Cole's Promise

USA TODAY Bestselling Author

Cheryl Harper

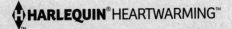

Recycling programs
for this product may
not exist in your area.

ISBN-13: 978-0-373-36807-5

Keeping Cole's Promise

Copyright © 2016 by Cheryl Harper

Printed in U.S.A.

Cheryl Harper discovered her love for books and words as a little girl, thanks to a mother who made countless library trips and an introduction to Laura Ingalls Wilder's Little House stories. Whether it's the prairie, the American West, Regency England or Earth a hundred years in the future, Cheryl enjoys strong characters who make her laugh. Now Cheryl spends her days searching for the right words while she stares out the window and her dog, Jack, snoozes beside her. And she considers herself very lucky to do so.

For more information about Cheryl's books, visit her online at cherylharperbooks.com or follow her on Twitter, @cherylharperbks.

Books by Cheryl Harper

Harlequin Heartwarming

Heart's Refuge
Winner Takes All
The Bluebird Bet
A Minute on the Lips

Visit the Author Profile page
at Harlequin.com for more titles.

I owe Dana Grimaldi, the editor who patiently works with me on every one of these books, the biggest thanks. She makes these stories and characters that I love so much shine. Thank you for all your hard work, Dana!

CHAPTER ONE

THE DAY THAT Cole Ferguson walked out of Travis County State Jail was twice as terrifying as the day he walked in. On that first day, he'd been unprepared to serve fifteen years for six counts of aggravated assault, but he'd been too young to understand how his life had changed. Both then and now, though, the threat of the unknown was enough to make a smart man shake in his shoes.

At twenty, he'd had zero sense and relied on a cocky certainty in his own skill to battle the nerves. Nearly eleven years later, he'd learned some hard lessons. No matter how bad things were, they could always get worse. In lockup, he'd followed the rules and never had to worry about food or where he'd sleep. As a free man, he stopped in the bright sunshine of a hot September day and wondered what he'd do if the one friend he had left didn't show.

Figure it out. There was no other choice

but to make his own way, head down, one foot in front of the other, for as long as it took.

They'd be his steps, his decision. He had control of his life again.

He'd imagined this day a thousand different ways, but raw nerves and the anxiety of overwhelming freedom were a surprise.

"Well, now, let's don't stand out here in the heat. Truck's running." Old Ephraim Walker was resting against the wall in the only shady corner beside the doors. Cole had been certain EW was as old as dirt when his grandmother had introduced them the first night he'd been dumped at her trailer "temporarily" while his mother looked for work. Apparently, she was still looking. The occasional birthday cards and Christmas phone calls had dwindled to nothing years ago.

"I thought you might have come up with something better to do on a day like today." Cole held out his hand. "Can't thank you enough for making the trip, EW."

"I shoulda waited inside with the air, but the place gives me the heebie-jeebies, like all the sadness done sunk into the walls and no amount of good news gon' get it out." He shivered. EW's shoulders might be slightly more rounded, but his hair was still white with a dark spot in the front, laugh lines still wrinkled his face and when he smiled, bright white teeth gleamed. "But you ain't got to worry about that place anymore." EW clapped a hard hand on Cole's shoulder.

Four years ago, the first Saturday his grandmother had missed her monthly visit, EW had taken her place and delivered the bad news. His form of comfort had been the same as his congratulations, one hand on Cole's shoulder. Since her death, they'd written now and then. His grandmother's old trailer was under EW's watchful care until Cole's release.

"Needed to get out of the house, don'tcha know? Fish ain't bitin' in heat like this no way." EW waved a hand in the air and headed for the beat-up truck idling in a parking spot near the front. Sweat was glistening on his brown skin by the time they slid into the truck's front seat. "No thanks necessary, young fella."

"Sure don't feel young." Cole's body might be stronger than ever, but there was no denying that the weight of his mistakes had aged him. Maybe time and space would lighten the load. Otherwise, he could only keep putting one foot in front of the other.

"Young is relative, son. You oughta learn

that." EW's rusty laugh was comfortable and reassuring. Cole's world had ended eleven years ago, but he'd made it out the other side and there was still something to laugh about. He sucked in a gust of hot air. He could do this. He'd done harder things.

There wasn't much to say as EW navigated the traffic around Austin and hit the two-lane highway that would take Cole home. The truck coughed and sputtered now and then, but the breeze blasting through the open windows covered most of the engine's knocks. His grandmother had told him more than once that EW could make an engine sing. This truck was long past its life expectancy but still rolling.

As they puttered through Holly Heights, EW took the scenic route. "Few things have changed." He pointed at Sue Lynn's diner. "Best things haven't, though."

The Shop-on-In was still displaying the weirdest collection in the large front window. Every street corner had a church. And not one person in the small crowd of shoppers doing business on Main Street turned to point at the prodigal returning to the scene of the crime. When they reached the edge of town, Cole tried to chase away the dread building in his gut.

"Old Gulf station closed. Got one of those fancy places what sells fried chicken and ice cream now." EW didn't glance his way as they passed a bright gas station with twelve pumps and a neon sign advertising lottery tickets.

This place was a drastic change from the old-fashioned filling station he'd tried to rob at eighteen. That place had had four pumps and made more money from cigarettes than gasoline. Thinking that he could get enough cash to help his grandmother pay for the heart surgery she needed from such a dump qualified him for the world's dumbest criminal contest. He would have been lucky to walk away with three hundred dollars.

Eleven years of his life and his grandmother's respect flushed away for three hundred dollars.

At least he hadn't shot anyone with the gun he'd borrowed from his best friend. Waving it around was bad enough. "World's dumbest criminal, for sure."

EW shook his head as he turned down the dirt road that led to the trailer park. "I'd say you don't have the natural talent for breaking the law. Better try something else this time."

"Good advice." The sizzle of anger tingling around his edges made Cole uneasy. If only EW could have given him that handy advice when he was a kid, Cole's whole life might have been different.

He had to keep his emotions in check. While he tried to douse the anger with gratefulness for all EW had done since he'd been in prison, Cole rested his arm on the hot metal of the truck door and studied the trailers. None of them was a palace, but the whole park was neat and clean. Whoever the neighbors were, they worked hard. The basketball goal at the end listed to the side over hard-packed red dirt. He and his friends had pretended to play games there every afternoon after school. They'd also cooked up some of the worst ideas in the history of dumb plans there, but that wasn't the basketball goal's fault.

EW held up a key ring and jingled the single key. "Left a surprise inside. Might help you figure out what comes next."

Cole took the key ring and struggled to form the right words to express his gratitude, but there was too much to say. EW had been a good neighbor for years before Cole went to jail. After, he'd helped Cole's grandmother keep the place up, and when she died, EW had been his only lifeline. "I don't know how to repay everything you've done, but…"

EW raised a single bushy eyebrow. "Keep your promise. Stay outta trouble. That's all. Until the day she died, your grandmama prayed this day would come." He shrugged. "And when you have the chance, pick me up some beer. Cheap beer. Lots of cheap beer."

Cole shook his head as bits and pieces of his grandmother's lectures floated through his mind. She and EW had disagreed on the importance of a good beer. She had no use for spirits of any kind. EW couldn't get through the day without a buzz.

And Cole was in no position to lecture. "Will do."

"Hope it's soon. A man gets thirsty in this heat." EW rubbed his mouth. "Figure you might need a ride, once you get your feet under you. Let me know." Then he tilted his head. "You got a driver's license still?"

Cole nodded. "Yes, sir. Need to renew it, since it's about ten years expired."

EW grunted. "You need to borrow the truck, rent's cheap." He winked and mimed drinking from a can.

Cole slid out of the truck and waved as EW's

truck lurched on down the road to his own trailer.

"Home, sweet home. Again." Cole scuffed one prison-issue sneaker in the grass as he tried to convince himself this was what he'd been dreaming of for years.

Except his grandmother was gone.

And there was no telling what memories would boil up today.

Unless he kept those memories and the emotions they stirred up contained, they'd destroy his chance at freedom. It would be too easy to do something stupid under the influence of grief or fear.

The sun was beating down on his head. The temperature inside the two-bedroom trailer might be worse, since there'd been no one to pay the electric bill for years now. Whatever his grandmother had left would have gone to taxes and the monthly rent on the spot in the trailer park.

Air-conditioning had been a luxury reserved for the hottest of days when he was growing up. Today would qualify, even for his frugal grandmother. As soon as he got a job, he'd crank the cold air in her honor.

Cole climbed the three steps leading to the door carefully. The railing he'd helped EW add listed to one side, and he wasn't certain the wood would hold his weight. "Rot. Wonderful." And a warning about what he'd find inside.

Before he yanked open the door, Cole closed his eyes. He'd never been good at meditation, not even after the class offered by the jail's shrink. Controlling his temper had been a problem when he was young and stupid and angry. At least prison had taught him *why* he'd want to learn how to keep his cool. It was the only way to keep his promise.

To help, he tried to picture his grandmother's face, not as she'd been during visitation or even as sick as she was the last summer he'd been home, but on the first night he'd slept in her spare room. Now he understood that she had to have known his mother was dumping him, but the joy in her eyes as she'd held out her arms had been real.

That joy. She'd never lost it. It dimmed, but it never disappeared.

"Come on. Don't be a wimp. It's four flimsy walls, and you can leave any time you like." His voice was loud. If any of the neighbors were watching, they had good reason to worry about the convict frozen on the front steps. At least they would keep their distance.

He squared his shoulders and opened the door. Once he was inside, he took a quick look around the tiny, dusty kitchen and cramped living room. Other than the stale air of a house closed for too long, the place was frozen in time. Cole left the door open and stopped at every window to unlock it and throw it open. A weak breeze stirred the yellowed white curtains as he dropped down on the ancient green sofa that his grandmother had hauled home one afternoon, a gift from one of the families she cleaned for.

The letters he'd written her from prison were stacked next to the photo album she'd always kept front and center on the rickety coffee table. He didn't open it. He knew what he'd find: every awkward stage of his life captured in a school photo or candid shot.

And next to that photo album was EW's gift, a stack of newspapers. Cole flipped through them. "Holly Heights. Austin. Surely there's a job in this pile somewhere." At some point, food would be a necessity. What little money he had would go toward the grocery store and getting the utilities turned on.

While he was still inside, he'd taken every course he could volunteer for. Only landscape design had been interesting. His reintegration adviser had gotten him guaranteed employment working for a landscaping company out of Houston, but he'd come home to Holly Heights. Would that be the second-worst decision he'd made?

Finding a job where every single employer knew he'd served time was going to be a challenge, no matter how well prepared his counselor promised he was or how big the tax incentive the government offered.

Quitting before I even start.

The thought sounded so much like his grandmother that he almost looked around. Surely there was a recorded message or her ghost.

Cole rubbed his forehead and snatched the first paper. "Let's see, Austin. What have you got for me?" As soon as he saw the first listing for lawn maintenance, he jumped up and dug around through the familiar junk drawer to find a pen. "Only a phone number. Wonder if EW has phone service."

After he'd circled five jobs, the realization that there was no way he could make it into Austin every day for work crashed around Cole's head. Half a second later, he'd balled the paper and tossed it as far away as he could. His fingers shook until he pressed them hard against his thighs.

So weak. The disgust tasted bad in his mouth.

No matter how good his intentions might be, the odds were still too high. He was going to fail.

The temptation to borrow EW's truck and go after the beer that would make EW happy and might numb some of his own panic washed over him, but Cole gripped the photo album hard with both hands and concentrated on remembering his grandmother's face.

The tears in Rachel Baxter's eyes hadn't fallen on their last visit, but her voice had wavered. "Promise me. You stay out of trouble."

They'd ended every visit the same way. Why did it even matter now? She was gone. His promise meant nothing. Robbing that new flashy gas station wouldn't net him much cash, but he'd learned how to navigate prison. This new old world? He was lost.

"Brought a turkey sandwich. Chips." EW shuffled his feet awkwardly on the yellowed linoleum. "Door was open."

"Good. I'm starving." Cole cleared his throat. "These papers are nice, but…" He shook his head.

EW didn't answer, just held out a plastic

bag with sandwiches wrapped in napkins. "One paper? You givin' up after one paper?"

Cole shoved half a sandwich in his mouth. Snapping in anger or whining after all EW's help would never do. "Nope." He grabbed the Holly Heights newspaper and flipped to the two-page classified spread. "Used car. House for rent." He shoved the other half of the sandwich in his mouth. Talking and chewing would have gotten him a smack on the hand if his Mimi were still here.

In the last column, he found it. A job listing for an assistant manager at an animal shelter. "Paws for Love." He glanced over at EW. "Know anything about it?"

EW wadded his empty napkin. "Down the road a piece, maybe two miles. Pet project for the new millionaires."

Cole waited for EW to either acknowledge his pun or explain the "millionaires" comment.

EW stretched lazily and shuffled through the papers to slide one out. On the front page, a full-color photo showing four beautiful women grinning with absolute joy caught Cole's eye. A surge of jealous bitterness shot through him, turning the sandwich into a hard lump in his stomach. "Local lottery winners Rebecca Lincoln, Stephanie Yates and Jen Neil celebrate the open house at Paws for Love." As he read the headline, Cole had a vague memory of them at Holly Heights High School, but they were a year or two ahead of him and they'd moved in different crowds. "And Sarah Hillman. Looks like some things don't change. Hillmans are still running this town."

He scanned the story about the shelter's reopening with new funding provided by the foundation set up by Rebecca, Jen and Stephanie. Sarah Hillman was listed as the organization's director and the day-to-day manager. That would be a problem. He expected a Hillman would set low priority to hiring people like him.

"Two miles..." He pointed toward Holly Heights.

EW shook his head and pointed the opposite direction. "Down the highway."

Cole tapped a finger nervously on the coffee table. He could walk two miles easy. It was only part-time, but it was a place to start and he had the skills listed. Flexibility. Experience working with animals. He could lift fifty pounds no problem.

"Good character." That might be the sticking point. Not that he didn't have it, but that he had no way to prove it.

"Take the truck." EW stretched in the seat. "Go in the morning. Won't know until you try."

"You'll have to come with me. Can't drive. No license." Maybe if he had a personal witness, they would listen.

"Might be better to take your chances without me." EW raised an eyebrow, and Cole understood exactly what he meant. Mimi had bragged on EW's skills with motors. The rest of Holly Heights viewed EW as the town drunk.

But Cole would enjoy having a partner, a little bit of backup, someone who believed when he wasn't so sure himself.

Relying too much on what other people thought was how he'd gotten mixed up with the gang that convinced him taking what he needed was the only answer. Not anymore. Going alone was the only way to stay out of trouble.

"I'll walk it. I can do it." The distance was nothing. Convincing Sarah Hillman to give him a shot would be the challenge. Finding a job was the key to everything. If he spent too much time sitting around this trailer with nothing to do but list his mistakes and fight the temptation to drown his problems, he'd be back inside Travis before the year was out. He didn't believe in fate or destiny, but this felt right. All he had to do was seize his chance.

CHAPTER TWO

REBECCA LINCOLN PUT the car in Park and checked the clock on her car radio. "Fifteen minutes early, right on time." The only other cars in the parking lot belonged to Sarah and Shelly, Sarah's right hand and the most important volunteer at the shelter. They'd both been at Paws for Love since sunrise, no doubt.

As she reached over to grab the floral tote she used to organize all the paperwork for the shelter, Rebecca hit the buttons to lower the windows a crack. Otherwise, the Texas sun would turn her car into an oven. She loved ovens but had no desire to sit in one on the drive home.

Whistling might be over-the-top, but it was a beautiful morning. On sunny Saturdays like this one, the bedraggled flower beds and dusty gravel lot in front of the building seemed twice as sad, but Sarah was slowly and surely changing every piece of Paws for Love for the better. With enough time, she'd hire someone to replace the peeling paint and plant bright flowers, and the outside of the building would reflect all the joyful work done at the shelter.

Time. That was all this place needed now. Smug certainty and a touch of pride at what her money had accomplished added up to a song in her heart. If Jen was there, Rebecca might hum a happy tune, to annoy her.

Before she could open the car door, Sarah stepped out of the building. "Good. You're here early. Can you cover the phone and desk for me? I need to call Will before Jen gets here."

"Sure. I've got the desk. This time next week, we'll have some real help for you." Rebecca was perfectly happy to spend some time behind the counter at the shelter. Sarah was ruthlessly organized, so it was easy to find the log of volunteers. Rebecca ran a finger down the list of names and hours. The kids she'd sent over from the high school where she worked as a guidance counselor had plugged right in. The satisfaction of correctly identifying and connecting kids with opportunities was nice. Every single one of them would have great extracurriculars for college applications.

That job satisfaction made it impossible to consider quitting her job, even after hitting the lottery.

Her phone chirped to notify her that a text had come in. Every time she heard it, she pictured a bluebird of happiness.

Booked the flight into Austin. It'll be good to see my kids in person. Her mother had taken to texting instead of calling, probably because she was too busy for long conversations. After a lifetime of charity work in Holly Heights, Rebecca's parents had moved to Florida, where they played golf. Lots and lots of golf.

Already planning the menu. Rack of lamb. I've always wanted to try it. Can't wait to see you. The farewell dinner for Daniel and Stephanie was going to be her inaugural dinner party with the new kitchen. Saying goodbye to her brother and her friend would hurt, but she was anxious to demonstrate what a smart investment the large check she'd write to the contractor would be.

Starving children, Rebecca Lincoln. Refugees. Go for chicken, something reasonable. We aren't fancy, you know that.

Her mother's reply shouldn't have surprised her, because she'd heard similar responses her whole life. But it did shave off a sliver of the good mood she'd begun the day with. Trying something new would have been fun.

While she waited for one of the shelter's volunteers to come up to the desk, Rebecca wandered over to the bulletin board to check out the photos Sarah had posted of all the dogs up for adoption. She bent to study the details for the cutest beagle on the board when the door opened.

"Welcome to Paws for Love." The last part of her greeting was strangled as a man stepped inside. His size, the ferocious frown wrinkling his brow, sweat shining on his face, everything about him shouted that he was out of place.

The loud bang of the door as he closed it behind him shook her.

And she was cornered. The sensation of being helplessly cut off flashed through her mind, a reaction from the first and last time she'd tried to stop a fight at the high school. Confident of her authority as an adult and school counselor, she'd stepped between two boys roughly her size and found herself pinned against a wall of lockers, one hard hand on her throat. In the seconds it took Eric

Jordan to come to his senses, she'd frantically clawed at that arm and wondered if anyone would save her.

This guy, he was twice the size of Eric Jordan. His shoulders strained against the ironed cotton button-down that had to be at least ten years old. His khakis fit better, but had the same crisp crease that showed careful attention. His white sneakers shuffled as he stopped in the center of the tiny lobby.

She'd been able to look over Eric's shoulder to see the watching crowd. This guy would block out the sun.

Rebecca put one hand over her racing heart and managed to say, "Can I help you?"

He fidgeted nervously for a second, shifting back and forth between the door and the shelter's ancient cash register. The too-tight sleeves of his shirt strained over hard muscles as he clenched a folded newspaper. "I'm here about the job." He wiped one large hand over his forehead.

As Bub, Sarah's goofy brown dog, came ambling down the hallway, Rebecca held out a hand to try to stop him. Bub had no guard dog setting; he was strictly a social ambassador, a lover, not a fighter.

"Hey, pup," the big man said, and bent

down on one knee. The ominous sound of a seam stretching beyond its limits whispered through the lobby. Bub, sensing another admirer, tipped his chin up for a scratch.

Man and dog communicated silently long enough for Rebecca to get her brain in gear.

"The deadline was Friday. We aren't accepting applications any longer." Her voice was the cold, we-have-rules-for-a-reason tone all educators learned early on. People who wouldn't follow directions were a pet peeve.

"I understand, but I'm asking for a favor, some leeway." He braced one hand on the counter beside the computer, and the whole base tilted. He scrambled to right it, but everything on top crashed to the floor. The clatter kicked up her heart rate again. Rebecca held out a hand to keep him from crossing behind the counter to clean up his mess.

"We set the deadline for a reason," she said, and crossed her arms tightly over her chest. "Everyone wants *leeway*. Why should we give it to you?"

"Are you the manager?" The guy wasn't going to take the first no. He didn't have to. She would have to stand there until *he* decided to go.

"I'm not, but she's very busy. We had quite

a few qualified candidates, so there's no real reason to ignore the deadline stated in the ad." Rebecca spoke slowly, determined to hold her ground. It was the fair thing to do.

"Please. I'll beg. Is that what you need, Your Highness?" The man squeezed the wrinkled newspaper so tightly it squeaked. "The heat. It makes me short-tempered."

Before Rebecca could figure out how to answer him, laughter eked around the closed office door.

He turned his head and considered the door. "If you're not the manager…" Rebecca darted around the counter to stand in front of the door. They couldn't hire him. He needed to leave.

When he moved closer, she regretted the decision. At this distance, the lines on his face were clearer. The fatigue and desperation in his eyes were impossible to miss. It was tempting to give in.

Very slowly, he put his hands on her tense arms and shifted her out of the way before he reached around her to the doorknob and gave it a twist.

Rebecca fell back a few steps to get some breathing room.

And the giggles slowly died out as Sarah

regarded her and the intruder. "Gotta go. Call you later," she said as she hung up the phone.

Before Sarah could ask or Rebecca could explain, the man said, "Cole Ferguson. I'm here about the job." He slid the crumpled newspaper on top of the stack of applications and stepped away quickly. One hand ran absentmindedly over his closely cropped hair and he glanced down at Bub. The dog rested against his leg and yawned.

Everyone but Cole Ferguson relaxed a fraction. Rebecca met Sarah's stare over the desk as Sarah mouthed, "Good people."

Anxious to get this guy back to wherever he came from so that she could regain her composure, Rebecca said, "I've explained the situation. Mr. Ferguson was just leaving." She raised her eyebrows at him and held a hand out toward the door in case he needed a prompt. He wasn't listening this time, either.

Cole Ferguson hadn't moved a centimeter when Jen Neil burst into the tiny office. "I'm telling you, she's got a business degree and experience with fund-raising. Why would we look for anyone else?" When she realized she was interrupting a conversation already in progress, Jen frowned. "Who's he?"

"He's interested in the job," Rebecca said,

"but he's just *leaving*." The way his feet were planted made it clear he wasn't budging.

Sarah waved a hand. "We've got the time. Tell us about your experience. It's obvious the physical part of the work will be no challenge." She coughed and then smiled brightly. "And I don't think we have the right candidate in this stack. No pets, Jen. Your sure bet has no pets, not one to tell me about." Sarah tapped the last question on the application. "How long is she going to be happy around here? The suit she was wearing when she brought in her application? Had to cost at least eight hundred dollars. Believe me, I know. If it were older, it could be my old suit snagged from the consignment shop. But this place is dog hair and cat scratches and wash-and-wear wardrobe. I need someone who can do more than make phone calls and look pretty."

"I guess you think you've got that covered." Jen raised an eyebrow.

Sarah stuck her tongue out and they both smiled. Rebecca wasn't sure whether Jen and Sarah were going to murder each other or run off to lunch together most days. After a rocky past, the two of them were tied together by two great loves: Will Barnes—Jen's stepbrother, Sarah's boyfriend and the man charged with matching their lottery winnings with worthy causes—and the need to rescue every stray in the Holly Heights vicinity.

Cole folded both hands in front of him and assumed an impressive, perfectly rigid posture. Did he have military experience?

"I worked with a program for three years. It's called Prison Partners. We trained rescue dogs from local shelters in basic obedience so that they could be adopted." He cleared his throat.

Prison? Rebecca did her best not to gasp and point, but her instincts had been right. There was no way they could hire a criminal.

He glanced around the room and rolled his shoulders.

"So that means you were *in* prison?" Jen asked, her eyebrows set in a firm, disapproving line.

Jen was the one who was convinced Rebecca would lose her millions to the first grifter who came along. Even if Sarah wanted to give the guy a chance, Rebecca and Jen could send him on his way.

Being aligned with cynical Jen was a new, unsettling experience.

"Yes. Just got out," Cole said in a rough

voice. "Aggravated assault. Tried to rob a gas station." Whatever else he intended to say was swallowed as he clenched his teeth and returned to painfully correct posture.

Sarah tilted her head to the side. "Yeah, it's coming back to me now. I vaguely remember my father telling me all about it. Your grandmother cleaned our house for a while."

Awkward silence filled the room until Bub heaved a disgusted sigh.

Everyone took a breath.

"Yeah. I imagine a lot of people in Holly Heights could say that." Cole tipped his chin up.

"Good character. That was one of the qualifications," Rebecca said, and pointed at the crumpled newspaper. "Remember? Trustworthy, honest." Not that there was any way to tell the character of any of the other applicants, but at least they didn't have prison experience.

"Yeah, well…seems you're the *second* criminal I've met," Sarah said with a shrug. "Big Bobby Hillman's headed for lockup as soon as the police track him down. Surely it won't be much longer."

Sarah had gotten pretty desperate for an update on her father. He'd embezzled money from his businesses and disappeared. The Austin police had been getting closer, but Hollister, the Austin detective who'd hounded her for so long, was no longer answering her calls.

Cole's posture relaxed. She, Stephanie and Jen had all changed their minds about Sarah Hillman since they'd gotten involved in Paws for Love. Apparently, understanding they had something close to being in common changed Cole's perception, too.

"Nobody was hurt in the robbery. Do I remember that right?" Sarah asked.

"Yes, ma'am. I did a stupid thing, but I've learned a lot since. I made a promise. No more trouble. Getting this job would help me keep it." Cole shifted back and forth and managed to make eye contact with everyone in the room except Rebecca. Bub gave his hand a slurp.

Something about the way his lips softened changed his whole face. Broody disappeared, replaced by humor and affection.

"We haven't even interviewed the others yet," Rebecca said. "What if there's the perfect person in that stack?" She held up both hands. "I'll get an application. If you measure up, we'll call you back." Offering a compromise wasn't the best solution here, but he wasn't leaving otherwise.

"Listen..." Cole stopped. His hands tightened into fists. "I know a guy with a record seems like a bad bet. Let me show you what I can do."

Sarah rested her elbows on the desk. "What did you have in mind?"

Cole straightened his shoulders, as if his confidence grew the closer they got to real work. "Show me your biggest headache. Give me an hour. I'll have him sitting on command." He patted his pockets. "But I'll need some dog treats."

If he was the kind of guy who made it a policy to always carry dog treats, Sarah would hire him then and there. The former mean girl had a weak spot the size of Texas for her animals.

"Our biggest headache barks when he's happy, sad, excited or bored, chews on everything that sits still for two seconds, has the attention span of a two-year-old and is the sweetest beagle you'll ever met," Jen drawled.

"Wait a minute. The deadline for applications was *Friday.*" Rebecca held up a hand, the breathlessness hitting again as Cole turned to study her. "We've got plenty of candidates."

"You know how much I love rules, Rebecca."
Sarah rolled her eyes. "Besides, if he can do
what he says he can, I want to see it." She held
out a hand to urge them all out into the hallway.
"Cole, I believe it's time you met Freddie. If you
want a test to prove your skill, he's your dog."

CHAPTER THREE

GETTING WHAT HE wanted when he'd set out on foot from the trailer park that morning made Cole feel good. Every step he'd taken to get to Paws for Love had been a sweaty, exhausting battle between his will and his fear.

Walking two miles in the hot sun was enough to force a man to concentrate on what mattered.

"Here's our cat room," Sarah said as they passed two large windows. Cats of all colors and shapes slept or scratched or ate or watched their audience disdainfully. "Have any experience training cats?"

He hated to disappoint her. Sarah's hopeful tone made him want to say yes, but the redhead, Jen, snorted. "Nobody *trains* cats. Cats train *us*." She was shaking her head as she motioned at Cole to continue walking down the hallway.

You can do this. You've worked with all kinds of dogs. Never with an audience like this one, but his pep talk succeeded in soothing some of the ridiculous jitters.

When he'd insisted he talk to the manager, he'd expected to be leaving in handcuffs. Superior Rebecca Lincoln could have called the cops. Touching her was a mistake. He could see her anxiety in her eyes.

That fear burned. Was that how his whole life was going to go? Another good reason to give people a wide berth. He'd get this job, do it well and go home. No need to make friends.

Only one thing could distract him from the doubt and fear of failure—a dog named Freddie who howled as if his heart was breaking the instant Sarah stopped in front of his kennel. He was white and black with a tan face and droopy ears that trembled as he poured out his heart.

"What's the matter, Freddie?" Cole asked in a deep voice. The dog broke off a building howl and tilted his head curiously, his tail wagging wildly. "You just wanted to say hello, didn't you?" Cole lifted the latch on the kennel as he braced himself. If he had to guess, Freddie was a jumper.

The slight hesitation to the dog's exit could be fear. "What's his story?" He held out his hands for Freddie to sniff.

"His owner died." Sarah rubbed one of Freddie's ears between her finger and thumb. "The family played hot potato with Freddie for a few months, but I don't get the feeling any one of them ever wanted him." She shrugged. "As soon as I reopened the shelter for adoptions, I had more than I could take, but Freddie was on borrowed time. The guy who brought him in threatened to dump him on the highway."

Cole heard someone curse under her breath. He glanced over his shoulder at Jen, the one he'd instantly pegged as the hard case in the group. Everyone else had turned to look at Rebecca. The princess cursed? Interesting.

Seeing that he was no longer the center of attention, Freddie picked that second to decide Cole was his new best friend. The dog lunged up, feet and toenails scrabbling on the concrete of the kennel. Cole managed to catch him and ease him to the floor. "Easy, boy. Things are going to get better."

Freddie immediately started a frenzied race around the room, baying at the top of his lungs. All the dogs in the other kennels answered until it was impossible to imagine a nice calm world with silent dogs in it. When he'd inspected the entire room, Freddie

hopped up and down against Cole's leg until
Cole picked him up to cradle him in his arms.
There, Freddie grinned, a long pink tongue
lolling out of his mouth while Cole pressed
his chin against the beagle's head.

All day. I could do this all day.

Cole shook his head as he scratched Freddie's
bright white chest. Then he realized the whole
room had gotten quiet. Losing track of what
was going on while he was working with a dog
wasn't that unusual. Looking up to see Sarah
and Jen blinking misty eyes at him was a once-
in-a-lifetime thing.

And terrifying. He'd learned to live without
emotion. Seeing it on their faces and feeling
it swirl in the atmosphere made him uneasy.
Restless.

"He's okay. I've got him." Cole bent to put
Freddie carefully down. "We should let him
run around outside for a few minutes. Should
help him concentrate." Maybe they'd stay inside. The women. That would be good.

"Have some treats," Sarah said as she
reached in a tin on the shelf beside the door
and handed Cole a few, bracing her feet to
keep from being knocked backward into the
doorframe by Freddie's enthusiasm.

Beagles were known for their appetites.

Freddie might have also faced some neglect. Attention and food would work wonders for this dog.

Sarah pulled open a door and stepped away. Freddie didn't move. His eyes were locked on the treats in Cole's hand. "Outside." Cole laughed as intelligent brown eyes darted to meet his. *No way, man.* That's what the dog's expression said. He was staying as close to the treats as he could.

With no other option but to lead the parade outside, Cole stepped out into the hot sunshine. Later in the day would be better for training, but this was his shot.

Freddie drifted a few steps away, drawn by all the new smells. Cole eased down on a picnic table and tried to ignore the eyes locked on his every move.

Pretend this is easy.

He crossed one foot over the other and winced at the tight pull of his shirt across his shoulders.

"Freddie." He whistled and waved a single dog biscuit in the air.

The picnic table kept him from being knocked over as Freddie launched forty pounds of muscle into the air. Cole caught him and set him down in the grass, one hand on the dog's back, right above his tail. Freddie eased to an awkward, hovering sit. "Good boy. You know your name." *And your favorite dog treat.*

He gave Freddie the treat and eased back, a signal to the dog to go on with his business. "I didn't have a chance to complete an application but…" Cole lost his train of thought when he noticed Jen and Sarah were both staring at him with hands clasped in front of them. Rebecca was sniffing, her lips a tight line. What did that mean? Was it a good sign or a bad one? "I had some training in landscape maintenance and design. I could help with that." He motioned at the second play yard, a wild mess of weeds that would need to be cleared before it could be used. "And out front, too." The sign was new, but everything else about the front of the shelter suggested the shelter director had bigger things on her mind than the flower beds. "If I get the job." That might sweeten his deal.

Sarah smiled brightly at Jen. Once they high-fived each other, he started to feel better about his chances of landing the probationary period. He repeated the same process with Freddie four more times, adding a "Sit" to each treat.

He had one last biscuit in his hand. This was it, his shot to show them he could work patiently with dogs like Freddie.

"You try it." He waved at Rebecca. "Let's see how he responds." Why her? He wasn't sure. If he had to come up with a reason, he'd say it was because Sarah and Jen clearly had experience with dogs, and he wanted to show that his training could work for someone who didn't. Mainly, he wanted to see what she would do. Everything about Rebecca was sunny, like her whole life went according to plan. A dog would shake that up. They were messy and she was clearly into neat.

Rebecca wiped both hands down her white shorts. "Freddie." She called him with a firm voice and then whistled like Cole.

He knew his eyebrows rose, but he was pretty surprised at the impressive whistle.

So was Freddie. The dog trotted up, spared Cole one glance and then stopped in front of Rebecca.

"Sit, Freddie." When the beagle carefully folded his legs and sat, they all cheered. Freddie's total time obeying the command had to be less than two seconds, but he was entitled to join in the party. Rebecca was still cheering when she dropped down in the grass and caught Freddie before he could lick her face.

She was giggling, her hair a curly halo blowing in the weak breeze, when she glanced up to catch Cole's eye. "I'm not sure he's cured, but you've made a good start, professor."

Was she teasing him? Cole's lips twitched in response, but answering her smile with his would be a mistake. She didn't trust him. That was for the best.

Watching her smile fade as she realized who she was talking to confirmed his own mistrust.

Anxious to get the answer he wanted, Cole rolled his shoulders and heard the whisper of another seam. The shirt he'd found in his closet had been too big at eighteen, a thrift-store find his grandmother had bought for his graduation. He fit the shirt now like he fit his old life in Holly Heights.

"I say yes." Sarah bent to run a hand down Freddie's back. "I like his style."

"You want someone with a green thumb," Jen muttered. "And a strong back. Also, a good way with animals." She sighed. "But a record, a history of bad decisions." Her lips twisted. "Sorry. I've got to say no. For safety."

Cole watched Rebecca's shoulders relax. She'd been scared to death they might hire him.

"I don't need a title. Forget assistant manager. I can just be a...worker." He clenched the wooden seat with both hands to keep from making embarrassing begging motions. "One week. I'll work for free for one week. And you call me extra help or something. I *don't* need the title. But I need this job." His mouth was too dry to say much more. "I need this place. I need this chance." The words tasted terrible on his tongue, but he was desperate.

Everyone turned to Rebecca. "We should do some interviews. And if he's the most qualified, then..." She shrugged. The way she studied the ground instead of meeting his stare was cowardly.

Cole was ready to mumble something about hoping they'd keep him in mind so he could escape, but no one was paying any attention to him. All the women were frowning at...Rebecca.

"I have to work with you, so *I'll* make the final call. Better not make me regret it." Sarah was shaking her head as she stepped around Rebecca and Freddie. "But I have two conditions."

Cole was already nodding when she held out her hand.

"You work for one month as a probationary period." Sarah held her hand up to keep him from shaking it. "*With* pay. And you start tomorrow. Very early."

"Great." Relieved and more optimistic than when he'd walked in that day, Cole whistled for Freddie. The beagle raced across the yard, ears flapping in the breeze, to lurch to a stop at his feet in an awkward sit. They still had a lot of work to do and Freddie would forget most of what he'd learned today, but he wasn't afraid. As long as the dog treats held, Freddie would be the perfect student. "Good boy." Cole scratched his ears and enjoyed the light wave of laughter that floated in the silence as Freddie flopped on his side to offer him his belly.

"He's gonna be a success." Cole scratched the dog and then said, "Let's go, Freddie."

Inside, the dog bounded from one kennel to the next, baying his hellos, and Cole picked him up to set him inside his own kennel. Freddie's expression was predictably heartbreaking. "I'll see you tomorrow, Fred."

Conversation was impossible with all the

barking and howling, so the group was silent until he stopped in the lobby. "Sunrise?"

Sarah wrinkled her nose. "It's best to start early in this heat."

"I'll be here." So much weight rolled right off his back as he stepped out into the gravel parking lot that it was easier to stand tall. Spotting EW and his truck idling in the lot was almost more than he could handle. Relief and gratitude and enough fear and remorse that this was what his life had come to all roiled in his brain and he wasn't sure whether to cry or hit something.

But he had an audience. The ladies working with Paws for Love were on one side. EW was on the other. So he took a deep breath of searing Texas air and got inside the truck.

"Thought you could use a ride." EW didn't glance in his direction but raised a hand in a wave to the ladies. "You got the job."

"I could have walked it, but yeah, I did." Walking was easy. Depending on EW or anyone would get him in trouble, but it was nice to ride in this heat. Neither one of them said anything else until EW rolled past the entrance to the trailer park.

"This definitely deserves a beer, EW, but let's not go to the new gas station." Cole wasn't sure he was ready to walk in those doors yet.

"Groceries, kid. Maybe some lunch." EW shook his head. "Too early for beer anyway."

Was EW done drinking? None of his business. "And a new shirt," Cole said.

EW nodded and that was it. Cole turned his face into the hot wind blowing in through the window because in half a second he was going to do something shameful like cry.

He had a job and a place to live. Nothing could stop him from keeping his promise now.

CHAPTER FOUR

REBECCA TURNED AWAY as EW's rusty truck puttered out of the parking lot. The cool air inside the building did nothing to chill the heat in her cheeks.

As soon as the glass door closed behind her, the silence in the tiny lobby was uncomfortable.

"So, that was all the business we had to take care of today, right?" Rebecca said airily as she retreated behind the counter to grab her tote. She wanted out. She did not want to examine her reaction to Cole Ferguson. The file of applications was easy to find, so she waved it and set it on the counter; then she bent and picked up everything Cole had dumped on the ground. "Great. I have a contractor coming to install the cabinets and new appliances, the moment I've been dreaming of for years."

"You have nothing else to say? What's with the personality transplant?" Jen asked.

Sarah leaned against the counter. "Explanation, please. You're the one who's all about saving the world and making a difference. You had an easy opportunity here and you... What would you call it?"

"Freaked. She freaked out," Jen said. She frowned and then straightened. "Did he threaten you or something?"

Rebecca dropped the tote on the counter. "No. Not with words but..."

Her best friends in the world immediately stepped forward. "Not with *words*?" Jen asked.

"I mean, no, he didn't threaten me. On purpose." Rebecca rubbed the throbbing spot right in the middle of her forehead. Her attempts at explanation were only making things worse. "He was completely polite but insistent."

"Because he was desperate. I've been there." Sarah nodded.

"Except you aren't the size of a large green superhero, complete with clothes ripping at the seams." Rebecca pressed both hands to her cheeks. "Sorry. He rattled me. I don't know what else to say. Add his history and it's a bad idea to have him around."

"But you saw how patient he was with Freddie." Sarah raised both eyebrows. "There's no way you feel the same way now."

Their confusion felt like disappointment to Rebecca. She was letting them down. Her role had always been to lead them to do the right thing, sometimes kicking and screaming. This time, she'd failed miserably. The sharp sting made it hard to find the right words.

"There's no rule that says bad people can't like dogs, you know." Jen smoothed her hair behind her ear. "Or even that dogs can't like bad people." Her own dog had come through some serious neglect and possible abuse with a firm love for people.

"Coming from you, the pessimist's view is no surprise," Sarah snapped.

"Oh, yeah," Jen said as she straightened to her full, unimpressive height. "And let's talk about you ignoring your board's direction. You didn't have approval to hire him in the first place."

"Well, you should have brought that up *then*, dear board member," Sarah said sweetly. "You or Rebecca could have played that card if you want to be sticklers about our board of directors. We have a done deal at this point."

Watching them glare at each other got old fast. "Sarah's right," Rebecca said. "She's in charge here and her offer was smart. A probationary period will help us all decide whether he fits." She still couldn't figure out how they'd make him go if he wanted to stay, but that was a problem for another day.

"Fine. I'm here to help Les and Shelly with the outdoor pens." Jen flexed her muscles. Les was the retired veterinarian who did most of the day-to-day care at the shelter. He and Shelly were an item. "Nothing like trying to teach a classroom of kids all hopped up on summer break the difference between convex and concave polygons to make me want to hammer something."

"I have bills. Bills, bills, bills," Sarah said with a sigh. "Save me some hammering."

Relieved no one was examining her failure closely, Rebecca clasped her hands together. "Once my kitchen is up and running, I'm planning a dinner party no one will forget. Rack of lamb or…something in one oven. Chocolate soufflé in *another*." Double ovens. It would be heaven, a luxurious, over-the-top heaven she could never have afforded without the lottery win. She could almost picture her mother's dismay.

"You need to get out more," Jen muttered.

"No one should get that excited over a kitchen remodel."

"We could all go out to eat so you don't have to work so hard. Daniel and Steph would love some Tex-Mex before they fly to Lima. Can you imagine? A whole year before they'll be back." Sarah shook her head. "And Steph's been so busy in Austin, I've barely seen her."

Rebecca didn't want to spend any time thinking about her brother and Stephanie being so far away for so long. Their work for HealthyAmericas, a program that matched doctors to underserved communities in Central and South America, was so important, but she loved having everyone close. Flying to Lima herself for a visit would take more bravery than she had and a prescription for really strong drugs.

At some point, she was going to have to see about getting both.

"But I love my new kitchen." Rebecca frowned. "I want to use it." For all the guilt she was experiencing over spending some of her new fortune on such a selfish project, she looked forward to using the new kitchen every single chance she got. The guilt could be overcome with the smell of baking bread. Probably.

Sarah and Jen shook their heads. Between them, they could barely boil an egg. What did they know of the joy of brand-new appliances?

At least they could poke fun at her without arguing with each other. "I'll be a little less rich thanks to the big donation they're taking to HealthyAmericas. Steph should be cooking *me* dinner."

Jen wrinkled her nose in disgust. "Nobody wants that."

"Think this dinner is actually about something else, like a big announcement?" Sarah asked and fluttered her eyelashes.

Rebecca snapped her head around so fast a sharp pain landed at the base of her skull. "Announcement? Like what?" An engagement? Stephanie and Daniel had known each other forever and Stephanie had been half in love with him all that time, but it had only been a few months since Stephanie blackmailed her way in to a trip to the Andes to see his work in exchange for a big donation. Surely they weren't that close.

Were they?

Rebecca shuffled through the junk in her tote to find her phone. With one quick punch, she had Stephanie on the line. "Are you and

Daniel getting ready to make an announcement?"

Stephanie cleared her throat. "No idea what you're talking about."

Confused about whether she should be relieved or disappointed, Rebecca said, "But you guys are good, right?" They seemed so in love. That had to be true.

"What is going on with you? Of course we're fine. Your brother is currently pricing an X-ray machine and happier than a pig in mud. I'm planning my first newsletter. We've got a website up. I'll email you the address. No worries, Bex. We're great. Any announcement…well, you'll be the first person I tell. I promise." Stephanie laughed. "Your brother just turned a nice shade of pink. We've only been 'us' in Texas. Daniel still expects me to wither up and die when we go back to Peru. Little does he know, I have plans. Big plans. Opening that office in Lima, setting up networks of doctors serving in the remote areas of the Andes…I'm going to be too busy for any withering." She was silent for a long minute. Rebecca wondered if there was some silent communication going on. "He's got questions, but me, I have the answers."

Rebecca eased back, aware of the tension

in her shoulders. Daniel had made a terrible decision and had gone around the Holly Heights hospital's rules to help a patient. His big head had caused him to say things there was no coming back from so he'd retreated. All the way to South America.

On this visit, he seemed happy. Fulfilled. Like he'd found the work he was meant for.

She didn't want him to blow a good thing with her best friend by being stupidly noble. Thank goodness Stephanie had things under control. She'd always been the brave one in the group.

Jen was a soft center covered by a hard shell. She'd fought for everything she had and used that fierceness to protect her friends and family whenever necessary.

The three of them had been friends long enough that they might as well be related.

They'd recently reconnected with Sarah and folded her into the group as easily as cream into coffee, and she was proving to be a savvy businesswoman.

Rebecca was the one who encouraged others, except for Cole—the one guy who'd caused her to collapse with the trembles—and dreamed of double ovens.

How depressing.

Get a grip. All of this is happening because of you.

"Well, okay. I'll get back to planning a dinner worthy of my two favorite do-gooders."

"Bread. Lots of bread," Stephanie said right before she hung up.

Relieved and sad at the reminder that they'd be leaving soon, Rebecca dropped the phone back in her tote. Everyone was moving or growing or changing. Stephanie had gone to Peru because of her. Sarah had a chance to save her shelter because of Rebecca. Even Jen had discovered the love of her life, a pit bull named Hope, in a roundabout way because of Rebecca. She'd stumbled with Cole Ferguson, but the fact that Sarah had been able to step up and do the right thing only showed the power of Rebecca's good influence.

Right?

"No announcement, but they're fine. On that note, I'm off to see my beautiful kitchen," Rebecca said and pasted on a happy smile. Sarah and Jen were bickering on the way down the hall to the outdoor pens. Sarah and Jen at Paws for Love, Stephanie and Daniel in Lima, everyone had work they had to get to.

Except for her.

"That's because my kids are scheduled for

counseling sessions already, and I've been prepping my best students for a full year for all their college entrance exams and forms." Rebecca dropped her tote on the hot passenger seat and slid in behind the wheel. "I'm prepared. I've *been* working."

Her own defense didn't do much to lighten the guilty load as she pulled into her tiny driveway. Bill Hayney was already unloading a beautiful refrigerator.

Today she was going to celebrate her renovated kitchen.

No one was criticizing her. Figuring out why she was so defensive should go at the top of her to-do list.

THE SOUND OF giggling girls on Friday afternoon reminded Cole that it was quitting time. The best thing about starting at the crack of dawn was being able to leave before school got out and the volunteers arrived. Over the past week, he'd settled into an easy routine at Paws for Love, one that limited most of his contact with actual people.

The Texas heat was bad enough to make a man daydream about avalanches and blizzards, but he was doing a good job.

"Here. Drink this." Shelly handed him a

tall glass of ice water, the condensation rolling down the sides in the most perfect way. "You worry me."

"I'm tough," Cole grumbled before he tipped the glass and drained it. The sharp cold brought on a brain freeze that was a tiny price to pay for the sweet burn of cold all the way down. He should have taken a break sooner.

As he flopped down in the shade next to the bench Shelly was seated on, he glanced over his shoulder to shoot her a thankful smile, but it died on his lips when he saw Rebecca and two teenage girls staring out the window. All three immediately disappeared and he wondered how long they'd been watching him work.

And why.

"I thought you'd left for the day," Shelly said. "Otherwise, I'd have brought *two* glasses of water."

When Cole realized he'd taken the glass of water she'd made for herself, he straightened up. "Oh, man, I'm sorry. When you offered it to me, I thought…"

She laughed and waved a hand. "You definitely needed it worse than I did. I'll make another when I go in. This place is starting to shape up."

"Yeah, I wanted to finish trimming the fence line before I left today." Leaving early was the best way to avoid conversation with... anyone. Avoiding Rebecca had been on his mind all week. He, Sarah and Shelly worked easily together, mainly because they gave him assignments and left him alone. Alone was how he liked it.

"Sarah's hustling to have your check ready before you go. Make sure you stop by the office on your way out." Shelly raised her eyebrows, almost as if she recognized his immediate struggle not to argue that he didn't need the extra effort.

The money? That he needed.

"Think she'll let me come in tomorrow?" Cole asked as he wiped his forehead. "I'm making good progress on that second yard. If I can get Les's help tomorrow, we can put in the gate Sarah wants."

"You know this is a part-time job, right? You've put in more hours than I have this week." Shelly tapped his arm. "You're making me look bad, kid."

"It's okay. Some of it can be volunteer hours. Free." Cole shrugged, surprised she was comfortable enough to tease him.

"Take a couple days off. That's what the rest

of us human types do after a long, hard week."
She sighed. "Soak in some air-conditioning
somewhere or float in the water or..." She
shrugged. "There have to be a million things
you'd like to do now."

That you're free.

Unfortunately, free time would be dangerous, give him a chance to think things he
shouldn't.

The cough and sputter of EW's truck
floated over the building to their shady spot.

"Sounds like your ride's here." Shelly
groaned as she stood. "And the new dog won't
wash himself."

"I'll be happy to stay and help," Cole said
as he rolled up off the ground. "EW won't
mind."

"Go. Get your check. Find some weekend.
There'll still be plenty of work here on Monday." She wrapped her arm through his and
pulled him to the doorway. "They won't bite."

He grunted as he yanked open the door.
She wasn't talking about the dogs. There was
no honor in pretending not to understand
what she meant.

"Nope. Just giggle and stare." He held the
door open for Shelly and followed her inside.
"It's a requirement of being a teenage girl."

She grabbed his sleeve and towed him down the hallway. "The good ones grow out of it."

Sarah and Rebecca were laughing at the way Freddie rolled back and forth between their two volunteers. One girl would scratch his ears while the other rubbed his belly. Then he'd roll to the other side so they could switch. He was a very happy dog.

When Rebecca covered her mouth to muffle her snorted laughs, Cole shot Shelly a look.

"Hey, he's a funny dog. That laughter is totally justified, grown-up or not," she said as her lips twitched.

She was right. This kind of laughter didn't fill him with uneasy restlessness. Listening to them filled his chest with a weird, warm lump.

Unfortunately, the second they realized he was there, everyone froze. Freddie's head jerked around and he did an acrobatic spring toward Cole. The instant before he skidded into Cole's legs, Freddie squatted into an imperfect sit, his tail wagging wildly, the bright white tip a blur.

"Good boy, Fred." Cole bent to ruffle the beagle's velvety, floppy ears and scratch under his collar. "Good sit. We'll work on sticking the landing next week. You be a good boy until Monday."

The weekend without Freddie and work stretched out like another kind of sentence, solitary without the confinement, and he wasn't looking forward to it.

He could work for free over the weekend. Just to come in and say hello to his second best friend in the world.

"Here, you guys take him out. See if you can get him to come when you call his name," Rebecca said softly to the two volunteers. She handed them dog treats and Freddie was ready for his next test.

Cole watched the white tip of his tail disappear through the door before he turned to go.

"I've got your check ready," Sarah said. She darted around them into the lobby and trotted in and out of her office. "Thanks so much for everything you've done this week."

Cole folded and refolded the check while he studied it. "Might be able to get to the flower beds next week." He forced himself to look up. "If you want. Gonna take some time to clear the old stuff out."

Rebecca was standing on the other side of the counter, right behind Sarah. She didn't look up from the papers she had in her hand. Too afraid he'd frown at her or something.

"Maybe. Let's talk on Monday." Sarah tipped her head forward. "You know you don't have to do everything this month, right?" She smiled. "You've been such a huge help around here. Next week, let's talk about a training program. We're having a big adoption drive in Holly Heights and it would be awesome to have some well-mannered candidates."

"Sure. I could draw up a schedule to work with more dogs than Freddie." He'd enjoy that. The new dog, a German shepherd mix, might have the smarts to become a service dog. Right now the animal was unpredictable, lurked in the corner of his kennel with watchful eyes. That made him dangerous. Some basic training would be needed before he could be evaluated, but Cole would like to give it a shot.

Sarah nodded. "Good, but I meant training me and Shelly. The volunteers." She glanced at Rebecca and cleared her throat. "So on the days you're not here, we can keep the process going."

Work with the giggling girls? The dread that swamped him was immediate. He'd never trained *people* to do anything except leave him alone. His hesitation must have been apparent.

"Please?" Sarah folded her hands together.

A Hillman begging him for help. Add that to the fact that she'd thanked him for doing his job and he'd be willing to try anything she asked. Cole nodded and shoved open the door.

"Hey, have a good weekend," Shelly called.

Cole waved his hand as he slid inside EW's truck.

EW raised two fingers and then backed out of the spot. "Running like the bogeyman after you, young fella. Everything okay?"

"Too much…niceness for one day." Cole hung one hand out the door and closed his eyes as the hot breeze dried his skin.

The prospect of staring at the walls of the trailer while the heat beat down on the roof didn't thrill him. Besides, he didn't need a lot of time to worry about what the next week might hold. He'd either pass or fail. Worrying wouldn't change a thing.

"Got any jobs you need help with?" he asked as he slouched against the seat.

"Yep." EW drove right past the entrance to the trailer park. When he didn't slow down at the closest gas station, Cole relaxed a bit. It didn't matter where they were headed. Anywhere with company was going to be better than time alone.

EW pulled into Junior's Bait and Tackle where a neon sign shouted We Cash Checks.

"Beer?" Cole asked as he opened the door.

EW pursed his lips. "Well, that's not a terrible idea, but get the bait first. Some Cokes. We're goin' fishin'. Found a nice shady spot yesterday that's bound to work."

Cool water. Shade. Silence. EW was a genius.

The uncontrollable smile that curled Cole's lips felt good. He'd worked hard for his first week out in the open. With EW's help, he might enjoy a weekend.

CHAPTER FIVE

"NOT A SINGLE WORD?" Sarah shook her head. "You *really* don't like him, do you?"

Rebecca blew out a frustrated breath. "Just... You won't understand this, but some people, normal people, can be intimidated by making conversation with others they don't know. We don't have anything in common. Besides, he was here for less than ten minutes."

And she'd been watching him for about five minutes longer than that, but nobody needed to know that part. When her students Alyssa and Madison had joined her at the window to see what she was staring at, she'd nearly died of embarrassment.

Then he'd caught them watching.

Rebecca was pretty sure she was actually a ghost at this point. No one could survive the flaming heat of embarrassment that had swept over her and live to tell the tale.

Up close, his power was scary. She'd been

amazed at how easily he'd finished the cleanup of the yard that would have taken her a solid month to slog through. He'd mowed and trimmed the huge expanse. The trash that had accumulated there when it was not being used had all been removed. And he'd done it in heat that made stepping outside a test of endurance.

Rebecca would never have imagined the man who'd barged in that first day could be so gentle with the animals.

Cole had doubled the shelter's capacity with his strength and focus and hard work. In one week, he'd made a change that was going to impact the shelter for years to come. Not just the shelter, either. Holly Heights would be better off, too.

She'd almost chased him away. Why? Irrational fear. How humbling that was to consider.

"What? Did I miss something?" Rebecca ran a hand through her curls self-consciously when she realized Sarah and Shelly were watching. She hadn't said any of that out loud, had she?

"We're waiting on you to finish the conversation in your head," Sarah said with a smirk. "What I said was that you have never once in the years I've known you had trouble making conversation with strangers. And we know Cole. So give me another excuse, but this time put it in the form of a question. Just for fun." Sarah started humming the *Jeopardy* theme.

Shelly was coldly patient. For the first time since Rebecca had met the older woman who'd kept the shelter afloat until Sarah stepped up, Shelly's mouth was pursed with displeasure. "That boy is doing the work of two men for this place, I'll have you know."

Hearing sweet Shelly, the grandmotherly type who enjoyed the cat room above all else, voice Rebecca's own thoughts made it hard to stand still. Rebecca wanted to duck behind Sarah or at least hold up both hands as a shield. Then Shelly glanced at Sarah. "I'll go let the first group of dogs out."

She narrowed her eyes at Rebecca and marched down the hallway.

"Oops. I should have waited until his biggest fan had left the room." Sarah shrugged. "We're one week in. Les and Shelly both believe Cole is better than Christmas, payday and a Cowboys win all combined."

Rebecca nodded. "Great. I'm glad. And I don't *dislike* him."

"No, you vibrate with *nerves* whenever he's around." Sarah braced both arms on the counter. "What's the deal?"

Telling Sarah about her disastrous attempt at breaking up a fight wouldn't explain all the reservations she had about Cole, but it might be enough to buy her some understanding.

"At school, I did a stupid thing. I tried to stop a fight between two boys." Rebecca squeezed the counter tightly. "Together those boys might make one of Cole Ferguson, but that didn't stop Eric from pinning me against the lockers, his hand wrapped around my throat. If he hadn't come to his senses, he could have hurt me. And...I don't know. That first day, when Cole walked in, he surprised me, rattled me."

Sarah reached over to squeeze Rebecca's hand. "That's scary, Rebecca. I had no idea, but Cole's just...a guy, no more dangerous than the veterinarians we work with or Will."

Except none of those guys had spent time in prison. Rebecca wanted to argue, but she'd already disappointed her friends enough.

"Listen, maybe it's a matter of time," Sarah said. "I've worked with him for a week and haven't seen one bit of anything other than

a man determined to work himself into…
something. Exhaustion, maybe. I don't know."
She sighed. "It sort of reminds me of how I
worked here in the early days. I wasn't sure
what I was doing, but I knew that it could
save me." Sarah blinked rapidly. "It did. *You*
did, with your money and support for this
place. And together we can do the same for
him. So…try, okay?"

Sarah Hillman, formerly the queen of Holly
Heights High School who had terrorized anyone unfortunate enough to cross her, was asking Rebecca to be nice.

The change in circumstances was dizzy-
ing. Rebecca had started her first charity in
elementary school. Her mother had volun-
teered them to supply a school in Africa with
shoe boxes filled with toys and basic toilet-
ries, so Sarah had convinced her fifth grade
class to perform chores in exchange for donations. She'd exceeded the goal by 50 percent.
Austin's homeless, wounded veterans, Ro-
manian orphans—Rebecca had raised funds
for them all.

All that work was part of being a Lincoln.
They did the right thing. Helping others was
all in a day's work.

Cole Ferguson needed some of that charity.

"I will. I will try." If she didn't, she'd be the worst sort of hypocrite.

"Okay, let's go see what Freddie has destroyed." Sarah rushed around the counter and wrapped her arms around Rebecca's neck. "You, you're awesome. You know that, right? No one cares as much as you do." Sarah squeezed her arm.

Rebecca nodded to satisfy Sarah. Then Sarah towed her down the hall by one arm and they were caught in a low-level circus in the shelter's play yard. Happy dogs were barking at something outside the fence, two Lab mixes were zooming in a breakneck game of chase, and it was almost impossible to walk, thanks to a begging hound anxious for a treat or a scratch, or any drop of attention.

As she and Shelly worked with the girls whose volunteer hours at the shelter would enhance their college applications to Baylor and SMU, Rebecca did her best to ignore the small voice whispering in her mind that she should be doing more.

This was important, but it was so comfortable. Writing checks was easy.

Improving Holly Heights was nothing like

serving as a doctor in Peru the way her older brother, Daniel, was doing. Stephanie was going to leave home to set up a network to help him. Even Sarah was out of her comfort zone with this shelter, although every day the leadership settled on her shoulders better.

If she was doing everything she could, Rebecca thought, she would feel better. Wouldn't she?

Talk about First World problems. The lottery winner is morose.

As they worked, Rebecca knew Sarah had one eye on her at all times. Pretending to be her normal self wasn't working. Even after the shelter closed and she did her very best not to study the entrance to the trailer park she passed on her way home, Rebecca couldn't get Sarah's words out of her head. *Just try.* Not even her nightly twirl and lovefest with her new kitchen could silence them.

The quartz countertops sparkled. The stainless steel commercial-sized refrigerator was quietly awesome. The double ovens were charming as she preheated them to prepare some of her famous cookies.

But all she could hear was Sarah's words. *Just try.* The memory of Cole's face as he said goodbye to Freddie that afternoon distracted her, and before she knew it, three dozen cookies were cooling on racks. Her top-of-the-line dishwasher was quietly cleaning her prep bowls while she rested against the counter in her beautiful kitchen.

Her phone dinged to announce an email—Stephanie's promised link to the new Healthy-Americas website for Peru. Rebecca clicked it and smiled as her brother's goofy grin took over the screen. He had his arms wrapped around a gaggle of boys who were clearly soccer fans. Every photo on the page showed volunteers working hands-on with kids who had limited access to medical care.

She read a short profile, so clearly written in Stephanie's voice that it made Rebecca tear up, about a boy they'd met at three years old and the progress he'd made after he received the vaccinations he needed. Rebecca realized Daniel and Stephanie would be able to watch that boy grow. They'd be his neighbor, see his life and the changes they'd made.

Her money was funding that good work. That improved her outlook for half a second.

While she puttered in her fancy new kitchen, Cole was… She had no idea. A man recently released from prison. What were his circumstances? He walked to work from the trailer park. EW picked him up every day. His old button-down had been replaced with the three-in-a-package T-shirts from the local discount store.

Rebecca covered her hot cheeks with her hands as an unexpected wave of shame swept over her. She had everything. Cole was doing his best with the cards stacked against him.

But he's a criminal. You work hard to have things you enjoy. The logical voice in her head wasn't sympathetic.

"And I live in my parents' house, work the job I love because I graduated from a college my parents paid for and spend obscene money on appliances. Then I drift through life, wallowing in my loneliness." The guilt tightening her stomach made it hard to sit still. "While I avoid Cole because he makes me feel…"

As Rebecca shoved a cookie in her mouth, she picked up her phone to call Jen, the only single friend she had left. After she lured Jen over, she could convince her to do something crazy.

She could take cookies to Cole. That would brighten his life and it was an easy thing to do.

Almost as easy as writing a check. The cynical voice whispering through her mind was new and unwelcome. It sounded a bit like Jen, too.

When Jen answered, Rebecca said, "I have cookies. Come get them." Once Jen was here, Rebecca would ask her to drive her over to the trailer park. The two of them together should be safe enough. She could make Cole's night better, smooth things over and get back on Shelly's good side, get rid of all the cookies that she'd eat all by herself otherwise and have a reason to bake more. So many wins with one simple plan.

"Can't tonight. The decorator Sarah recommended is demanding to hear my *vision* before he'll take the job and paycheck," Jen snapped. "Save me some."

"I need to get out of the house. Take a ride with me." Rebecca dropped her head back to stare at the ceiling. "Or I'll bring them to you. Are you unpacking?" Luring Jen out to the car would be easy enough, and she had to get out of the house. The rosy glow of the setting sun covered the ceiling in pink.

"No, I have so many magazines still to destroy while I create my *design board*. I hate decorating homework. I'll call you in the morning. We'll shop for my new house's kitchen, okay?" Jen ended the call before Rebecca could argue. She almost called Jen back.

"Nope. If she wanted company, she'd tell you." Rebecca paced in a circle around the beautiful new island she'd had installed. It had four outlets and a prep sink. The cost had nearly knocked her backward when her contractor showed her the bid.

And if she spent a minute longer staring at the outrageously expensive gifts she'd given herself, she'd melt down.

Was she brave enough to go to Cole's trailer all by herself?

No, but she was desperate to uncoil the knot in her stomach.

Before she knew what she was doing, Rebecca had pulled down a tin covered in happy sunflowers and loaded it with cookies. She could deliver them to Jen, no matter how pathetic it might seem. If she got roped into unpacking or whatever do-it-yourself project Jen had tackled, so be it. At least she wouldn't be running the movie of her regrets through her mind on a constant loop.

Delivering the *next* batch of cookies to Cole in the bright light of day made so much more sense anyway.

One turn through town meant she was nowhere near Jen's new place on the highway headed out to the state park. Instead, she was going toward the shelter. And Cole's trailer park.

"Just try," Rebecca muttered as she turned in. If worse came to worst, she could say she was visiting EW. Her father had taken his Cadillac in to EW's garage every three months like clockwork until EW sold the place. She could remember his old waiting room clearly. He'd favored wildlife scenes and gospel music instead of blaring country tunes and talking heads of twenty-four-hour news channel like the dealership she frequented in Austin.

Of course, EW wouldn't remember that from fifteen years ago. And no one would believe her story.

The growing shadows didn't help the trailer park. Everything seemed scary in the twilight, especially the three kids standing under the basketball goal. At this distance, making out their faces was difficult, but the one standing directly under the goal could be Eric.

"Such a terrible idea, Rebecca," she muttered as she squinted at the nearest lopsided mailbox. "Don't be ridiculous. No one attacks a woman carrying a tin of cookies."

This is not your smartest plan. The kid had wrapped his hands around her neck.

Should she even get out of the car?

The door to Cole's trailer opened, spilling a golden rectangle of light down the steps.

Busted. She had no choice now.

Rebecca stared at his expressionless face, willing him to come down the steps and cross the tiny yard. She'd roll down the window and hand him the cheerful tin with a conciliatory smile and a finely worded apology without leaving the safety of her comfortable, four-door sedan. Then she'd throw the car in Reverse and return to the safe side of Holly Heights.

But her telepathy failed. Cole pressed one shoulder on the doorframe and waited.

Rebecca shook out her clammy hands before turning off the ignition. Holding the tin of cookies like a peace offering and a shield, she slid out of the driver's seat.

REBECCA WAS WEARING her petrified expression again. Whatever she'd been watching down at the end of the street had better be some kind of monster. Otherwise, he was doing it again without lifting a finger.

Scaring a woman with his breathing and standing upright.

If he ever wanted female company, this would be something he'd have to work on.

"I should have called." Her breathless voice was hard to make out, but she repeated herself as she stopped in the light at the bottom of the steps. "I'm sorry. The polite thing to do is to call."

"No phone." Cole didn't move from his perch at the top. If he did, she'd drop the tin and run for the safety of her car. He had a feeling whatever was inside would be compensation for whatever little digs her visit made to his confidence.

"Oh, you don't have a phone." She bobbled the tin and managed to catch it. "I would have had to yell really loud then."

Her joke hit hard on the ground between them. He didn't smile.

"These days, everyone has a phone. I didn't…think." She cleared her throat. "So far, this is going well, am I right?"

"No air-conditioning. No television. Nothing to drive." Cole straightened. "Want me to go on? I do have running water. The lights work. And I'm not locked behind bars, so I'm making progress."

"I brought cookies." Rebecca shrugged. "A peace offering."

Cookies. The only choice homier and more downright small-town America would have been apple pie. This woman with her golden curls and frilly apron—she must wear it so often she'd forgotten she still had it on—was standing there with baked goods in her hands.

And shaking in her shoes.

The whole situation was nuts.

"What will scare you less? If you tiptoe forward and deposit them on the bottom step or if I come down to get them?" Cole muttered. If she'd brought something else, like spinach, he'd have closed the door in her face. He avoided her at work. How dare she come here like this? "I'm not up for visitors."

He wanted those cookies. He'd investigated all the cookies in the discount store's bakery but walked away. There was no sense in spending good money on something that would disappoint him. The need for his

grandmother's sugar cookies would go un-
fulfilled.

Whatever Rebecca held might soften that
blow.

"I have something to say to you." Her voice
broke on the last word, ruining her delivery.
Rebecca's shoulders squared off and her chin
snapped up. "I am coming inside and you will
listen. Then I will give you the cookies."

Whatever mental pep talk she'd given herself must have been powerful. The teacher
voice was enough to make his lips twitch.
Instead of breathy nerves, this time he could
hear steel and no-nonsense "do what I say or
you will regret it, mister."

She was good at faking confidence. He had
to admire that in anyone.

Cole stepped out of the doorway and did a
courtly sweep of his hand. "I wouldn't dare
argue with that tone or the boss's boss." Then
he raised both hands and backed slowly into
the living room.

He watched her face carefully, certain he'd
see distaste or dismay. Seeing how the other
half survived would be good for her.

Rebecca's march didn't slow down until
she was standing in the center of his grand-

mother's tiny kitchen. She did a measured spin to take it all in and then slid the tin on the empty counter.

"I used to have the same refrigerator." When she met his stare, her lips flattened. "Put your hands down. I'm not here to rob you." The small flush that bloomed in her cheeks the second she realized she'd said "rob" to a would-be robber should have been satisfying. But it made her blue eyes brighter.

"Of course not. Nothing here to steal." Cole lowered both hands. "But I don't want to scratch my chin and scare you into screaming bloody murder."

Rebecca crossed both arms over her chest.

"Especially when you might have dropped the cookies."

Her eyes met his, and some of the grim determination on her face faded.

"You don't have a weapon, do you?" Cole asked. "If I sneeze, are you going to pull out a handgun and stand your ground?" He lowered his hands.

"Just cookies. A tin of cookies that I can toss out the door at any second."

He wondered if she knew her shoulders

were raised so high that they brushed her golden curls.

"Wasted home cooking. That would be a shame. I might actually cry." *Instead of sitting on the verge of tears like the biggest wimp in Texas.* Whether it made him mad or sad, too much thinking brought out the worst in him.

That didn't mean he was up for visitors, though.

"That almost sounds like the truth," she said as she shifted from one foot to the other. "You haven't even tasted them. What if I'm a terrible cook?"

"Frilly apron like that, I figure you must have some skill." If he could still grin, he would have at the way her head snapped down to check if he was telling the truth.

"Great." Rebecca closed her eyes. "Exactly the good impression I was hoping for." She reached behind her to untie the apron, whip it off and fold it carefully before placing it on the counter. Her khakis were still spotless and the white shirt she was wearing was the same one she'd worn to the shelter. There was not one wrinkle in the cotton.

Millionaires probably had a staff dedicated to making sure they didn't wrinkle.

Showering off the fish smell before he put on his new pair of shorts and one of the three clean T-shirts he owned had been all Cole could manage after the long day.

"Why are you here?" Cole asked. She still didn't trust him. He wasn't sure she realized she was leaning toward the door even as she did her best to pretend she was in control.

"I made cookies. I wanted you to have some. You've done such a good job this week." Rebecca clasped both hands in front of her. Her eyes darted to meet his before she returned to studying the linoleum.

"That's what you came to say? Good job?" No way. Cole knew better.

"This is me making amends. For…when you came in to apply for the job. It's clear you were the best man for the position." She smiled. "And I'm welcoming you to Holly Heights."

And now she was here to make herself feel better. With cookies and a frilly apron and spotless clothes and a superiority that she'd been born with.

Cole grunted. "Well, Your Highness, it's difficult to express my gratitude for the effort. I have the job. No hard feelings." He hadn't done anything wrong, except talk over her and insist on an interview. She thought her expression of remorse was a big gesture, no doubt.

But she had a stubborn streak. She pressed her lips together. "Fine, I understand I have no reason to be so…"

"Afraid?" Cole said. He didn't want to re-hash his history, but curiosity was building. Where was she going with this?

"Right. My only excuse is that I had a… run-in with a student, ended up with his hands around my throat. When you came in that day, it surprised me—"

Cole held up a hand. "I get it. First rule of prison life is not to sneak around behind a man. Good way to get hurt." And even when he'd made his presence known, Stitch, his cell mate, had reacted violently when Cole caught him off guard. Fight or flight was powerful, especially when a person's only choice was fight.

"Except this isn't prison. You weren't sneak-ing. And there was no reason to…" Rebecca pursed her lips. "Freak out."

"I respect fear." Cole shrugged. "Better than most, I get being afraid. And I should never have put my hands on you." He had no explanation for why he had except desperation. This soft, sweet woman wouldn't understand desperation. "The kid. What happened?" Why was he asking? The situation had zero to do with him. He wasn't getting involved with anyone, much less her.

"He realized the mistake he was making, I think." Rebecca squeezed her eyes shut. "He might be your neighbor. When I drove up, I'm sure it was Eric standing under the basketball goal."

"Ah, another reason to shake like you were about to meet with a serial killer when you opened your car door." Cole shoved aside the curtain to look out the window. The same three kids who'd loitered under the goal almost every night that week were in their usual spot. "Don't know them, but they spend a lot of time right there. Days *and* nights." He didn't add that that was where all his trouble started. The plan to steal his grandmother's station wagon for a joyride had hatched right there and ended with a long walk to town and his grandmother having to pay a tow truck to pull it out of the mud. His first taste of alcohol had been under that goal.

Ricky Martinez had shown him the handgun he'd "borrowed" from his stepfather there, too.

Maybe he shouldn't have felt the wave of nostalgia for the goal. The kids might be better off if he knocked it down.

"I haven't seen him at school since that day." She shook her head. "Why didn't it occur to me that he hadn't *been* there since then? It's been more than a week."

"Seems like that would be a relief." Cole let the curtains drop. A weak breeze lifted the fabric before it settled. "Just like me avoiding you was my gift to you. Accept it and move on instead of invading my space with a peace offering I can't refuse." He shrugged. "Assuming those cookies are any good."

"It's my job to assist these kids and make sure they have a plan for the future," Rebecca muttered as she jerked the lid off the tin.

His input was unnecessary. She was talking to herself.

She sighed and held out the cookies, her mouth downturned.

"Forget about me and those guys. Nothing but trouble that direction. Focus on the kids you can help." Cole picked two of the biggest cookies and then set the tin on the table next to his grandmother's photo album. A split second later he realized he should have shut it before confronting Rebecca. He'd been trying to distract himself by flipping through the pages. Sixth grade had been a rough year for him. If she got a load of that school picture, she'd die of laughter instead of fright. "Those girls headed to college appreciate your help. Save yourself some aggravation. Work on them. Leave the rest of us..." *Behind. Where we fall. In the dust.* He wasn't sure what words finished that sentence.

He took a bite as she slammed both hands on her hips. Wrong thing to say.

"I'm supposed to help them *all*. And that boy needs his high school diploma." She paced in a line back and forth in front of the coffee table, her fingers twisted together in a tight knot. "Loitering like that is only going to lead to trouble."

"No argument here." Cole nodded as he took a bite of the chocolate chip cookie. Then he closed his eyes to savor it. Nothing tasted like homemade.

"So, what are we going to do about this?" Rebecca stopped pacing to wait for his answer.

He couldn't be bothered. They weren't his grandmother's sugar cookies, but they were heaven.

When the first cookie was gone, Cole realized she was waiting for him to say something. "What?"

"I asked what we're going to do about Eric. Those kids. Out there." She pointed at the window in case he couldn't add all the clues. "We have to do something. Good people don't walk away when they can see someone needs help. What should we do tonight?"

"Nothing. You're too scared to say boo to them and I've got all I can handle keeping a roof over my head." He broke the second cookie in half and held a piece in each hand.

"Unacceptable." Rebecca pursed her lips. "Try again."

He thought about arguing. The firm set of her jaw indicated she was ready to go a round or two.

Cole sighed, set his cookie down and stood abruptly. If that didn't send her on her way, he'd be shocked. He held both arms out in a trick he'd learned to make himself seem bigger.

More dangerous.

The more he said with body language in prison, the fewer bruises he'd picked up.

She didn't retreat, but something about her posture shrank. Her hands were clenched in white-knuckled knots. Standing her ground was costing her.

"I'm not going to panic. Not again. No one who hums when he bites into a chocolate chip cookie is going to hurt me." She tapped her chest. "I make the best cookies in Holly Heights."

Cole pressed one hand to his chest and dropped down on the couch.

"Also, that's a dirty trick, using my fear against me." Rebecca's disappointed face wasn't quite as powerful as his Mimi's, but it was hard to ignore the guilty feeling he'd always gotten when his grandmother gave him the same sad eyes.

"And now we know it doesn't work," Cole muttered. "When did that happen?"

"Possibly it was the sight of your knobby knees." Rebecca tilted her head, a bright smile chasing away clouds of worry. "Now I know your weak spots." She blinked so innocently as she said it that he studied her face. She was teasing him? They were alone. She had no safety net.

He didn't smile but watched her until she got that nervous V in the middle of her forehead.

Her smile faded as she stepped closer to the door. When she had one hand on the doorframe, she stopped. "You could talk to them? Tell them they should be in school?"

Cole shook his head slowly. "Not going to happen. I made a promise. No more trouble. They are trouble." *She* was trouble.

Rebecca nodded slowly. "If I leave my phone here, will you call the police if things get out of hand when *I* go tell them they should be in school?" She snapped her fingers. "I could pay you in more cookies." Her enthusiastic smile told him she'd won plenty of cooperation previously with charm and baked goods.

For a split second, the idea that she was trusting him to have her back, even from *way* back, by being her phone call lifeline amused him. Her opinion of him had taken a small turn, at least. Then he realized she honestly thought baked goods could fix everything. How naive. And insulting.

"You've done your good deed, so your guilty conscience should be taken care of. Go home. Call their parents. Help the kids who want your help." Cole waved another cookie. "Write a cookbook or something, but learn the lesson that kid tried to teach you. Don't stick your nose in his business and you'll be okay."

Now get out. He didn't say it. He didn't have to.

He expected an argument. Instead, she pointed at the tiny photo his Mimi had framed and hung over the sink. "Is that the county fair?"

Cole frowned as he tried to follow the conversation.

"It looks like the building where they do all the craft and food judging." Rebecca bent to study the photo. "Someone should have brushed your hair."

"Someone did. The tousled hairstyle was in." That sounded like a criticism of his grandmother. She'd done her best to hold him down and make him presentable. It wasn't her fault he'd taken that as a challenge. "And yeah, that's my grandmother and me at the fair."

"Blue ribbon. For what?" Rebecca asked.

Cole rubbed his aching head. "What does it matter? Baking. She won a ribbon for baking sugar cookies, but she's dead, so you don't have to worry about losing your cookie queen title."

Even he was surprised at how angry he sounded. Instead of arguing or telling him to shove his head in the toilet, Rebecca turned and disappeared into the dark night.

If she gets hurt by three boys when you could have stopped it, you'll have nothing in this life left to redeem, idiot.

Cole lifted the curtains. The boys had disappeared.

He hurried over to the door to see Rebecca's taillights fading as she drove out of the trailer park.

Good. This was not his problem. Those kids would learn their hard lessons.

Cole slammed his door shut and locked it before he turned to see Rebecca's neatly folded apron on his grandmother's counter. "Probably has a frilly apron for every day of the week. She'll be fine."

Cole studied the tin of cookies and considered walking down to EW's to offer him a couple. The guy had been his lifeline so far. Without him, Cole wouldn't have stood a chance. That burned, irritated him because he'd been so certain he'd be better off by himself. There'd been no beer runs, but it

was a matter of time until EW let him down.
Still, that afternoon had been nice, normal,
a glimpse at what life could be like. Too bad
EW hadn't taken him fishing at seventeen.
How different his life might have been.

*What if you could do that for one of those
kids? What if that is all it takes to make a
difference?*

To drown out the little whisper that sounded
a lot like Rebecca's voice, Cole snatched up
another cookie. "There's absolutely nothing
wrong with my knees," he grumbled.

He was certain he'd be replaying her visit
long after her peace offering was gone.

CHAPTER SIX

On MONDAY, REBECCA stubbornly refused to acknowledge the arrival of the man who'd ruined her weekend. If Eric and his friends had still been under that basketball net when she'd left Friday night, she would have been angry enough to tell him exactly what she thought of his behavior and order him back to school.

Just because Cole Ferguson had told her not to do her job.

But Eric had disappeared and she'd seethed the entire drive through Holly Heights. When she'd gotten home, she'd realized her favorite apron was still on Cole's counter, so she'd eaten the remaining cookies in retaliation. The sickness that came afterward could have been from too much sugar or the recognition that she'd been following his advice without realizing it. Instead of investigating Eric and his absence, she'd breathed a silent sigh of relief.

Now she had to face the jerk who'd forced her to confront her own cowardice.

And none of this was his fault. The jerk.

"Come in and have a seat." Sarah waved vaguely toward the couch that Bub had claimed as his own. When Cole approached, Bub hopped up on the couch and barely waited for him to sit down before he collapsed in a furry, boneless heap across Cole's legs.

Animals were supposed to be such great judges of people. Rebecca tightened her lips. The fact that Bub was right *so far* was another reason to feel like the world's biggest failure.

"It's time to finalize the plans for the first annual adoption drive in the center of town. Getting approval to set up in the town square took every bit of leverage I have left. This has to be awesome." Sarah leaned back in her chair. "We'll stake out my lucky sidewalk spot to attract attention and focus on two things—adoptions and donations." She shrugged. "And if we can find anyone else to volunteer around here, I'll be ecstatic."

"'Many hands make light work,'" Rebecca said with a nod. The pious tone of the quote tasted funky in her mouth. How much holier-than-thou could she get? And nerdy. Jen's snort spoke volumes.

This was not the first time Rebecca wished her mouth came with a rewind button, but the heat flooding her cheeks was worse. Not only had she said something ridiculous, but she couldn't even pretend she didn't know she'd done it.

One quick glance at the couch showed that Cole was doing his best to memorize Bub's face. He wasn't paying a bit of attention to her.

The jerk.

The unexpected blessing took a second to appreciate.

That was long enough to see the look he darted her direction.

"With Brenda's help, the bake sale is going full speed ahead," Rebecca said, anxious to move away from her seconds-ago self. Bake sales were Rebecca's area of expertise. Brenda, Jen's mother, was an amazing baker. She'd seized this challenge with both hands. "That will help with the donations. Les has worked up some cards for the dogs and cats currently ready for adoption. We'll attach one to each dessert to give people a reminder of the sweet faces waiting for them."

Jen held up a hand. Rebecca slapped it in a victory high five, feeling a twinge of guilt for taking credit for what had been Les's inspiration.

"We're going to do another fashion show," Jen said. "Chloe insists. We've been working on costumes every weekend. We'll take some photos. There's a calendar waiting to be made and sold." The first fashion show at the shelter's open house had been a big hit, but Jen and her niece, Chloe, had thrown it together at the last minute. With weeks to plan, this show could be epic.

"I'll make sure that goes in the press release I'm sending out to the local papers and radio stations." Sarah made a note. "Cole's going to draw up a list of basic training for the dogs we'll be taking to the event. Cats..." She shrugged. "Cats will be cats. We'll have a large pen and crates for them. The dogs will be out on leashes, rotated in and out of kennels by volunteers." Sarah tapped her pen. "We have two weeks. Before that Saturday, the dogs need to walk calmly on leashes and it would be nice if they could sit on command."

"With enough volunteers and practice, we can make that happen." Cole cleared his throat as everyone turned to him. "*I* can make that happen?"

"You train the volunteers. We work *together* to make it happen," Sarah said. "We've got to have more help. Shelly, Les and I will be running adoptions. Brenda and Rebecca have the bake sale. Even if I rope in Stephanie, Daniel, Will, Chloe and the four Saturday volunteers to show the dogs, we're going to be scrambling."

"None of the juniors I reached out to wants to add volunteer hours. Not yet." Rebecca crossed her legs. "They'll change their tune in the spring when planning for college gets real."

Sarah scrubbed her hands down her face. "Should we hire help?" The question was loud in the center of the quiet room. No one wanted to spend money that should be going to helping the animals if they could come up with another idea.

"Make sure I'm on the list. I'll be there," Cole said matter-of-factly, as if it was a given.

"You'll have to take a day off during the week," Sarah said, and pulled out her calendar. She scheduled all the shifts at the shelter carefully to stretch resources as far as she could. "*After* we get the volunteers going on the basic obedience training." She bit her lip as she ran her finger down the calendar.

Her small frown almost convinced Rebecca to offer to cover more help out of her own pocket. No one could accuse Sarah of wasting the shelter's money. She worked around the clock, hours that were not reflected in her paycheck most weeks.

"Call me a volunteer that day. No problem," Cole said. He brushed a hand across his forehead when they all turned toward him. "It's no big deal. I want to."

"Okay, but let's keep searching for help," Sarah said, her shoulders drooping. Rebecca was reminded again of how often she had to make choices between imperfect options.

Cole nodded. "How many dogs?"

"All of them." Sarah shrugged. "I can't pick and choose, so we're going to take them all." Her lips firmed as if she expected an argument.

"And we can only do things the hardest way possible," Jen muttered.

"They all deserve a shot. At the open house, we weren't ready. We will be this time." Sarah pointed. "This time, we have Cole. A trainer."

Rebecca understood where Sarah was coming from, but she had her students to protect. At least one dog needed to stay at the shelter. "Major should stay here," Rebecca said softly. "He barely lets Shelly inside to clean his kennel. We have to let him out in the yard alone. He has behavior issues, Sarah. Picture all the little kids rushing around."

"He's better. Cole is making him better." Sarah straightened in her seat. "Tell them, Cole."

Cole tugged on the neck of his T-shirt. "He is doing better, but…"

Sarah raised an eyebrow.

"He might need more help than we can give. There are rescues specifically for German shepherds that might help." Cole rubbed a hand over his mouth. "But I'll keep working with him. We can decide closer to the day."

"Fine. And you're up for working with Jen and Rebecca today to show them how the volunteers can help us get the dogs ready?" Sarah asked.

Cole tapped the tiny clock on her desk. "For an hour or so. EW will be here on time today."

"But I'm out for this afternoon," Jen said as she stood and smoothed her ruffled skirt down. "Previous plans."

"Are you going to tell us what they are?" Rebecca said slowly.

"Interior designer's coming to review my

homework. Then he's going to start the plans on my house. I'll be glad to see some progress." Jen turned on one heel and pointed at Cole. "Landscaper, right?"

Cole blinked, obviously struggling to follow Jen's leaps, as well.

"You know how to do more than mow and trim," Jen said as she nodded.

"Yeah, I studied design, too. Outdoor architecture, how to plan beds for all seasons, things like that." Cole gave a quick glance at both Rebecca and Sarah.

Jen grunted. "Good. I might have a side job for you. We'll talk later." Then she sailed out of the office without saying goodbye.

Rebecca frowned at Jen's retreating back until she left the shelter. "What is going on with her?" Rebecca asked.

"She hasn't settled into this money thing yet. Working with an interior designer? Can you even imagine what that conversation must be like? I warned her he was the best, because she insisted on the *best*, but that he would not be easy to work with." Sarah rolled her eyes. "If she keeps using fewer words than normal, we're all going to have to learn sign language."

With nothing left to discuss, there was

only the dread of spending time with Cole. He didn't have a high opinion of her. Being together more often might not improve that situation. At least Sarah would be there.

"Should we get started?" Cole asked as he stood, his gaze fixed firmly on Sarah. Tight lips and the frown equaled grim determination. He wasn't excited about the prospect of teaching Rebecca anything, either.

That tightened the knot in her stomach. She'd done her best to make amends. Very few people had refused to let her off the hook when she'd done her best to apologize. She was nice to everyone. He should give her a second chance.

As Sarah stood, the phone rang. "You guys go ahead," she said, and waved both hands. "Paws for Love. This is Sarah."

Rebecca didn't have to hear the person on the other end say a thing. Sarah's immediate goofy grin was her uncontrollable response anytime Will Barnes was near.

"We should get started. She'll be here for a while." Rebecca marched down the hall to the room lined with kennels. "Which dogs should we start with?"

Cole pulled down two leashes. "Grab Princess. I've got Freddie. And you'll need a hand-ful…" His words trailed off as she knocked off the lid of the treat container with one hand. The loud clatter of the metal against the concrete floor was a good sound track for her jumbled emotions.

Cole didn't say anything, but his loud sigh spoke volumes. After her pockets were filled, Rebecca marched over to the kennel in the corner where Princess, a sheltie mix, pawed anxiously at the gate. "Hey, girl, want to go for a walk?" Instead of jumping or indicat-ing she was ready, Princess scurried to the back of the kennel and sat, her legs shaking. Rebecca glanced over her shoulder. "Now what?"

"You saw how I worked with Freddie to get him to come to me. Apply treats. This is part of it." Cole calmly held the end of the leash while Freddie ran in widening circles, baying his excitement. "We'll wait for you outside."

As soon as Cole and Freddie—and his loud excitement—were outside, Princess seemed to relax. Rebecca remembered how it felt to be cornered. A little space was all the dog needed.

"Boys. They're so much trouble, aren't

they, sweetie? Some of them are too loud. Others are way too quiet." Rebecca snapped the leash on Princess's collar. When the dog pressed harder against the wall of the kennel, Rebecca broke a treat in half and held it in her hand. It took a minute, but Princess eased forward to snatch it away. "Good girl, Princess." The dog darted anxious glances at Rebecca as she crunched. "Look, another treat, Princess." Slowly, Rebecca backed up and coaxed the dog out into the room. Instead of pulling at the end of the leash, Princess hung back, too timid to explore. The loud commotion of the other dogs seemed to be too much.

Given the choice between Freddie's enthusiasm and shy Princess, Rebecca would pick the beagle, but the fear in Princess's eyes was hard to ignore.

Rebecca slowly encouraged the dog toward the door, using her name and half the treats in her pocket, and as soon as they both stepped outside, both of them sighed with relief. Freddie was doing a perfect imitation of a dog with good manners. Cole's frown said he was already short on patience.

"To encourage her to walk with you, start with the leash in your left hand and a treat in the right. Let's walk, Freddie." Cole demonstrated with Freddie. The two of them headed off across the grass and made it look so easy.

"What do you think, Princess? Can we do that?" Rebecca smiled down at the dog, who was licking her lips nervously. When she held up the dog biscuit, Princess tilted her head and everything got serious. Rebecca did her best to mimic Cole's stance.

"Let's walk, Princess." The dog dragged behind Rebecca until she was forced to stop.

"Show her the treat. Lower your voice." Cole glanced down at Freddie. "Let's walk, Freddie." The two of them moved in sync in a small square.

"You know, it's not fair to judge us on less than ten minutes' work," Rebecca snapped.

"Who's judging?" Cole stepped back. "You're the one getting all worked up. I'm not anywhere near you, either."

Rebecca rolled her eyes and then bent down to scratch Princess behind both ears. "We can do this." She stood up, put two treats in her right hand, showed them to the dog and said, "Let's walk, Princess."

Lowering her voice was not quite as successful as she would have liked. Mainly, she sounded like she was fighting a cold, but Princess managed to strut alongside her, her nose half an inch from the treats at all times. "Good girl, Princess."

Pride and contentment tangled together in her stomach, making it impossible to control the grin. She and Princess were doing it. Not smoothly, but they were working together. Both of them were learning something new, like a team. It had been too long since she'd done that, picked up a new skill.

How much more powerful this must have been for Cole in prison. At the reminder that Cole was watching her, Rebecca immediately got so nervous she couldn't have spoken if the building was on fire. Princess ducked behind her leg to peer out at Cole and Freddie.

"Good. Give her a treat. She did it." Cole backed up. Freddie, in a fit of showmanship, did the same thing.

Rebecca paused. She'd never seen a dog go in reverse.

Cole waited for her to look at him. "Since I know you need your breathing space, Freddie and I are going to practice over there. Just keep doing the same routine. At a nice, easy pace."

Rebecca wanted to inform him she knew what she was doing, but there was no good reason to be so annoyed with him. He hadn't done a single thing to make her feel awkward.

She was bringing every bit of awkward to the situation herself.

"All right, Princess, let's see what we can do." Every time she gave Princess the command, the little dog perked up and did her best to follow orders. Eventually, they were able to walk from one end of the play yard to the other without the dog falling behind. "Good girl. One more time."

When she gave the "Let's walk" order again, Cole murmured from behind her, "Lower your shoulders. You look like you're prepared for a fight. Dogs understand those nerves." His large hands pressed down on her shoulders, the warm weight easing some of her tension and replacing it with a weird awareness.

Rebecca gasped for breath and did her best not to show it.

"Sorry. Didn't mean to scare you. Again." He stepped back. "We should let them off the leash to play. They've both done well."

"Want to run free, Princess?" Rebecca

asked as she knelt down to loosen the dog's leash. "Go for it. Don't let Freddie boss you around."

She and Cole watched the dogs investigate all the new smells in the play yard. Was it time to give in to peer pressure and adopt a dog? A cat might be easier, but it wasn't difficult to imagine coaxing Princess around the block. She wouldn't provide much security, but the little dog would be company. Since her friends were pairing off, finding a sidekick who'd never leave her had taken on some urgency.

Freddie was busy, running up and down the fence with his nose pressed to the ground. Every now and then, he'd woof. He was on the job. No one would sneak up on her if Freddie was in charge.

"I'm only following orders. Not trying to boss you around." Cole eased away from her to prop one foot on the fence. "It's a bad idea to ask me to work with anyone."

Rebecca exhaled loudly. "Nope. You're doing your job. We need you to do your job. I just…"

He raised his eyebrows but didn't answer.

Eventually, Rebecca mirrored his stance,

one foot on the fence post. "You made me so mad on Friday. I wanted to let you have it. Give you one of the perfect retorts that have been popping through my brain since I left your trailer." Why wouldn't they come when she needed them most? Delivering the best set-down three days later was more pathetic than righteous.

"Go ahead. Yell, even. If it will make you feel better." Cole's resigned voice would have made her smile if they were on better terms.

"No. But…" Rebecca kicked a clod of grass. Complaining about his attitude didn't seem appropriate. He was doing his job well and she'd invaded his space. Why was she so mad at him? "You were diplomatic about Major and his chances of adoption in Sarah's office."

"I don't want to disappoint her," Cole said, "but I understand your concern."

"It's a safety issue. I don't want everything the shelter is doing here to be derailed by bad press. If we can work with Major and get him ready, then…" Rebecca bit her lip. "Okay." She didn't believe it would ever work. Some dogs were beyond their help. "I could contact the rescue groups you mentioned."

Cole nodded. "Sure. Pass the problem on to someone else. Smart."

Rebecca had to replay the words in her head for a second before she could react. "It was *your* suggestion. Remember?" Now was the time for a biting answer, and she couldn't find one. Again.

"Yeah, I remember, but I'm also working with him, giving it my best shot before I throw in the towel." Cole walked away from her.

She was almost certain he was shaking his head as if he couldn't believe how out of touch she was. "Hey, wait."

Cole stopped but he didn't turn to face her.

"I'm the only reason we're here," Rebecca snapped as she jabbed a finger in the direction of the run-down building. "Giving all this money away. I'm the one who gave Sarah a shot. I believe in this shelter."

"But not me. Or Major—at least, not if it gets scary." He nodded. "Good for you. Don't get directly involved. Shows good, safe judgment."

Instead of marching off, he propped his hands on his hips and waited.

If she could gather enough air in her lungs,

she might have exploded, but she stood there with her mouth dangling open.

"You want to talk about people who cut their losses?" Rebecca poked him hard in the chest. "You're the one who's certain his problems are bigger than anyone else's."

"Yeah, for good reason." Cole stared hard at her finger until she stepped back.

The exhilaration that swept over her when she realized she'd stood her ground made Rebecca dizzy.

"I have real problems, not a guilty conscience that keeps me from sleeping soundly in my tower."

"Is this because I didn't jump up and down and say 'yes, hire the convict'? Is that why you're so angry? Still? I apologized. There were cookies."

Rebecca had no idea how to handle anger like this. Even her students hesitated to lash out when she did her best to be supportive.

"It was rude of me to drop in." This wasn't easy for her, especially when Cole said nothing. "Okay, I admit it. I was focused on how I felt more than doing the right thing. There. I'm apologizing again."

Cole studied the grass at his feet. "Yeah, fine. I get it."

"Do you? Because I have no idea what's happening here. Are we enemies?" Rebecca ran her hands through her hair. She'd never had an enemy before. She wasn't sure she'd even had a real critic. All she'd ever done was what people expected of her.

"No, we aren't. Just stay…away. I'm not your project." He waved a hand. "I don't need your charity, no matter how it looks to you, and I sure don't need a cause to keep me awake at night."

Confused, Rebecca straightened. "Charity? What are you talking about? I haven't given you anything but a peace offering. Never mind that. Are we really fighting again because I suggested you should do something to help me help those boys?"

"No, we aren't fighting, but I haven't joined the Rebecca Lincoln fan club. It'll be okay. You don't have to make another unexpected visit. I made a promise to stay out of trouble. Easiest way to do that? Keep my nose to myself instead of sticking it where it doesn't belong." Cole crouched down and ruffled Freddie's fur. The beagle had had enough of exploring and now was ready for his next treat. "I have trouble sleeping as it is. I don't need to waste time staring at the ceiling, wondering if anything you said had a bit of truth to it."

The small zing of pleasure that shot through Rebecca was illogical but impossible to ignore. Cole didn't like her, but he couldn't ignore her, either.

She dropped down on the bench in the shade and caught Princess as the dog jumped up next to her. "Maybe those kids aren't a practical use of my time, but they need me more than anything. You pointed out that I was letting my own comfort get in the way. That's unacceptable. I'm going to stop in to visit Eric this week. I'll talk with the truancy officer. If we can get him back in school, he could still graduate."

"And then what?" Cole asked. "If you get him to graduation, what's going to happen to that kid the next day? He's not going to college." He braced one hand on the post and studied the play yard.

"The community college has all kinds of technical programs. Maybe he'd like to study culinary science." Rebecca jerked at Cole's harsh laugh.

"Right. I bet Eric spends a lot of time dreaming of cooking." He shook his head. "You're the only person who does that."

"How do you know?" He hadn't been around her long enough to say that. One plate of cookies did not a habit make.

Of course, she had the habit. But he had no proof.

"Just judging from the grief Sarah and Jen give you." Cole shook his head. "That kid doesn't dream. That much I can tell you. Not of anything."

The sharp pain in her chest at his words caught her off guard. How could he say something like that? "Everyone has dreams, Cole."

"You sure about that?" He didn't glance at Rebecca but studied Freddie's face as if the answers to all of life's questions could be found there. Instead of trembling with fear because the big man held him, Freddie licked his hand and sighed happily.

"I *hope* everyone has dreams," Rebecca said softly. She couldn't imagine going through life without plans for the future. Life was hard.

The sweetness of dreams big and small mattered.

Maybe it was renovating a kitchen, doing a job she loved or even taking a trip to see one of her best friends during the summer break. Rebecca had dreamed big and accomplished some of those things.

"How do we make it possible for those kids to dream, Cole?" She scratched Princess and stared out over the immaculate play yards. "That's what I should be doing right now instead of…"

Cole shook his head. "You'd have to change their lives from day one."

"We can't help every kid, but we could help one. Or two. Right?"

"You're going to do what you want. Obviously." Cole stood and Freddie followed, ready for his next lesson and dog treat. "I'm going to make it through today. Then I'll worry about tomorrow. Those kids? They're a problem for…never. I can't imagine any day when I'll have the time, money or—" he waved his hand "—*energy* to dream for myself, much less a kid. I know too much about what Eric has waiting for him. He's got to learn to trust only himself and what *he* can do. Usually, that takes a hard lesson. A smart woman would never let herself in for that sort of pain."

This time Cole did meet her eyes. She wasn't sure what she expected. Anger, maybe. He seemed to have anger to spare.

His eyes were dark and impossible to read. "Work with Princess to teach her to come when she's called and sit on command. Do those three things—walk, sit and come— every day, but don't overwork her. Dogs have short attention spans and they need time to rest."

Rebecca licked her lips and frantically tried to find a topic to prolong the conversation. She didn't want this to be a world where anyone had to live without dreams and hope for a better future. He worked hard. Cole Ferguson deserved to believe in his own future. But he was done with the conversation.

"Let's walk, Freddie," he said. Instead of going back and forth in front of her in the shade, Cole headed for the sunshine. Unless she insisted on following, he was going to do the rest of his training away from her.

"Hey, Cole?" She waited for him to turn. When he did, there was no sign of irritation on his face. Instead, it was blank. "You and Freddie, you make a great team."

Cole couldn't see how Freddie's perfect posture mirrored his own, but it was one of those images Rebecca knew she'd never forget.

"This is my job. I can work with any dog." Cole ran a hand down Freddie's back. "He's the first of many."

Right. And the man could tell himself that forever, but Freddie was a dog that would stick with him. He and vocal Freddie were too perfectly matched for it to be any other way. Opposites really did attract.

"I'm going to take your advice. Sort of." She nodded. "I'm going to work on one kid at a time. Use small steps."

"My advice was to stay out of it, but whatever," Cole muttered.

"And if I have any ability to do it, time or money or whatever it takes, I want to teach Eric to dream." She sighed. "I want the same thing for you. Without the hope of something better, this life is too hard."

He didn't respond, but his retreat to the farthest corner of the yard spoke volumes. She figured if he'd told her what he really thought, she might never recover.

Did she have the right to meddle in his life? All she wanted to do was prove that…

"Oh, Princess," she said softly. "I have to prove that I'm right."

He deserved to dream. And even if she had to face her fears with Eric, he deserved to graduate. Whatever he did with the rest of his life would be up to him. But she was going to help him figure it out.

Had no one done that with Cole? How different his life could have been if someone had asked him what he wanted most and then helped him get it. She could be that person for Eric.

And Cole… Well, she wasn't sure where to start with Cole, but she wasn't giving up. Not yet.

CHAPTER SEVEN

MAKING IT THROUGH a "lesson" with blessed Rebecca Lincoln observing had been torture. While she was watching him, he'd stomped around like a circus bear trained to walk on his hind legs. He'd snapped like that bear, too. Telling her he didn't have any dreams made him sound like the biggest waste of life there was, and he hadn't realized his mistake until he noticed her big blue eyes locked on his face.

If he'd ever wanted to paint himself with a target, he'd discovered the most reliable way to do so.

Make a bleeding heart feel sorry for him.

He could have asked her to give him twenty dollars and she'd have emptied her purse out and apologized for not doing it sooner.

Golden curls. Blue eyes. She should smell like cotton candy or bubble gum. Something pink. Touching her had been a huge mistake.

"Rough day?" EW asked calmly as he

pulled out of the parking lot. "Door 'bout slammed off its hinges."

Cole tried counting as the doctor inside Travis had counseled him after his first ill-conceived attempt at arguing with a guard.

"Yeah." Admitting that was bad enough. He did not want to get into the why. "Busy. Boss's planning a big event in town weekend after next. Need volunteers. Want to spend a Saturday walking dogs?"

"Could do that." EW nodded and drove the rest of the way to the trailer park in silence.

Some of the irritation of facing Rebecca again faded. He'd hesitated to throw in EW's name when they were listing possible volunteers. Were they friends? How far did EW's charity extend?

Each day, his resolve to shut everyone out was tested by this…whatever it was he had with EW.

Cole was already dependent on him for holding on to the trailer, rescuing him from prison, daily rides home from work and saving his sanity.

The sight of two kids loitering under the basketball goal again reignited Cole's temper.

"She thinks I ought to do something to

help those kids. Help them *dream*." The word twisted his mouth and it was satisfying.

EW put the truck in Park in front of Cole's trailer and waited.

"Can you imagine? Like I'm some kind of mentor or something. A life coach. Those kids are nothing but trouble. I don't deal with trouble anymore." Cole grunted and waved a hand at the goal. Neither of the boys was paying them any attention. They had their heads together, talking.

Probably plotting some terrible plan.

"The short, beefy kid, Mike, his parents split up three years ago," EW said. "Daddy never came home from Afghanistan. Mama never recovered, but she works hard at the hospital. Drives a Honda." He lifted one finger off the steering wheel. "Black kid, Eric, lives with his older sister. Neither one of them is old enough to be on they own. Usually, they's a third one, got carroty-orange hair, just showed up. Don't have his story yet."

Satisfied with his contribution to the conversation, EW stretched his legs out.

Confusion made it a challenge to figure out EW's goal with the roll call, so Cole settled on, "I have chocolate chip cookies. Homemade. Want one?" Since he'd been rationing them like precious jewels, eating one a day, offering to share them was evidence of his growing maturity and kindheartedness and complete lack of self-preservation.

But he was only prepared to share a few. Whatever annoyances came with crusader Rebecca, the cookies were good.

EW pursed his lips and then opened the truck door. He raised a hand when the boys turned together to watch them.

Cole ignored them. He was going to continue to ignore them until he forgot about the anger in Rebecca's face after he told her to focus on kids with a future.

When they were inside, Cole studied the air conditioner. The electricity was on, but he hadn't taken a chance on the decrepit window unit yet. As long as it *might* work, he could anticipate the day when he turned it on as a special reward.

EW watched him for a second then held out his hand for the cookies. After he'd picked two, the biggest left in the tin, he said, "Dreams is important, young fella."

Cole rubbed his sweaty forehead, caught off guard that EW and Rebecca would be on the same side of the issue. Then he couldn't contain a harsh laugh. "You have got to be kidding me."

EW slowly shook his head and bit into the cookie. He chewed and said, "Good."

"How can you believe in dreaming, EW?" Cole opened the refrigerator door to enjoy the tiny splash of cool air. "You're going to breathe your last breath in this trailer park." And soon. How old was the guy anyway?

"Could be a dream come true," EW said. "Time was I thought I'd have no home at all. Held on to it, though. Wasn't easy." He chewed his cookie slowly.

Cole didn't want to ask questions. This was none of his business.

"Why are you still here, EW? You had a business." A life. A hope for more than this trailer park.

"Yeah, well…" EW shook his head. "Lost a wife. Things got real difficult after that. Didn't cope the best way, either. Took me a while to figure it all out again."

"That's what I mean." Cole pointed. "That *difficult* part. Once you've been there, how do you think dreams are possible?"

EW put the last bite of cookie in his mouth and chewed thoughtfully, savoring every bite as he brushed off his hands. "Not worth living without it, kid. Could be it's dreaming of a fried fish dinner and a cold beer, but that makes every hot day easier to get through. Sometimes a cookie shows up you didn't expect."

"Seems like it would be better to tell those kids to toughen up. Aim lower. Get jobs now and keep them so that they can run the AC now and then." That was what Cole should have done. If he'd gone out and gotten a job at eighteen, he could have helped Mimi with expenses. All he'd seen then was easy, fast money. He'd been too impatient to consider real answers. None of the consequences had factored in, because he'd never imagined they'd apply to him.

He knew better. Showing those kids what a ruined life looked like would be a better gift than encouraging them to dream, no matter what EW thought.

"Could be." EW tugged his earlobe. "When people ask for help, you've got two options. Give it or don't." When he looked at Cole, he didn't have to add how many times he'd decided to give it.

Every time Cole had asked, EW had helped. Why? Because he could.

Rebecca had asked for his help. Could he give it? Not in the way she'd intended.

He had all the tools he needed to *help* those kids prepare for real life in five minutes or less. Right that second, he could try scaring them straight and then forget about Rebecca and her ridiculous convictions.

"Fine." He braced one hand on the door and shoved it open.

"Take the cookies." EW motioned with his chin at the dwindling stack. "Might help 'em listen. Can't hurt."

Unable to argue with the man who'd saved him from Travis, Cole stomped over and grabbed the tin. He quickly moved the smallest ones to the top of the pile. As soon as he stepped down on the packed dirt of the road, the boys huddled under the goal turned to face him. Smart. Keeping an eye on the guy higher on the food chain might not save them, but at least they'd stand a fighting chance.

The beat-up car belonging to the third kid EW hadn't been able to name turned into the trailer park as Cole reached the road. Instead of passing him, the kid driving made a U-turn and headed for the highway.

He and EW exchanged a glance. *Good.*

EW's watching, too. Whatever that kid was up to, he didn't want an audience.

Instead of asking questions when he reached the boys under the basketball goal, Cole held out the cookies. "Here. Have a cookie." EW's grunt convinced him he might need to work on his approach. "I'm your new neighbor." He motioned with his chin toward the trailer.

"You never heard of stranger danger?" the biggest kid, Eric, asked. His mouth was a tight line, but if Cole had to guess, he was weighing his shot at outrunning Cole, not attacking.

"Now, Eric, it's a homemade cookie." EW's slow drawl caught the kid's attention. "Mebbe you can take a chance on it."

"From a convict?" The other kid had a nervous tic, a tapping hand that kept an erratic beat against the side of his leg. "No way." He darted two steps back.

"More for me." Eric took the cookies. Before he had a chance to take a bite, the kid snatched one out of his hand. Would they fight or laugh it off?

The whole short exchange reminded Cole of his old group. Ricky Martinez had been the meanest of the gang, but he'd preferred to hang back, watching and waiting for a weakness. Most of the time, they'd been tight, friends because they didn't have anyone else. Once or twice, he'd been pretty sure it was kill or be killed with Ricky, though. They'd had an epic fistfight right under this goal. With friends like that, he'd learned early on to watch his own back.

"You can go now." Eric took a bite of the cookie and waved his hand. "We've got business."

The heat of anger at the kid's dismissal shouldn't have surprised him. This was going as expected. There was no helping these kids. They already had their own, terrible plans. If he asked what they dreamed about, he'd be jumped in half a second. The law of the jungle didn't leave any opening for sentimental speech.

EW didn't move. Instead, he held up both hands. "Hit me."

Cole turned to see Eric and Mike exchange confused frowns.

"Throw me the ball," EW said slowly. Eric shook his head as he bent to snatch the basketball. He gave it three hard bounces and then tossed it to the old man.

"One game. Ten baskets. We win, you spend

some time volunteering at the animal shelter. You win, you can have the rest of the cookies." EW twirled the ball and watched Eric.

Cole knew his confused face matched Eric's. EW had to be eighty years old. While he was locked up, Cole had spent a lot of time scrabbling on a half court, so he could take on Eric and Mike by himself, but all three of them would be bruised and bleeding when it was over.

But now they were in it. He'd play to win, even if he had to go dirty.

Cole barely managed to snatch the ball out of midair before it bounced hard on his nose. EW closed his eyes as if he couldn't believe Cole's reflexes.

Mike snorted. "How about we *take* what we want? You need to go rest somewhere, old man."

EW pursed his lips.

Eric held up both hands. "I need community-service hours to make a judge happy. This shelter job count?"

Cole dribbled the ball as he considered that. "Don't see why not."

"Got nothing to lose, then." Eric bent low, both arms out to guard the basket. "Let's see what you got."

The cockiness of youth didn't surprise Cole. Man to man, he and Eric were about the same size. What Eric didn't know was that Cole had been honing his one-on-one skills for years. Before Mike made up his mind whether he was in or out, Cole dodged past Eric and dropped the ball in the goal. "One basket down."

EW's wheezy laughter caught them all by surprise. "Gonna be easier than I thought. Never expected Cole to move so fast."

"We split everything down the middle," Eric said as he pointed at Mike. "Win or lose." Mike nodded, they moved out to half court and for fifteen minutes, all Cole could focus on was keeping Eric away from the basket. After Mike and Eric scored three quick goals, he started to worry. Play got rougher, and the noise level doubled.

"Pretty good trash talk for a kid," Cole said with a grunt as he wiped blood off his lip. He was almost certain Eric's wild elbow had been an accident. "Making your teachers proud."

At least the kid was panting hard as he braced his hands on his knees. "Yeah. Top of my class in insults."

While he, Eric and Mike battled basket for basket, EW moved slowly along the perimeter. The guy might have made a basket, but Cole was afraid he'd knock him over with a pass.

"Last point," Cole said with a gasp. He had to make one more basket. Then he could go inside, take a shower to wash off the sweat, dirt and blood. It had been a long, long time since he'd felt this good.

Eric and Mike immediately rushed him, and he tossed the ball to EW. All three of them stumbled to a stop as EW launched the prettiest shot, the ball rising and falling in a high arc to drain the goal.

"Nothing but net." EW bent to pick up the tin he'd placed carefully outside the court area. "See you Saturday." He was whistling as he meandered slowly toward Cole's trailer.

"Guy's a ringer," Mike muttered.

Cole would have laughed, but he needed every bit of precious air. "Just smarter than the rest of us." When he could stand, Cole held out his hand. "Good game."

Mike shook it quickly and then collapsed in a heap against the goal.

"Rematch." Eric straightened with a groan. "Now that we know what he can do, we need a rematch."

Cole offered him his hand. "Sure thing."

When Eric shook his hand, he added, "Come by the shelter before Saturday. I know they can help with your community-service hours."

Eric dropped down beside Mike. "Maybe."

Cole decided that was the best he could hope for and limped toward his trailer. About halfway there, the nagging voice kicked in so he spun around. "But only if you're in school, Eric." He nodded. "We can help, but only if you're in school." Without waiting to see how that landed, Cole finished the unbelievably long trek to his place, winced as he climbed the stairs and ignored the smug expression on EW's face.

With two punches of buttons, stale but cold air trickled into the living room. Cole dropped down on the ragged carpet and closed his eyes. "You almost got me killed."

When the silence could no longer be ignored, he cracked one eyelid. EW was propped against the counter, a cookie in his hand. "What if we'd lost?" Cole asked.

"No way they could beat me." EW brushed off one shoulder.

Cole thought about arguing that he'd scored nine out of the ten times, but it didn't matter. "How'd you know?"

"I'm that good." EW brushed off his hands. "And so are you."

"You've never seen me play basketball," Cole said as he toed off his shoes. If basketball was going to be a regular thing, and it would be because all the worries of the day had disappeared, he needed better, cooler clothes.

"Yeah, I'm not talking about ball." EW's wheezy laugh surprised Cole again, but it was nice to hear. "Two choices, young fella. You either help or you don't."

Cole tried a disgusted sigh. Being out-flanked was something he'd better get used to.

"Thing I learned about saying no when someone asks for it is you gotta live with that for the rest of your life. You and I both know it ain't easy to ask for some kind of help." EW waited for Cole to acknowledge that, and it was impossible to pretend he didn't know what the old man was talking about. Every bit of help he'd gotten since he'd come home had been necessary but still pinched whatever pride he had left.

"I said no a lot back in the day." EW rubbed a hand over his white hair. "Too busy to be bothered. And I'm sorry for it." This time,

EW stared hard at the photo over Mimi's sink, the one of her and Cole together at the fair. Was he wondering what might have happened if he'd stepped in to try to change Cole's path? "Regret can kill a man or at least whatever he does to try to escape it. If he's lucky, he gets a chance to make it right. If he's not, his only choice is to swallow it, even if it eats him from inside."

The tense silence in the trailer was broken only by the wheezing window unit until EW tugged his earlobe and straightened.

"Now that you know how it feels when you do help, won't be so hard the next time," EW said and then made his escape.

EW was right. He'd made the effort. Sort of. And it had been as easy as a brawling basketball game that he'd repeat every day if the kid would give him a chance. That was how much better he felt.

The anger and irritation had evaporated, leaving something else behind. Cole stared up at the ceiling as he tried to find the right name. Peace maybe? It probably wouldn't last, but maybe he could do it again.

If the kid showed to help out at the shelter, Cole would lay out all the grim truths about being behind bars. The danger had been less about violence than he'd expected, but being contained twenty-four hours a day was never going to be anything other than a punishment.

He already lived with enough regret. Drinking away his days to forget one more was no way to live a life. Not for him or EW. So he'd try to warn Eric, and if he had a chance, he'd make sure EW understood how grateful Cole was that he'd saved his life this time around.

CHAPTER EIGHT

ON WEDNESDAY, REBECCA realized that she was going to have to apologize to Cole again at some point. After Sarah had called to tell her that Cole had found them two more volunteers, as long as they'd provide the community-service credit, she'd had no choice but to get Eric back to school. At first, she'd considered stalling. Technically, Sarah should have discussed adding volunteers with court-ordered community-service sentences with her board of directors.

But Sarah had pretty much seized the reins of Paws for Love and she'd mow down any dissenters if needed. Holly Heights' mayor had flat-out refused Rebecca's request to run the adoption event in town, but he'd folded like a wet newspaper under the force of a determined Sarah Hillman. It was a good thing they hadn't called the Paws for Love leadership position Supreme Ruler of the Universe. Sarah would have had every house in the world ruled by both a dog and a cat by the end of the first year.

Cole had done his part, something she'd been certain would never happen. Sarah had made all the calls necessary to get the shelter approved for court-ordered community-service hours through the local judges and for volunteer hours needed for work programs. Adding those hours to the ones covered by Rebecca's high school volunteer program would make it easier to expand the shelter. Something else they could thank Cole for.

If she didn't take the baton and move Eric further along the track to graduation, she'd be the biggest hypocrite in Texas.

So this was one time she'd have to get out of her office, get some dirt on her hands, to make a difference.

Take that, Cole.

Her phone rang as she parked in front of the Jordan trailer. In the light of day, the whole trailer park was different. These were homes. People cared about them. There were wind chimes hanging from the trailer next door. The Jordan trailer's small porch was covered in potted plants, most of them…green. She didn't know a thing about plants.

"Hello?" Rebecca checked the rearview

mirror to make sure her curls were in some sort of order as she answered the call. She did not check to see if Cole was home.

"Hey, Rebecca, I've had an emergency," Carl Montoya, the school's truancy officer, said quickly. She was lucky to understand that much. The crying baby in the background wanted to be heard. At six months old, Ruby Montoya was pretty good at making that happen. "Ruby is teething and Monica called for reinforcements. Can you reschedule?" Carl's voice was distracted and the screaming seemed to be growing louder.

"Sure thing, Carl. I'll let you know." As Rebecca ended the call, a young woman stepped out on the porch. Eric's sister was wearing the polo Dinah at the Shop-on-In had recently instituted as the uniform in order to give the place an updated feel. The fact that Backstreet Boys lunch boxes filled the display window because she'd gotten an excellent bargain on them didn't stop Dinah.

"Hi," Rebecca said as she slid out of the car. She clutched her briefcase in front of her and offered her hand. The girl's firm handshake indicated she was used to handling meetings like this on her own. "I'm Rebecca Lincoln, Eric's counselor."

"I figured. Debbie Jordan. Have a seat." She pointed at two chairs that were nearly hidden in the foliage. "It's too hot to talk inside."

"You have a nice porch here. Are you the green thumb? Every plant I buy has a short life expectancy." Rebecca settled carefully and noticed the tray of iced tea. "Oh, good. I was thinking as I drove up that I should have brought along a bottle of water. It's too hot for September." She picked up a glass and sipped sweet tea strong enough to knock her flats off. "Yum."

Debbie laughed as she sat down, her hands knotted firmly together. "Eric made it. I haven't managed to teach him that it shouldn't make your mouth tingle after you drink it. I keep working on it. And yes, these are all my babies. When it gets cold, I move them inside. It's like living in the rain forest without the fear of being eaten by a big snake." Her eyes darted to meet Rebecca's and they both grinned.

It was hard to imagine this petite girl trying to teach the boy who towered over her anything. Rebecca thought of how uneasy she still felt every time she turned the corner by the science classes at the school.

Not a girl, Rebecca. She's running a house all by herself. Debbie Jordan was nervous, but she wasn't afraid. She met Rebecca's stare without flinching. "Help me get him in school."

Caught off guard at this proactive opening, Rebecca took another sip of her tea. Some parents wanted to make every problem *her* problem. Eric's sister was asking for help. "Is Eric here? I'd like to talk to him." Rebecca licked her lips nervously. "We can reschedule if you'd like. Mr. Montoya had an emergency and couldn't make it."

Debbie snapped a few dead leaves off the nearest plant and stuck a finger in the dirt. "He's inside. If there's any way to do this today, I'd like to go ahead. Getting time off isn't that easy. I had to get someone to cover my shift, and we need the money." She bent to grab a watering can and poured a steady stream over the plant closest to her. Was this her way of handling stress?

"He thinks he could go to work instead of school." Debbie shook her head violently. "When I point out that he hasn't even done that yet, that he's going to be short on community-service hours to report and that standing around under the goal with the

creeps he calls friends is not in any way improving his life…" She stopped. "Well, you
can imagine we don't make it far down the
road back to his senior year."

"Have you talked about the community
service lately?" Rebecca asked as she stifled
the urge to ask what Eric had gotten in trouble for. It didn't matter.

"He did some early on, picking up trash,
but it's like he doesn't care. He's dead set on
enlisting," Debbie said. "He's the only family I've got. I want him here."

One careful sip of the iced tea gave Rebecca a second to consider the proper answer.
"It's a fine thing to want to serve your country. If Eric hopes that's his future, I can help
with that, too." The army recruiter would do
a back flip if she called to say she had a kid
who wanted to talk with him. Debbie straightened in her chair and Rebecca could see her
cooperative spirit draining rapidly. "But—"
Rebecca put her hand on Debbie's clenched
fist "—we still have a year. He needs a diploma. I should have talked to him sooner.
I'm sorry."

"Why didn't you?" Debbie crossed her legs
and gave one irritated kick of her foot. "Could
have saved me a whole lot of shouting."

That was the question that had been bothering Rebecca for days. She had no good answer. She could mumble things about budget cuts and too many students and Eric's lackluster grades and so many other excuses.

The truth was that she'd missed Eric. He'd fallen through the cracks of her system and she had to fix that fast. How many others was she missing while she sat in her office? "I'm going to do better for kids like Eric."

"The ones who aren't smart enough for college, you mean? No amount of volunteering is going to help me." Eric stepped out on the porch. "You can go."

Debbie popped out of her seat. "Watch your mouth." She brushed lint off his shirt and then gently touched a spot on his face. "I mean it."

He was a foot taller and outweighed his sister by at least forty pounds, but the kid wilted around the edges. Whatever cocky swagger he had evaporated instantly. "Okay, sis." He could have shouted, argued, stormed off or worse. Instead, he ducked his head. Eric might be nearly a man, but he loved his sister too much to disrespect her.

Were they all alone in the world? Rebecca quickly tilted her glass to hide her stinging eyes. Her strangled cough as the powerful tea hit the back of her throat made an excellent cover. Some of the tension on the small porch disappeared as she patted her chest and tried to catch her breath.

When Debbie backed up, Rebecca was impressed by the glare on her face. If it had been aimed her direction, Rebecca would already be in the car, reversing down the dirt road.

"Your counselor made a special trip out here. You will listen." *If you know what's good for you.* Debbie dropped down in her seat.

"Or what? You'll throw me out?" Eric snorted. "Nobody buys that."

"Or I will make you very, very sorry. I have blackmail, Eric. Don't make me pull out the pictures of you dressed for Halloween." Debbie's smile had a touch of evil. "Think your gang will be impressed with your lustrous wig?"

"I was *five*, a kid." Eric said each word loudly and clearly.

"*That* time." Debbie raised her eyebrows. "And you still are a *kid*."

Rebecca scooted forward. Was Debbie going to say more about these costumes? Why did she care? Hard to say, but Rebecca was riveted. Should she mention the drama program at the school?

When Eric glanced her way, there was murder in his eyes. Hoping that was aimed at his sister instead of her, Rebecca rubbed her forehead. "There's no need for that, right, Eric? You've got some time to figure out the future. For now, we'll get you back in school and knock out your community-service hours. That way, whatever happens next, you have a clean slate."

"Why?" Eric held both his arms out. "Why would you help me?"

"It's my job. This is what I love, helping kids." Rebecca smoothed her hair behind one ear. "And I'm usually pretty good at it, but I need to do better."

He shook his head. "I mean why would you help *me*?" He met her stare and then looked away. Rebecca glanced quickly at Debbie to see that his sister had no idea what Eric was talking about.

"I discovered you've missed school. That's all. Standard operating procedure is to work with the truancy officer to get you on track." And that was all she had to say about that. If the kid hadn't told his sister about the fight, then she wasn't going to get into it here. Things were going so well.

"Have you thought about it, what you want to do after you get your diploma?" Rebecca shifted her folder and bag around.

"Eat. Sleep." He rubbed his forehead. "Nothing else."

Debbie laid her hand on Rebecca's arm. "Cars. The kid lights up like a Christmas tree every year when we get the muscle car calendar in the mail. You know, the one the dealership mails out? Drool. I'm not kidding."

Rebecca couldn't tell whether Eric was blushing, but he fidgeted with the rough edge of the railing and rolled his eyes.

Almost like a kid who'd found the toy he wanted but was afraid to ask for it.

"Cars." Rebecca tapped her file. "The community college over in Baxter has a two-year program where you could get an associate's degree in automotive service technology or a technical certificate. The job placement's excellent, too. You might consider that in addition to the army." If only Bobby Hillman hadn't gone into self-destruct mode. She'd have had a real connection to a man with four different dealerships. "Tomorrow, let's talk about your grades and getting you back on track. You stop by my office. After your last class. That you attend." Rebecca pointed and waited for Eric to nod.

"Fine." Eric didn't move, but his attitude shifted. Instead of defensive, he seemed... younger. There was the faintest bit of hope on his face.

"And get him started on the volunteer hours," Debbie said as she shook her head. "Kid needs one hundred by January." Her side eye was as impressive as her mean glare.

"Well, I don't know if you know this," Rebecca said, and cleared her throat, "but I work with the animal shelter down the road. Paws for Love is the name." Why was she so nervous about this? Eric and Debbie needed her more than the shelter needed him. "Your neighbor Cole Ferguson works there."

"Yeah, I lost a bet." Eric rubbed the dark spot on his jaw. "And a pretty intense pickup game. I gotta do some volunteering to help out."

Debbie surged up to inspect the bruise on Eric's jaw. "Did someone hit you? Did that *criminal* hit you?"

Rebecca stood up and moved closer to the porch steps. Defending Cole from assault might be her next challenge.

"Accidental elbow. Mike's." Eric brushed Debbie's fingers away. "I'm fine, but Cole thought the shelter might have some hours for me."

Rebecca noticed the way he clutched his sister's hand and squeezed it. Debbie instantly relaxed. Whatever their story was, the two of them were tight.

"Come by after school. Talk to Shelly. She'll be waiting." Rebecca slowly walked down the steps. "The day after tomorrow. Tomorrow we're going to talk about your future."

Eric sighed loudly and jumped down to stand next to her. "Fine." With all this space and bright sunshine and the power of his sister nearby, Eric Jordan didn't scare her. That was a nice discovery. Here, he was one of her kids.

"If you could do anything, what would it be?" Rebecca couldn't let the idea of someone living life without a dream go. It couldn't be true.

"Buy a car." He braced both hands on the railing. "That's it."

Rebecca nodded. "You know, I understand that. When I was sixteen and riding the school bus, all I could imagine was that one day I'd have my own car and I wouldn't miss that noise one bit."

Eric shot a glance at Debbie. She snorted. "Yeah, I hear her." She waved a hand between them. "We've had this conversation a million times."

"Eric, walk me to my car?" Rebecca said as she offered her hand to Debbie. "I'm sorry you had to miss your shift. I imagine getting the hours from Dinah can't be easy. I think she sleeps behind the counter of the Shop-on-In."

"Yeah." Debbie nodded. "But her daughter's planning a monthlong tour of Europe. Dinah will have to have extra help so she's anxious to train someone now."

"Cece's taking her to Europe? Wow." Rebecca tried to imagine talking her own parents into a trip like that. The argument would be heard in outer space. When she'd won the lottery, she'd started sending her father links to nice houses on golf courses. At first, he'd played along.

Then she'd gotten a snippy phone call from her mother because no one needed houses like ones she was choosing for them. They were perfectly fine in their two-bedroom bungalow and any child of theirs would spend her money on something more important. There were children starving all over the globe, after all.

"She's going to be the babysitter, but a trip to Europe could convince me to sign up for nanny duty." Debbie's wistful voice convinced Rebecca that both Jordans knew how to dream. Whether they *believed* they could make their dreams come true was another question altogether.

"Other than working at the Shop-on-In, what kind of things would you like to do?" Rebecca asked. Debbie frowned at her. "I mean, if I hear something, I could pass it along. Dinah's great, but that's not going to get you to Europe."

"I should go buy a lottery ticket." Debbie raised an eyebrow.

So that conversation was done. No problem.

"All right. I'd like to talk with you next week, but I'll drop by the store. We can catch up on a break and you won't have to miss the hours." Debbie should be in college or starting her own career. Where were their parents? Did she have any help?

And what could Rebecca do about it anyway?

So many problems had no solution.

At her car, Eric shoved both hands in his back pockets. Rebecca pulled on her best expression of authority. "If we do this, you're going to come to school. Every day."

Rebecca waited with one hand on the car door, her nerves making it difficult to stand still.

Eric stepped back. "I will."

Rebecca had to clear her throat. "Good."

He shifted forward and then back. While she waited on him to decide whether or not he was going to speak, Rebecca tossed her bag on the seat. Finally, he said, "I'm sorry. I didn't know it was you."

Rebecca studied the greenery on the porch as she tried to figure out the right way to answer that. Softly, she said, "I accept your apology, but it shouldn't matter who it was. You know?"

He nodded once. "Won't happen again."

His face was serious, caught somewhere between a frightened kid and an angry man.

"You and Debbie, you seem tight." Rebecca dropped her briefcase beside her bag and watched his sister snapping off dead leaves. "Where are your parents?"

Eric rubbed a hand over his mouth. "Gone. Car accident. Three years ago."

Rebecca willed away the tears that sprang to her eyes. He said it so matter-of-factly.

"That's when the trouble started," he said as he ran a hand down his nape. "With me. Doing the wrong thing. Whatever I do, it goes wrong. She'd be better off if I left, but I can't do that, not without a job."

Rebecca inhaled slowly. "You better not let her hear you say that, young man." The urge to hug him was nearly overwhelming. Instead, she patted his shoulder. "Debbie and I both think there's a better choice than you quitting. Give me a chance to find it, okay?"

He lifted one shoulder as if he didn't care, but Rebecca studied his face carefully. This time she could see the color of embarrassment on his cheeks, so she offered him her hand. "We're going to make a powerful team, Eric Jordan. Wait and see."

Eric hesitated and then carefully wrapped his hand around hers. He didn't agree or disagree, but there was the gleam of interest in his eyes.

In her experience, that interest was all she needed to get a kid on track. This was going to work. He'd been beaten, but Eric wasn't lost yet.

After she slid into the driver's seat, Rebecca thought about stopping at Cole's place to gloat. He'd said she was wasting her time, but she could make this happen.

Driving past his trailer took strong will. All the windows were up. He had to be home. She could say she was stopping by to pick up her apron and then casually work into the conversation her coming victory.

Or she could go home and make some notes on what she needed to do next for Eric.

There would be plenty of time to gloat later.

CHAPTER NINE

COLE HAD BEEN able to avoid any uncomfortable run-ins with Rebecca all week long, mainly because she hadn't visited Paws for Love. He was still getting the crick in his neck because he hadn't quite learned to relax.

But today, it was like she was doing her best to make sure that he saw her. He and Eric had finished weeding out the front beds over the weekend, so he hadn't seen the kid except in flashes as he trailed behind Les, the veterinarian, for two days. That was fine.

Eric had been smiling the last time he trotted in to answer Les's call.

Shelly had taken over organizing all the volunteers training the dogs, so he was free to leave on time, but he'd wanted to at least make a start at planning what he'd plant in the beds in front of the shelter. Sarah would have to give him the go-ahead and come along to write a check for any supplies, but he needed to draw something up.

When he'd started landscaping design classes inside, he'd done it out of boredom. Then he'd discovered the satisfaction of physical work mixed with the chance to build something new. Imagining what the front of Paws for Love could look like with some time, money and hard work was…fun. That wasn't something he'd expected—to have fun while he worked. The idea made him uneasy, but he was still anxious to get started.

When Rebecca had parked, he'd suddenly become engrossed in the composition of the gravel filling the bed. Nothing was going to grow there but weeds and dust. If Sarah wanted anything green, they'd have to build beds with better soil. Coming to that conclusion took about two seconds. Waiting for Rebecca to go inside the shelter had seemed to take a lifetime. When she'd stepped inside, he'd inhaled an easy breath.

But now it was time to leave and he wanted to stop in to ask Sarah about the proposed visit to Travis to watch Prison Partners in action, but *she* was inside the office with Sarah. If he stuck his head in, he'd have to be polite. Since he still hadn't recovered from his unexpected effort with Eric, he wasn't ready to play nice.

Do the job.

Cole held his hand up to knock, hesitated, then tapped lightly on the office door. When Sarah called out, he stepped one foot over the threshold. "I'm leaving. I drew up an outline of what the flower beds out front should look like." He held the paper between his finger and thumb as if it were covered in germs. "Should I leave it here?"

Sarah waved him forward. "Let me see." She took the paper and the room was completely silent as she studied it. One quick glance at Rebecca convinced him that she was waiting on her chance to pounce.

"Is EW coming to pick you up today?" Rebecca asked as she crossed her legs. Today she looked like a spring garden in a flowing dress that had pink and yellow flowers on the skirt—a fairy-tale princess who'd landed in a Texas meadow. If she broke out into song, he wouldn't be surprised.

The poetic direction of his thoughts was unsettling.

At least he didn't say it aloud.

Cole nodded and did his best not to shuffle his feet. "Far as I know."

"Cole and EW have been doing some fishing," Sarah said. "Cole mentioned the possibility of a fish fry in the shelter's future. What do you say to that?"

Rebecca blinked slowly as she considered. "Sounds delicious. I'll make…something."

She smiled at him and he had no words. There was nothing to say to that, but everyone seemed to be waiting for his answer. "Cookies are always welcome."

The gritty tone made him sound like he'd slept on a bar stool. Something about her brought out the worst in him. The rumble of EW's truck was as welcome as the song of the ice-cream truck when he was ten. He was going to escape.

"Is this a drawing of a cat with a halo?" Sarah asked as she pointed to a spot in the center of one of the beds.

Cole had forgotten he'd included that. "Yeah, there's a place we pass on the way to the creek that has metal yard art." He waited for her to nod. "I thought a dog and a cat would add a touch of fun to the front of the shelter." He tugged the neck of his T-shirt and wished he'd left the drawing on her desk when she wasn't around. "Kids would love it."

He *thought* they would. What did he know about kids?

Sarah sighed. "Oh, Cole, you get me." She

tacked the drawing to a bulletin board on the wall next to her desk. "Don't know how we're going to convince the board of directors we need yard art, but I want it so desperately now that I'm going to get it." She clasped her hands together and tilted her head at Rebecca.

Rebecca's easy laugh made it impossible to worry about his cat drawing anymore.

"I'm still waiting on a confirmation for the next Prison Partners graduation ceremony," Sarah said. "I had no idea it was so complicated. I had to provide a list of names of people who'd be coming so the organizers could perform background checks. And I scanned the rules David sent over."

David Thomas ran the state program and oversaw every graduation. Cole had worked closely with David the last few months he was in. It would be nice to shake his hand as a free man.

"No open-toed shoes. Don't wear white. Nothing with a low neck." Sarah glanced at Rebecca. "We'll need to talk before we go. There are a lot of rules." Sarah yanked open the drawer beside her. "Got your check."

Cole took one giant step closer and reached for the check. "See you Monday."

He nodded at Sarah, avoided Rebecca and

took more giant steps until he was in the lobby. He almost took a deep breath of relief but he realized Rebecca was on his heels. Cole managed to get the door open without pawing at it like a circus bear but stumbled as he tried to keep it open for her. Smooth. He was so smooth.

Rebecca wrapped her hand around his forearm. "Are you okay? You should sit down." Her tiny frown reminded him of all the times his concerned Mimi had placed her hand on his forehead to test his temperature. "You spend too much time out in the sun. Sit. I'll get you some water."

He was close enough to see EW's face through the windshield. No way was he going to delay his escape, even if it was nice to have someone fussing over him. He didn't need the attention.

"Just clumsy. That's all." Cole opened the door. "You want to talk to EW?"

She didn't protest, but the worry was still there. *Get in the truck before you break your neck, idiot.*

"No, but I wanted to catch you before you left today." She didn't let go of his arm as a smile bloomed slowly on her lips. "I was so right. About Eric. Admit it."

Cole glanced down at where she'd tangled her fingers through his. At some point, whatever fear she might have had disappeared. Probably about the same time she did her victory dance in the end zone.

"I blame EW for that." Cole fought the urge to grin back at her. The wicked pleasure in her eyes was hard to resist.

"Oh, I owe him my thanks, then," she said, her eyes alight. The little dance she did made her skirt twist around her knees, and she squeezed his hand. "Unless you want it. Thank you. That kid is glowing this week. You don't want to get involved. I can understand that. But don't you ever forget what you've done for one kid." She tapped her chin. "I'll have to remind you."

When she teased him like this, he might as well be any normal guy. That was seductive.

She tugged on his hand but didn't let go. "Now I need to tell EW thank you."

When they reached the truck, Cole let her hand slip away and ignored the regret that hit.

"Afternoon, Miss Rebecca." EW propped his hand on the steering wheel. "Hot enough for you?"

Since he wasn't the focus of her attention, it was nice to watch her smile at EW.

"You bet. I sure don't want it to get any hotter." She fluffed the curls on her neck. "Seems September ought to be nicer than this."

"Won't be long now." EW's voice didn't betray any curiosity or impatience. Whatever life had handed the man and whatever patience he'd started with, at this age, nothing ruffled his feathers.

"Eric told me about the epic basketball game," Rebecca said as she leaned against EW's window. "Seems I have you to thank for our best volunteer."

"Well, now, I do enjoy a good game, so that's my pleasure," EW said with a courtly dip of his head. "Far as I know, Cole did the rest."

Rebecca lunged through the window to wrap her arms awkwardly around EW's neck. "Very reluctantly, if that's true, so you must be a good influence on them both."

EW chuckled and patted her arm. "Tell your daddy he better be taking good care of that Caddy down there at the beach."

Cole studied EW's face, but it was too hard to tell if he was blushing. Had to be. If she'd wrapped her arms around him that way, the heat would have swamped his face immediately. Which was so stupid.

She was enthusiastic. And beautiful. But mostly, she was grateful and determined.

Eric was lucky to have her pushing behind him, and Cole was relieved she had a new project to work on.

"Oh, I will tell him, Mr. EW." Rebecca patted the truck door as she stepped back. "Thank you."

Eric and Les walked out of the shelter. Through the windshield, Cole could see Les grip Eric's hand in a hearty shake.

"We taking the kid home, too?" Cole asked.

"Nope. Fishing." EW grunted with satisfaction at Cole's shaking head. "Gonna need the help if we're doing up a fish fry."

As Cole slid out of the truck to let Eric climb into the middle, Les propped his arms on EW's door. "Kid's a natural. Whoever directed him this way did us a favor."

Neither he nor EW answered and Eric rubbed his forehead in response.

Rebecca stuck her head in the cab. "A natural? Assisting with medical procedures?" The gleam in her eyes was focused as she switched from Les to Eric, and Cole could already see the wheels turning. "What do you have to say to that, Eric?"

The kid's shrug might as well have a bashful grin. That was all boys that age knew to do with that pleased and horrible feeling of flattery and happiness. Cole could vaguely recall the sensation.

"I haven't done much." Eric pulled hard at his dirty T-shirt.

"You know Major? Dog loves this one." Les pointed excitedly. "And he was so patient with Snowball. She ate too much after we found her in that abandoned lot. Threw up all over him. Kid calmly sponged off and went back to scratching her ears and telling her she was a good girl. That's something you can't always find."

Silence filled the cab of the truck, but Rebecca was nearly vibrating with her pleasure. If the kid thought he wanted to be a veterinarian, he was out-of-control dreaming, but she could already see it in her head.

"Puke happens," Eric mumbled.

"Yes, it does," Les said firmly. "Good doctors don't let that stop them. Neither did you." The older man raised his eyebrows. "I'm just saying…"

He stepped away and raised his hand to wave. Rebecca did, too.

EW backed away from the shelter. Cole watched Rebecca through the windshield. When she mouthed, "Thank you," he felt it like a shot to the gut. He hadn't done anything. There was no need for thanks. He wasn't getting involved.

At the highway, EW cut a glance at him out of the corner of his eye. "You two cozying up?"

Cole snorted. "Nope. Never."

EW's "mmm-hmm" made the corners of Cole's mouth curl.

"Different to see you and little Rebecca Lincoln on the same side." EW passed the trailer park. Eric pretended he wasn't there.

"Little?" Cole asked. She wasn't. She had a year or two on him and he was ancient these days. Naive? Yes, but a fully grown woman capable of making trouble wherever she went.

"Remember her swaying to the music in my shop while her daddy waited for his oil change. Seemed like an angel then, never cried or whined like other kids. And I swear the waiting room was neater after she left than when her and her daddy walked in."

"So she's always been perfect." That didn't

surprise him, but some of the weird warmth he'd felt at the connection between them disappeared. He was as far from perfect as he could get and still be free. If she was a warm sunny day, he was black clouds and a cold front. How long could the two of them move in the same space without causing a storm?

"Naw, just been told she should act perfect. Kids is kids on the inside." EW stretched. "Hope this one can bait his own hook."

"I can, but I ain't no kid," Eric said as he straightened in his seat. "Don't make the mistake of thinking I am."

EW snorted. "Mad enough for a grown man, too."

"Maybe I am," Eric mumbled.

"What you got to be mad about, young fella?" EW asked.

"Life," Eric mumbled.

"Wise man once said 'puke happens,' and this wisdom you can't argue with," EW answered. "Might as well brush it off and get on with living, you know?"

Cole could feel Eric's building eruption, and it was too much for him. "Puke happens. It's not the worst motto I ever heard." He couldn't contain his laughter at the way

Eric grinned and ducked his head. "Tattoo that somewhere so you won't forget it."

"You wait and see. You follow Miss Rebecca's advice. Everything's gonna work out." EW glanced over at Cole.

"Which one of us are you talking to?" Cole asked.

EW smiled and hummed a happy tune.

Eric met Cole's stare and they both shook their heads.

"The guy's never wrong," Cole muttered, and ducked his head to let the hot breeze ruffle his hair. If he'd had to guess how this week would go down, none of the last hour would have been involved. Holding Rebecca's hand. A pretty girl's teasing. Laughing. It was nice to know that life could send a good surprise now and then.

CHAPTER TEN

REBECCA DID HER best not to stare out the window as she stacked up the new T-shirts she'd ordered for everyone who'd be working the first adoption drive in the town square, but it was nearly impossible. The weather had turned to fall in a snap, and all her volunteers were feeling the relief of cooler temperatures and the excitement of the upcoming event. Outside, Cole was running a doggy boot camp, drilling Shelly and the volunteers on their commands with each new group of dogs that made it out in the play yard. And he was a benevolent drill instructor.

That was the part that was so surprising. She'd expected him to snap and frown and send her sensitive teenage girls into meltdowns. Instead, he corrected gently. From her spot in the window, she couldn't hear what he had to say to the kids holding the leashes, but more than once, she'd seen an eager nod and a grateful smile on a face after he'd walked away.

And the dogs loved him.

"Good thing those tails don't sprain easily. We'd have an epidemic out there." Les braced a shoulder against the wall. "Guy's good with volunteers and animals." He whistled. "Would not have guessed that the first day I met him. He didn't have much to say."

Rebeca shifted the neat stacks she'd made and pulled out a large. As she offered it to Les, she said, "I know Sarah and Shelly are glad to have him around."

"Hard to imagine him doing something so reckless as robbing a gas station," Les said.

Rebecca glanced at Les and then at her neat piles as she tried to decide whether she agreed with him or not. She'd seen anger and impatience on Cole's face.

But she'd also witnessed his incredible patience. And stacking both on opposite sides of the scale, the outcome was heavily in patience's favor.

Did that mean she trusted him? Rebecca considered the group in the play yard again.

She must believe he was in control of all that power because she trusted him to speak to her kids without monitoring every word.

Shelly was out there, but that would never have been enough to keep Rebecca away.

She wanted to trust him.

When had she changed her mind about him?

Rebecca paced as she considered that change of heart. Eric. It had to be connected to the way Cole had reached out to Eric. What man at the end of his rope would make time for a kid because an irritating poodle like her was nipping at his heels? A good man.

She believed Cole had a good heart. That made all the difference.

As the training session ended, so did the silence. The door opened and the group of chattering teens and excited dogs ended all conversation. As soon as each volunteer returned his or her dog to the kennel, Rebecca handed over a shirt.

"Everyone's got the outline for Saturday's event, right?" Rebecca waited for every head to nod and watched Cole try to sidle around the edge of the room. "Cole, I have your shirt." He froze in the doorway and then slowly turned back. She picked up a shirt and held it tightly. "Volunteers, make sure you sign your sheets for the week. We want everyone to get the credit for the work."

Shelly clapped. "Follow me, team!"

After Shelly and her workers filed out, Rebecca waved the shirt. Cole held out his hand.

"I should have done this earlier," she said. "I've been trying to catch you all afternoon."

He crossed his arms over his chest. "Well, you have me."

"Try this one. It's the largest size we ordered, but if it doesn't fit, I'll have another one made for you. You won't have it for tomorrow, but it will make a great uniform and it will be nice to have when we go to the prison. We'll look extra professional." *And I'm babbling.* The discomfort of talking about his shirt was ridiculous. She'd have said the same thing to any other volunteer, but something about their previous conflict made her sorry to call out his size. At some point, the fight-or-flight response had tempered, but she couldn't help reacting strongly to his presence. Now when she caught sight of him unexpectedly, she might still have trouble catching her breath, but she wouldn't call her reaction fear.

Cole took the shirt and tapped it against his hand.

"There you both are," Shelly exclaimed as she buzzed into the room. "I'm so glad you haven't left yet." She squeezed Cole's arm. "I'm afraid we have another job for you."

"I'll be happy to do it," Cole said easily. He didn't ask what it was or explain that he'd already worked three extra hours that day in order to check up on the teenage volunteers. Again, Rebecca was reminded how lucky they were that Sarah had overridden her concerns and hired the man. "Whatever I can do to help out."

"Les and I were going to load up the van with Rebecca's things for the bake sale tonight once he picks up the cakes at Brenda's house. Then, in the morning, we could unload all the baking in the square before you and Eric need to start loading the dogs." Shelly bit her lip. "But Les had an emergency call. His daughter's horse isn't well. As soon as he finishes at Brenda's, he'll drop the van off here. I could load it all by myself but…" She clasped both hands under her chin. If Cole had been wavering at all, Rebecca didn't see how he could possibly ignore the plea in Shelly's eyes.

"Go with Les. He might need help. I'll take care of getting Rebecca's stuff." Cole's hand hovered near Shelly's arm, but he abandoned the pat. He didn't touch anyone if he could help it. Rebecca had never realized she was paying such close attention to his movements.

What did that mean?

And what did it say about her that she could still remember the feeling of his warm hands easing the tension in her shoulders? Sure, that had been about the dogs.

Hadn't it?

"It's a lot to do on your own. You'll need to put gas in the van. Rebecca will help you load her cookies at her house, of course." Rebecca was prepared to nod, but Shelly never glanced her way. Her agreement was a given. "I'll grab the gas card. You'll need to go to the big flashy station. You know, the one down the road?"

Whatever else she said was lost as Shelly charged down the hall.

Because she was still watching him so closely, it was easy to see the minute Cole's amused acceptance faded into something else, something darker. She wasn't sure what had caused the grim line of his lips or why she wanted to understand it so badly, but it was impossible not to offer him a way out.

"I can do this if you'd rather not, Cole," Rebecca said quietly. "I've already made so many cookies the entire town of Holly

Heights will gain five pounds." Her teasing smile faded when he didn't respond. "Let me do it." She wasn't afraid to drive the van. She'd never done it, but the streets of Holly Heights were no challenge.

His eyes snapped up to lock on her face. "Afraid I'll steal the van? Or I'll try to make some fast money again? I mean, gas stations are kind of my thing." He strangled the rolled-up T-shirt. "My job. I'll do it."

Rebecca held up both hands. "Okay, Mr. Sensitive. No one was making any accusations. Take it down about three notches." She rested her fingers lightly on his forearm and both of them froze. Rebecca snatched her hand back. "Sorry. Don't touch. It's one of the cardinal rules for educators."

He grunted what might have been a laugh on another planet. "I'm only surprised you didn't faint from the shock. Me, angry. You, in danger. Right?"

"I'm never going to live that down, am I?" Rebecca muttered. She clenched her teeth in a fake smile and said calmly, "Listen. I understand you don't want to deal with the gas station. That's all. I didn't mean to imply anything else. I was trying to help."

"Yeah. You're always trying to help. I get

that. I'm okay. You can find another project."
There was no anger or bitterness in his tone,
but the slump of his shoulders convinced her
that there were a dozen other emotions bubbling inside him.

Not that he'd share any of them with her.

"EW could come along." This time, her
hand hovered above Cole's shoulder.

"Yeah." Cole shook his head like a man
chasing away bothersome thoughts. "Sorry
I snapped."

Their eyes connected and breathing became a real struggle. Stripped of anger and
mocking defenses, his warm brown eyes were
beautiful. This close, she could see the little boy grinning from that photograph with
his grandmother waving a bright blue ribbon. The urge to wrap her arms around that
little boy and this man who needed someone
to… She wasn't exactly sure what *he* needed.

"Prepare yourself. I'm coming in," Rebecca muttered, and then carefully wrapped
her arms around his chest.

For half a second, she thought he'd push her
away. Instead of slipping his arms around her
in the universally accepted "return a hug" response, he held them out at his sides, so stiff
she might as well have been hugging a fence

post. Just before she stepped away, he gingerly ran a hand down her back. Every new inch he touched came alive, and the electricity that flowed from his hands to hers was surprising. She would have looked at him to gauge whether that touch was enough to rattle him, but he muttered, "Lemons" and settled his hands on her shoulders.

Rebecca stepped back. "And lemons to you, too." If that was a newfangled way of cursing enemies, she could get on board quickly.

Cole rubbed his nose. "Of course you smell like lemons." Then he turned on his heel and fled the room as if she might run after him, trailing her lemony scent all the way.

Rebecca straightened the small stack of remaining T-shirts as she considered his reaction.

Trying to make sense of his disgust at citrus scents was a lot easier than figuring out how she could stand so close to Cole Ferguson, close enough that she could have pressed her ear to his chest to hear his heartbeat, and feel so comfortable. If Cole was on her side, nothing would ever be able to frighten her again.

Not that it mattered. Cole Ferguson would

be keeping his distance if his reaction was anything to go by.

And she was out of time to replay the conversation in her head. She had to get home.

After a quick update with Sarah on the status of the volunteers and the bake sale schedule, Rebecca hurried through Holly Heights. She hadn't had a chance to ask when Cole would stop by. Or to give him her address. Or to do anything except freak him out with a hug.

She'd already finished twenty dozen cookies that she and Brenda would divide and price early in the morning. Thirty had been her goal, so she pulled out her mixing bowls and pans. If she had the time, she could finish the last ten dozen and send them on with Cole. If not, she could take care of packing them in the morning. Every cookie she made was a contribution to the dogs and cats at Paws for Love.

And to her friend Sarah's success.

And to Cole's, not that he'd thank her for it.

"But which ones to make?" Her chocolate chip cookies were the most popular, but she was out of the chips. "Sugar cookies. I have everything I need for those." But she didn't have a sugar cookie recipe committed to memory. Her mother's old standby cook-book, recognizable only because it was held together by rubber bands, was the answer.

Rebecca opened the pantry and studied her shelves of cookbooks. The thing about loving to bake and everyone in town knowing was that she tended to collect new cookbooks for every holiday, birthday and end-of-school gift exchange.

Given that she'd started her own collection before she could drive, Rebecca had more cookbooks than Texas had cowboy boots.

The line of tattered collections from blue ribbon winners at the state fair over the years caught her eye and the picture of Cole and his grandmother immediately flickered through her mind. Could she find that recipe? Would he thank her or hate her if she managed to track it down?

"You probably can't even find the recipe." There were so many books to choose from, but each one had the year stamped on the edge. Her best guess had Cole at eleven or twelve in the photo. With a hasty calculation, she pulled down the year she would have been twelve. The listing at the front had zero sugar cookie recipes.

"Forward or back?" Rebecca pulled the

previous year off the shelf and tried not to puzzle over why she was wasting time on this. Her mother's favorite cookbook was easy to find, mainly because it sat front and center for easy access. The sugar-cookie recipe inside was tried and true.

It took five more books for her to find the sugar-cookie recipe. She refused to think about Cole's age. He was *younger* than she was. "Rachel. His grandmother's name was Rachel." And all she knew about Rachel was that she'd lived in the same trailer, cleaned houses and loved her grandson. "And she could make a mean sugar cookie." That was enough.

Rebecca pulled out the ingredients and poured herself into preparing the batter and loading up the cookie sheets. She was congratulating herself on choosing double ovens for maximum baking impact when the doorbell rang.

In an instant, the calm satisfaction that always overcame her in the middle of a baking spree evaporated. Cole had arrived. No one else could be on the other side of that door, mainly because almost everyone in Holly Heights would open the door and come inside. That was the kind of house her mother had had, and Rebecca had never seen any reason to change that.

But Cole would not be certain of his reception.

And she was not going to be overly weird about this. She pulled out a clean cookie sheet to check her reflection. No dusting of powdered sugar on her nose. All of her hair was still there, but she couldn't tell where it was, thanks to the distortion of the metal sheet. None of that mattered anyway. She still smelled like lemons.

With a fine layer of vanilla on top. Maybe he'd like that better.

"Doesn't matter what he likes," Rebecca muttered as she brushed her hands down the red gingham apron that had replaced her favorite floral one. She made tight fists in the fabric, reminded herself he was just a guy and yanked the door open.

CHAPTER ELEVEN

NO MATTER HOW hard he'd lectured himself on the way over, Cole still couldn't do anything but stand on her front step, speechless. The only break in the constant mental pep talk had come at the gas station. As it happened, he'd been too distracted by her hug to panic as he'd turned into the same parking lot he'd tried to rob a million years ago.

Pumping gas had taken some trial and error to figure out the prepaid card and the buttons, but he'd managed without calling too much attention to himself. For the first ten seconds, he'd been certain the owner of the gas station would come out and threaten to call the police, but this wasn't the old Gulf station. Whoever had built the modern neon multipurpose rest stop was comfortable in a city like Austin or Houston and had zero worry about the ex-convict pumping gas for a van filled with cakes.

Then he'd leaned against the van and puzzled over why she'd hugged him in the first place and what he'd do about it at this point.

Pity. Had to be. A gesture of encouragement for her pet project, the pitiful soul who didn't have a dream. That was the only explanation thirty dollars' worth of gasoline had provided. Once he'd decided that, he went from confused to irritated. The short drive into this old, established neighborhood close to Holly Heights Elementary hadn't changed his mood. When he was a kid riding the bus, this place had seemed television-sitcom perfect.

When she opened the door, he tipped his chin up and waited. He wasn't going to be her project.

"Hey, I wasn't sure when to expect you. I have one last batch in the oven, but we can load the rest if you like." Rebecca smoothed her hands over her apron, a white-and-red-plaid number that reminded him he'd managed to throw the one she'd left at his house on the front seat.

She wanted to pretend they were friends or something. This wasn't the mansion he'd buy if he hit the lottery but they still lived in very different worlds. Cole silently held out both hands.

Rebecca didn't answer, but her expression was crystal clear. *Is that the way it's going to be? Fine.*

She stepped back and pointed at the tubs lining one wall of her small but top-of-the-line kitchen. The sparkle off all the stainless steel was nearly blinding.

Relieved to find that the cookie load was manageable, Cole picked up the two tubs easily and ignored her disgruntled sniff. Walking got easier when he left her behind in the kitchen. He slid the tubs into the only remaining space in the back of the van. Whatever else she had would be riding shotgun. That was an intense amount of baked goods produced by two women. He wasn't sure whether to be impressed or afraid, but the shelter would gain a nice sum from the sale. What must it be like to have talent like that? Cole shook his head as he grabbed the apron from the front seat.

His grandmother would have been mightily impressed with Rebecca Lincoln.

Instead of ringing again, Cole opened the front door to her small, comfortable house and stepped inside. Rebecca was muttering to herself when he paused inside the doorway to the immaculate kitchen. The only signs that she'd been working so hard were the finished cookies and the tower of cookbooks stacked haphazardly in the corner near the oven. The ding of the oven timer snapped her out of her rant. If he had to guess, that was to his benefit.

"Get your head together," Rebecca muttered as she pulled open the top oven and nearly grabbed the pan with her bare hand. Cole realized he'd been poised to launch into action, one hand held out and the word *Stop* trembling on his lips. Instead, she placed one hand over her heart and carefully slipped the other in a dog-shaped oven mitt. Of course.

He should announce his presence. The pleasure he was getting from watching her work, completely unaware that he was there, was dangerous.

"Smells good in here," Cole said, his voice rough and too loud in the silence. She didn't jump. She wasn't quite as unaware of him as he'd imagined.

He liked that.

Rebecca slid the cookie sheets on the island countertop and slipped off the oven mitt. "These need to cool."

Cole nodded and shoved both hands in his pockets, afraid to step closer and com-

pletely out of his element. "Nice place here."
It was. Everything about this room screamed
high-end. It was too bad he couldn't come up
with a logical reason to explore the rest of the
house. Seeing the differences in the way they
lived should make it that much easier to get
the tempting scent of lemons out of his head.

"It's a kitchen. You like kitchens, don't
you? That's where food comes from." Rebecca picked up a spatula and carefully loosened one of the cookies, concentrating hard
enough that he wondered if she was avoiding
looking his direction.

"Is that where food comes from?" The urge
to make her look at him put a teasing tone of
wonder in his voice. He wasn't sure where
that came from, either. Flirting was not an
option. "I had no idea. Mine doesn't do this.
It mainly makes sandwiches."

Their eyes met as Rebecca held out the
spatula. She wasn't happy, but some of the
tension around her eyes had disappeared.

"Yeah, that has a lot to do with the person
in charge," Rebecca said as she watched him
gingerly take the cookie.

"Sure, but the expensive equipment can't
hurt." Cole motioned with an airy wave. "You
were slumming in my kitchen, weren't you?"

He pointed with his chin. "Your apron. Poor thing thought it had been abandoned."

Her clearly fake smile made him want to push harder.

"Good thing I rescued it, brought it over to the nice side of town." Cole waved vaguely at the kitchen. "Don't see places like this much in Holly Heights, I bet. Surely not in the trailer park."

Rebecca tipped her chin down. "I grew up here. I know what fits in Holly Heights."

Some of it, maybe.

He should go. Spending time on this side, with her, would bring nothing good.

"You know, I've done a lot for this town, and not only since I won the lottery," Rebecca said. Her lips were curved in the kind of smile a shark might wear when it scented fresh chum. She was half a second from letting him have it. "If I want to spend something on myself, why should I feel guilty? I don't, by the way." She slapped a towel down on the clean counter and rubbed. Hard. "You should have seen it before. The stove was green. The refrigerator was…not stainless steel. I had no island. You think I could have made thirty dozen cookies for the shelter in the old kitchen?" She took a deep breath. "It would have been a lot harder."

Her lips were a tight line as she pinched sugar and scattered it over the tops of the cooling cookies.

She had a point. In her place, both Holly Heights and a new kitchen in his old home would have come very low on his list of things to spend money on. Cole cleared his throat and then took a bite of the cookie in his hand. That one bite took him back in time. Way back. "This...this cookie is almost perfect, almost exactly the kind of cookie my Mimi used to make."

He made the universal good cookie noise as he watched Rebecca fidget at the counter. She opened her mouth a couple of times and thought better of whatever she was going to say. Was she still hung up on the appliances?

"Can I have another? I was afraid I'd never find a cookie like this again. It reminds me of her. Mimi."

And it did. Funny how something so simple could call up all the times she'd celebrated large and small occasions with him in that tiny kitchen. The ache in his chest was a surprise. He would have held an imaginary hat in both hands and tried a meek, begging stance, but she slid a plate with four cookies on it across the island like a saloon barkeep. Then she reached over, grabbed a book and plopped it down in front of him.

"Rachel Baxter" jumped off the page. This was his grandmother's recipe.

"It should taste exactly the same," Rebecca said as she rested her elbows on the counter, "because I followed the recipe to a tee."

This close, he could see a fine sprinkling of white powder down the side of her nose. The urge to wipe it away was strong.

"Yeah, but she left off the secret ingredient," Cole said, and wondered when his voice had gotten so rough. "She never would have allowed that to escape the family." He crammed one cookie in his mouth to chase away the emotion that bubbled in the center of his chest. Crying over a cookie would be so ridiculous. There was no way it was going to happen.

Then he noticed the way Rebecca ducked her head. She was fussily arranging the cooled cookies in the remaining tub. She'd done this, gone to this trouble, for him. "Brown sugar. That's the secret." Cole cleared his throat and waited for her to turn and argue with him. They did much better when they were at odds instead of…whatever uneasy dance this was. He didn't know what to call it. He should be happy she'd stopped dodging him or retreating, but coming toward him was taking him off guard.

"You sprinkle it with the other sugar. Over the top." Cole bent to try to catch her eye. "I'm not sure you'd even notice it was there, but Mimi loved brown sugar. Put it in everything."

Why had she made these? Because she was determined to improve him? He fiddled with the dachshund oven mitt she'd discarded along with the hot pan. "Was this a gift from Sarah?"

She pursed her lips and nodded. "How'd you guess?"

"She's dog-crazy. I'm not sure it occurs to her that not everyone in her life is the same." Cole pointed at the remaining cookies. "These are great. I don't know how you managed to find it but…" He couldn't even figure out how he wanted to end that sentence. *Thank you? Don't do it again? I'm an emotional wreck and can't handle it when people do nice things for me so save us both some awkwardness and go back to watch-*

ing me like a wild animal that's wandered in through an open door?

"Brown sugar, hmm." Rebecca shook her head. "I would have had to do some guessing to discover that." She plopped both hands down on the folded apron he'd dropped on the counter. "Thanks for returning this."

"I sure didn't need it." Cole bit into a sugar cookie, braced this time for the nostalgia and the sweet memory of opening his lunch bag to find one packed carefully in plastic wrap. They hadn't had much, but whatever she could do to show him she cared, his grandmother had done happily.

What an idiot he'd been to throw away any of the time he might have had with her.

The hard lump in his throat should have made him mad, but he was too tired and too ragged at this point.

"This reminds me of a lot. Happy times. Thank you." Cole pointed at the stack of books. "Looks like you had to do some searching. You shouldn't have." That wasn't what he meant, but it sounded much better than "Why would you spend time on that for me?"

"I know. It's embarrassing how many cookbooks I own. I should go through them and pare my collection down to what I use. That space could go for actual food then." She held out both arms. "But I love them. My mother started my collection for me when I was still too short to reach the countertop. The hardest part was putting together how old you were in the photo and what year you were born. After that, it was easy." She wrinkled her nose. "Younger than me. That hurts a little."

Cole grunted. "If it counts, I feel like I should be retiring any second." He rolled his shoulders. "Although, every day I might be getting younger."

Their eyes met and she nodded. "Good. I'm glad."

"If you decide to get rid of them, you could donate them to the shelter for a yard sale. Then you'd be doing something good with the things you love." Cole ran a finger over the smooth edge of the countertop. He should get up. He'd done everything he had to do. Loaded the van: check. Dropped off the apron: check. Avoided any conversation about why she'd hugged him: check, check, check. He had an early day tomorrow. They both did. He'd be doing them a favor if he got up. Now.

"Good idea. Make sure you pass it along to Sarah and don't be a bit surprised if your task at next year's adoption event is running a rummage sale." Rebecca's voice was shaky. Was she afraid again? He should go.

Why didn't he want to get up? Suddenly, leaving felt like saying goodbye to home. And that was insane. His home had never once been this nice.

"You know, I could show you how to make those cookies," Rebecca said slowly. He wondered if she'd expected those words to come out of her mouth. "I'm convinced sweet treats make life worth living. You could put on the apron. Fifteen minutes and some secret ingredient later, and you'd never have to wait to have that memory. You could make it for yourself."

Tempting. It was like she could see all the way into the tightest corner of his heart and understand what he regretted most wasn't the time he'd spent in jail, but what he'd lost in time at home. Who would he have been with someone like her in his life at sixteen? Someone who believed he deserved not only to have a dream but to pursue it?

She was dangerous.

"Some other time." He tapped the apron. "I'm not sure this is my color."

"Too frilly? An insult to your manliness?"

Rebecca raised an eyebrow. "This one's much nicer than the canvas one you wear at work."

"The one at work is a tool belt...with pockets. For tools." He opened the apron and draped it over his chest. "This one's got daisies on it." He met her stare, the laughter in her eyes filling that strange bubble in the middle of his chest again. "I'm more of a daffodil man."

She frowned. "Unexpected floral knowledge. You're all kinds of contradictions."

"That could be true, but I had some training in landscape planning...inside." Cole crossed his arms over his chest, almost satisfied to remind her that he wasn't her typical visitor. "Remember?"

"Right." Rebecca licked her lips. "Well, the offer stands. If you'd like to add baking skills to your résumé, let me know."

This was a terrible idea, getting comfortable talking with her like this. The two of them might as well live on different planets.

"What caused the change of heart?" Cole asked. "Why aren't you pale and trembling right now? We're all alone." He carefully watched her face. He wasn't sure what he expected, but he honestly wanted to understand how she could go from panic attack to hug attack.

She stacked the remaining tins and he was pretty sure she was going to pretend not to hear his question. Then she sighed. "Honestly, I'm not usually an idiot, Cole. I know I can say that and you have no reason to believe it, but this thing between you and me, the fear, it has no real reason. Even Eric... When I had a chance to talk to him, I could see he's a kid. A big, strong kid who made a mistake."

"Right, but a smart woman would be on the lookout for the next mistake." Cole bent forward. "That *mistake* could be life or death for you." He hated to consider that. He was in control of his anger. Eric was, too. Most of the time anyway. Who knew how many other kids with hair-trigger tempers roamed the halls with her? And she honestly believed the best of every single one of them. It was a miracle she was still in one piece.

"I'm not going to live my life expecting people to make mistakes. I refuse." She tilted her head to the side. "And I'm not going to live with my own mistakes any longer, either. I should have helped Eric long before his senior year. Most of my good works have boiled down to writing checks. Maybe that doesn't make me a hypocrite, but it does taste bad in my mouth now. My brother is living his life helping other people. Sarah has changed her whole world in order to make the difference she wants. I can't even drive into a trailer park without hyperventilating. That's sad. I'm not going to live with that mistake anymore. I'm not going to preach helping others while I'm too scared to physically *act*."

Whatever he'd expected her to say, none of that would have been included. "You're too good to be true. You get that, right?" But it wasn't exactly that, because he still liked her. He shouldn't like her if everything she'd said was true.

"It's easy to believe that if all you know is—" Rebecca ruffled her curls "—what the town says about me or what I'd say about myself most days. The real me is about frivolous kitchens and the easy way out."

Cole wasn't sure if his eyes bugged out or not, but the whistling in his ears could be steam escaping or the breeze caused by whipping his head around. He did know his jaw dropped open. "That's the real *everyone*. You expect to be better than human?"

"I could have lived with the old kitchen.

I did for a long time. There's not so much different between yours and my old kitchen. Families used them. There was love there." She ran a hand down the stainless steel refrigerator. "But I'd mourn losing this lovely."

The hard laugh couldn't be contained. "I thought you were crazy to insist everyone have a dream, but now I know there's something not right in your head. Again, I say lower your expectations. For yourself at least because…" He shook his head. He wasn't sure whether he should call her a martyr or try to reason with her. Either way, he wasn't the man for the job.

"I better go." His head was already aching from trying to follow her train of thought. More talking would not help. He slid his hands under the tins and turned to leave, but he paused at the door. "You feel guilty for winning the lottery?"

He honestly couldn't wrap his head around it. She put her money down, played the same odds everyone else did. What was there to feel guilty about?

"I had a good life, Cole. My parents love me. My brother is annoyingly good at everything, but how can anyone complain about that? I have a job I love. What did I do to deserve this?"

Cole set the cookies down and rubbed his hand over his head. "So I was a bad baby, I guess. That's what made my father leave and my mother leave and…" He met her stare. "Is that what you mean? We only get what we deserve? Sure, jail I deserved. I did something stupid. But…the rest of it?"

"Of course not." Rebecca rounded the counter and put a hand in the center of his chest, right over the hand pressed against his heart. "It's not the same."

"Sure it is. Good things happen. Bad things happen. Some are the result of a choice, but for the most part it's all just…the way it is." Cole rolled his eyes. "Don't worry about the good things. In my experience, something bad's headed your way to cancel that right out."

Rebecca tugged at his hand and then laughed. "Thank you for those cheerful words."

Cole laughed, too, the sound unfamiliar, but the tight knot in his chest loosened. "I'm just saying, I've been on a pretty solid roll lately. I'm not feeling one bit of guilt, either."

"Yeah, okay," Rebecca said as she rolled her eyes. "Because your life is over and you're only marking the days."

Cole tried to loosen his hand, but Rebecca held on. "I'll stop worrying about wasting this money on the kitchen if you'll think of one thing you'd like to have. We won't call it a dream. We'll call it a goal."

Rebecca Lincoln, lit by the overhead glow and gleaming surfaces of her beautiful, comfortable kitchen, was a vision. Her ruffled apron and the smell of cookies in the air was a ridiculous amount of home, sweet home. In that second, it wasn't difficult to imagine one thing he'd like to have.

A kiss.

Thinking the words changed the atmosphere between them. His focus on her lips might have been clue enough for Rebecca. Her grin faded, but she wasn't afraid of him. If he pulled her close, she'd kiss him. He wasn't sure how he knew it, but the instinct was there, no matter how long it had been since he'd stood in the same spot with a beautiful woman.

"You gonna write me a check to cover it?" He wanted to make her mad, to back her up. Instead, she wagged her head as if she was sad about his pitiful attempt.

"You don't have to tell me what it is, whatever you're thinking of, right now." Rebecca's husky voice broke the tension between them.

"Why did you do it? Why go to all the trouble to hunt down the recipe and make those cookies for me?" He had to know the answer. Until he heard it, it would be impossible to breathe properly.

"I wanted to do something nice for you. Because I like you. You're a good man doing a hard thing and I wanted you to have something sweet." She shrugged. "No sneaky motive or plan to pull any strings. That's it. You deserve good things, Cole."

Confused, Cole studied her eyes. She meant every single word. A good man?

In a crazy, breathless rush, Cole wrapped his hand around her wrist and leaned in to press his lips against hers. It was so fast, it might not even qualify as a kiss. But…when he stepped back, her eyelids were heavy and his head was filled with the scent of lemons.

And more than anything, he wanted to do it again.

What a huge mistake.

Afraid he'd be unable to control the impulse if he hung around much longer, Cole picked up the tins of cookies and made a straight shot for the door. Even without the lemon scent, he'd know she was right behind him. He had the feeling that for the rest of his time on this earth, he'd know if Rebecca Lincoln was close by.

CHAPTER TWELVE

It had been a while since Rebecca had such a close call with a kiss, and she'd never felt as awkward as she did about running a bake sale in the middle of Holly Heights. That brief brush of his lips had been on her mind all night, but she still wasn't sure what to do about it. On Saturday morning, she'd arrived bright and early, just as Cole and Eric had unloaded the last stack of cakes. Before she could figure out what she wanted to say to pretend that everything was cool cool cool, Cole had held up two fingers in some weird wave and disappeared with the van.

"We should have coordinated better," Brenda muttered as she glanced up. The stack of cakes was impressive unless they wanted to be able to see over them to talk to people. "A town this size does not need this much sugar. We'll be having episodes—people hopped up on baked goods. It'll draw national attention."

"Well, if we can sell them all, we'll know

exactly how powerful we are," Rebecca answered. "Thank you for working so hard to help out. I know Sarah appreciates it."

"Certainly didn't do it all for Sarah. That girl made Jen and Will miserable in high school. They might have called a truce, but mothers have long memories. She seems to be making my boy happy now, but I'm keeping my eye on her." Brenda offered her the cashbox. "Jen said she'd help with the baking, so I was happy to do it. Since it takes serious arm twisting to get that girl in the kitchen, I didn't want to miss my chance."

Rebecca tried to imagine how smoothly that must have gone. "Is your house still standing?"

Brenda snorted. "Barely. And if she doesn't stop yammering at me about selling it and moving into the castle she's building, I'm going to change all the locks and forget how to answer the door when she visits."

"She wants to take care of you." Rebecca studied her tubs and tins of cookies. "Think we ought to break this up? Make some smaller sets?"

Brenda pulled out a box of plastic bags. "You bet."

They worked quickly and were ready for

business right on time. The Paws for Love van rolled to a stop at the corner of the town square. All the volunteers had been working on building small pens and the kennels for the cats, but they converged on the van. Of course, Cole towered over the teenagers and other workers, so it was easy to track his movements.

And then she could hear the bay of an excited beagle.

"Sounds like Freddie's here," she murmured. How well would Cole handle anyone interested in adopting Freddie? It would be hard to see the little dog go. Some dogs came in and left before the staff all got attached. Freddie, because of his story and his personality, would be missed, and not just by Cole.

After a minute she realized Brenda was watching her closely, her lips twitching. "What?"

"Oh, I'm interested to see which dog has you wrapped around his or her paw." Brenda smiled brightly. "Or is it the man? Who is he?"

Rebecca laughed breathily in an attempt to pretend that Brenda was being absolutely ridiculous. "No way. I was wondering if I needed to go over and help. That's all." She stacked more plastic bags in front of her. "That's Cole. He works at the shelter."

"Works at the shelter" didn't even begin to cover everything he did, but if she raved over his training skills, his work ethic, how patient he was with her students, Brenda might suspect Rebecca was spending too much time thinking about Cole. That suspicion would spread like juicy gossip always did, until her friends were all demanding details.

"You guys ready?" Sarah barely looked up from her clipboard. "We've got about ten minutes." She turned to study the dogs lined up with their volunteers and then spun around. Her eyes doubled in size. "Oh, my bakery, there is a lot of sugar on that table."

"Some of it's gluten free." Brenda held up a finger. "Those should be marked. Dinah will be interested. I can sell her two of my chocolate pound cakes. She won't even believe I figured out how to make them so tasty." She hustled away to track down her permanent marker.

"Everything under control?" Rebecca asked casually. She wasn't sure why she expected Sarah to be able to read her confusion over Cole and the kiss on her face, but it seemed important to act like nothing was wrong.

"Yes. Jen has the volunteers prepared for the fashion show. Stephanie's working with the kids who'll be walking the dogs through the crowd. The bake sale is—" Sarah motioned helplessly "—running amok, but you and Brenda will make a killing." She sighed happily. "For our first event, this is going to be awesome."

Rebecca focused on Sarah's face so that she wouldn't slip up, give any of her confusion or wonder about the brief kiss away. "Last night, Cole had the best idea. For next year." She cupped her mouth with both hands. "Rummage sale. We can take donations, run the town's biggest yard sale right here on the court square."

Sarah's eyes brightened. "That guy. We could totally do that. I wonder if I could get Dinah to donate one or two of her storage units rent free. We could accept donations all year long and store them. That way we could price them as we go. Some things could even be sold online to collectors." Sarah tapped her pen to her lips. "Do I want to know how he came up with this idea?"

Rebecca frowned. "What do you mean?"

"Guy's got, like, three shirts. I can't imagine he was planning to donate any of his stuff." Sarah glanced over her shoulder. "Oh, man, there's my old frenemy Cece. I was hoping to keep our interactions to near misses all day long. Better for my ego and indigestion."

Rebecca checked behind her. "She's caught, talking with the mayor. He doesn't seem too pleased."

"That's his permanent expression. Changing it would require surgery." Sarah tilted her head and blinked her eyes, the perfect picture of patient waiting.

"What?" Rebecca asked as she busily restacked perfectly stacked baked goods.

"You. Cole. Did you kiss and make up?"

The word *kiss* sent a shot of panic straight down Rebecca's spine. Did it show? Of course not. There was nothing to show.

"I'd love it if you guys started working together instead of leaving the room anytime the other one shows up. It's exhausting when I have to track you both down." Sarah raised her eyebrows.

"We were talking about my cookbooks and I mentioned I needed to get rid of some." But not the one with his grandmother's recipe, of course. If that story made the rounds to Stephanie and Jen, she'd never hear the end of it.

Sarah didn't seem convinced, but before she could ask another question, Les jumped onto the tiny gazebo that sometimes served as a stage. "Welcome, folks! Our fashion show will start in one hour. In the meantime, we'd like to introduce you to Paws for Love's volunteers and stars, the cats and dogs. We'll be moving through the crowd. If you see a pet you'd like to meet, stop us. And when you're ready to adopt, Sarah—" Les scanned the crowd, one hand over his eyes for shade in the bright sunshine, until he saw Sarah's wave "—will be happy to help. And we have enough baked goods to feed the entire state of Texas so be sure you hit the bake sale table."

The high school band started playing. Before Rebecca could ask if Stephanie had pulled in a favor to get the band director to agree, Cece Grant was on them.

"Well, ladies, you've managed to pull together something…sweet for your first event." She gave Sarah air kisses. "I do hope you'll remember your agreement to scoop after your dogs. Can't have a mess in the middle of town."

Sarah narrowed her eyes. "No, we couldn't have that. I still remember the letters to the editor from last year's Christmas parade. Let's see…who was in charge of that?" She pretended to think.

"Thanks so much for stopping by, Cece," Rebecca said. "Do you see any baked goods you must have?" There was no need to guess who'd been in charge of the Christmas parade. Cece was in charge. Since Sarah and the Hillman money had dropped out of service, leaving a large hole in the civic duties and budget, Cece had filled the gap. As the wife of the town's best, busiest lawyer, Cece enjoyed having money and the power that came with it. Ever since high school, she and Sarah had been locked in the battle for supremacy. Since Bobby Hillman had run away with all his money, Cece had capitalized on her chance to take Sarah's spot, the one she'd abused so much in high school, at the top of the pyramid.

"Oh, dear, no. I could never *buy* anything here. You must have an iron will or an impressive metabolism," Cece murmured as she studied the table. "If I'd made that many cookies, I'd have gained at least five pounds. I'm afraid my pants are getting tighter the longer I stand here." She smoothed her hand over her hip and her expensive slacks, the diamond on her finger winking in the sunlight.

Sarah's snort was impressive. Cece didn't even look her direction. "Of course, I'd have to ask Maria to do the actual cooking for me. I burn ice." She trilled a laugh and braced her hand on Sarah's shoulder. "We're hopeless, aren't we?"

Sarah didn't laugh. The corner of her mouth might have been lifting in a snarl. "In the kitchen, maybe."

"Right, right. You have this new career." Cece shook her head. "So impressive the way you've gone from the top to the bottom to…" She shrugged. "Here. It seems we're meant to run into each other on this sidewalk."

Since there was nothing to add to that, Sarah said, "I should be going. Make the rounds. Scoop the poop." She bared her teeth, but it was no smile.

Cece nodded. Rebecca watched Sarah walk away with dread. She'd never learned to trade thinly veiled insults like Sarah did with such skill. Cece could skin her alive. Rebecca turned to call for backup, but Brenda was busy selling baked goods.

"Darling, you and I, we're friends, aren't

we?" Cece said, a faint line appearing between her brows.

Uncertain of what the safest answer might
be, Rebecca shrugged awkwardly. They were
acquaintances, but she didn't want to make
Cece Grant an enemy, either.

"I'm amazed at how you've taken up with
the black sheep of Holly Heights." Cece shook
her head slowly.

Annoyed at her tone, Rebecca searched the
crowd milling in the square. Cole was easy
to find. If he hadn't towered above all the
kids milling around with dogs on leashes, the
black cloud over his head would have been
a beacon. He stood with Freddie's leash
clutched in one hand while he glowered over
the proceedings. Maybe he was only concentrating, but the complete lack of people in his
general vicinity suggested there was a frost
in the air around him. Poor Freddie wouldn't
stand a chance of meeting new friends as long
as Cole held his leash.

Was that the plan?

Cece's quiet laugh drew her attention to the
more immediate problem.

"What can I sell you, Cece? Every dollar
goes to support the animals." Rebecca had no

intention of defending Cole. There was nothing to defend.

Cece glanced over at Brenda, who was doing a stellar job and drawing kids in. The parents were forced to follow and nearly every visit converted to a sale. When it was clear no one was paying any attention to them, Cece murmured, "When I said black sheep, I meant Sarah, darling, but I suppose she *was* the black sheep of Holly Heights. Now she's been dethroned by the new criminal in town. Poor girl. She's had a difficult year, falling from the top of society to the bottom and now she can't even hold on to that place of distinction." Cece sighed. "She's always been the perfect adversary, someone I could go after without feeling the slightest twinge of guilt. But you... that's not who you are. You're all sweetness and goodness and kindness. Right?" Cece blinked.

Rebecca wasn't sure whether to agree, because that was who she'd tried to be, or toss one of Brenda's three-pound pound cakes in her face. If any more condescension had dripped off Cece's tongue, she'd have to dry a puddle.

In the awkward silence, Cece said, "Just a bit of warning, then. Sarah's friendship you might recover from. You're doing a good deed, after all." She glanced at Cole, who hadn't changed his position a fraction of an inch. "But consorting with a criminal? I don't know that you can recover from that."

"We work together, that's all. He's an asset to the shelter, something I can't say about everyone I know who'd like to call herself my friend," Rebecca said slowly. "But I do appreciate your concern. Now, how many of these cookies would you like?"

Cece sniffed. "I'll make a donation. I can't have this in my house." She turned and sauntered down the sidewalk, her sights clearly set on Sarah. At some point, Sarah would give her the killing set-down and Cece would retreat. Rebecca had watched it more than once and had done her best to analyze how it worked. She'd never master it.

"Hey, do you have change for a twenty?" Brenda asked and popped the crisp bill in her hands. Rebecca opened the cashbox and offered her the change. Then she turned to the patient family next in line. "Do I have any chocolate chip cookie fans?"

The crowd was steady until the fashion show. Every time Rebecca could look up, she checked the adoption table. Sarah, Les and Shelly weren't swamped, but the steady stream of people and pets was heartening. Every animal that found a home saved two— that lucky cat or dog and the one still stuck out on the street. By the time the fashion show was over, her cookies had been decimated and even Brenda's wall of cakes had dwindled to manageable levels.

"I never would have thought we'd sell all this when we started this morning," Brenda said as she braced her hands at the small of her back. She waited tables a few days a week at Sue Lynn's, but standing in one place was hard. Rebecca mimicked her stance and nearly groaned aloud at the stretch of tired muscles. From their spot, they couldn't see the fashion show, but laughter bubbled up every now and then, confirming that the town was enjoying Jen's work.

"That granddaughter of mine built an Elvis costume you would not believe." Brenda was bouncing as she straightened the wads of bills she'd shoved in an apron pocket during a crush of buyers. "I'm not sure what kind of career that is, making dog costumes, but Chloe is inspired."

"The theater, costume design or even something like set design or merchandising.

If she has an eye for color and the imagination to build things, there are all kinds of things she might want to do." Rebecca was doing her best not to watch Cole, who stood at the edge of the crowd, faithful Freddie in a nice sit next to his feet.

What if Freddie wasn't adopted today? He'd return to the shelter and Cole wouldn't lose one of his few friends.

But Freddie would miss out on a big opportunity. Cole, if he was thinking about it correctly, wouldn't want that. He'd want Freddie to have a home.

"Can you handle the table for a bit?" Rebecca said. "I'll send some help over, okay?" Without waiting for Brenda's response, she stepped out from behind the table, crossed the street and managed to sneak up on Cole. He didn't even glance her direction when she stopped next to him.

"Nice apron you got yourself there," she said by way of witty repartee. She gave the edge a tug. "No flowers at all. I'm surprised." She thought he might ignore her completely, because his focus didn't waver from the fashion show.

Then he looked down. "Holds my stuff. It's a tool belt, not an apron. No flowers needed."

Then he bent and scratched Freddie's ears.

"How come Fred missed out on the run-way?" Rebecca asked. She was working her way around to the problem slowly. So very slowly.

"Jen thought he should wear an Elvis costume," Cole snapped, the disgust quite evident in his tone. "He's not a… I didn't think he'd enjoy being a clown like that." Since Freddie had rolled over on his back and was kicking both feet in the air, Rebecca imagined that Freddie believed he actually was a clown.

But the glower on Cole's face suggested he would not laugh at the observation.

"Could you help out at the bake sale table? I need to take some photos." Rebecca waved the camera. "I can take Freddie with me. I'm not sure he should be that close to so much real food. He'd either eat the profits or lose his mind."

Cole studied her face as he considered her request. "You know, I'm not stupid, even if you think I need your concern and your up-standing example of doing good. People won't approach me because I'm scary. You want to see if you can find him a home. Why don't you say that instead of…handling me?"

His fierce scowl was a good reason to step back, but she refused to do it. "I was trying to be sensitive because it's clear you love this dog, you jerk."

"Don't be ridiculous. I'm doing my job. You saw a chance to pull my strings, is all, but I'm not your charity and I'm not controlled by my emotions. That's the part you don't get." Cole rolled his eyes. "Fine, but watch him. He's done pretty well with the crowd, but I don't want him to get overwhelmed."

Rebecca saluted and peeled Freddie's leash from Cole's tight grip. "Sir, yes, sir. And maybe think about another reason I would want to help you, you jerk."

Rebecca was irritated at him all over again, mainly because she only wanted to help a friend, but Cole would never accept her friendship.

They could still be friends with a little kiss between them, couldn't they?

Cole slowly stepped away from Freddie, who seemed to believe he was destined for a grand adventure at the change of control.

"All right, Freddie. Let's walk." A great dog like Freddie deserved to find his home. If she managed to do it today and Cole ever realized how he'd broken his rule of not getting attached to this little dog, he might never forgive her.

CHAPTER THIRTEEN

COLE HOVERED NEAR the end of the bake sale table until the woman counting out the cash looked up. She didn't startle, but the wariness in her eyes was confirmation that he'd made the right decision. If he'd crossed around behind the table, she'd have yelled for the police.

And that expression made it easy to see the family resemblance. While he'd worked with Jen on training the dogs, he'd outlined his landscaping suggestions for her new house, but not once had her suspicious frown lightened. Her mother had the same frown.

"Rebecca sent me over to help while she takes photos." He motioned vaguely at the spot where he'd left Rebecca. She and Freddie had already moved on, and he could no longer see them in the crowd. That was a good thing. This separation from Freddie had him nervous and he didn't want to embarrass himself by staring at Rebecca's lips. It was time to forget the kiss. "I'm Cole."

The petite woman nodded. "Yeah, I know." She tipped her chin up. "I'm Brenda, Jen's mother."

"Nice to meet you." Cole nodded. Offering her his hand would open him to rejection. He'd learned to avoid those opportunities when he could. "What can I do to help?"

She ran her hand through dark hair. "Honestly, we need to start clearing. There's a lot more trash than I expected and so many tubs." She motioned at the nearly empty table. "But we've sold a crazy amount of sugar today. Sarah's going to have the cash she needs for improvements."

And salary. Always a good thing.

"Looks like I can start filling in the flower beds," Cole said. At some point during the night when he was carefully *not* thinking about Rebecca, her kitchen, her thoughtful gesture of digging up his grandmother's recipe or her lips, he'd listed everything he wanted to do at the shelter.

Then he'd realized he should be careful. He might work himself out of a job once all the heavy lifting was completed.

But there were still the beds. Les wanted some outdoor kennels for observation. And then…maybe he'd actually work part-time at the shelter and try his hand at building a lawn-care business. He could ask Sarah if it would be okay to put up a sign, a small one with the name of his business and phone number once he got the flower beds at the shelter fixed. Jen's house could be his second project, his second sign. It would be hard to do on his own, but he could talk EW into helping out. Or Eric.

Asking for favors is no way to keep your promise. This was the problem with spending so much time with people. A man might start to depend on them. When they let him down, he'd have to climb twice as far.

"Earth to Cole." Brenda waved a tub. "Can you start picking up?"

With a grunt, Cole took the empty tub and followed directions. Before he'd finished stacking the empty containers, Brenda had sold all but two of the cakes and one of the bags of Rebecca's cookies. He was digging around in his tool belt for cash when Rebecca popped back up at the table. "Success!" This time she surprised him and every bit of change he'd squirreled away in his pockets rattled across the table.

She laughed. "Sorry. I snuck up on you."

He shook his head and picked up the scattered change with fingers that felt too big for a human hand. "No problem. I wanted to get some cookies before the last ones are sold." He held his hand out to Brenda, who recounted every nickel and dime before dropping it in the cashbox she'd been nearly sitting on top of since he'd walked up.

"Take a cake or two. Half price." Brenda said it without much warmth, but the sentiment was nice. "Go for the one with the pink sticker. Fully loaded with gluten."

Cole glanced at Rebecca, who picked up a cake and handed it to him. He'd be a fool to say no. "I'll drop these in the van. We'll have plenty of room." The number of dogs and cats they'd adopted out was impressive. He didn't know the final count yet, but the number of volunteers milling around without leashes in hand was a good indication.

Rebecca handed him the digital camera. "Can you put this in your tool belt? I don't want to lose it and Sarah's busy."

Surprised at how easily she handed the valuable camera over while Brenda maintained her death grip on the cashbox, Cole took the camera and dropped it in the center pocket of his apron, then noticed the furtive cut of her eyes. He realized she was watching the adoption table. Freddie was acting like a maniac, jumping at the end of his leash every time a new person walked by, but the older couple talking so earnestly with Sarah was paying no attention.

And that was why Freddie had lost his manners. He wasn't the center of attention.

"They want to adopt him."

The immediate rush of anger and the urge to move surprised Cole. He put one hand on Rebecca's shoulder to ease her out of his way. Instead of going along, Rebecca wrapped her hands around his arms and planted her feet. "Stop. Wait."

Cole stared hard at the couple, who'd done nothing wrong except pick Freddie. And then ignore him, but that…

He took a deep breath and met Rebecca's stare. "I'll stop the adoption if that's what you want, but think for a minute. Is that what you want?"

No. It wasn't.

He didn't want this panic or the immediate sensation of having something he loved ripped away, either. Cole braced his hands on his knees and forced himself to breathe through the anger and grief.

How could he have been so stupid as to get attached?

Rebecca pulled him away from Brenda and the bake sale table. "The Scotts walked the town square with me. They'd had their eyes on him since they showed up, but they were afraid to approach you."

Then she wrapped her hand around his forearm, which drew his attention to his own hands. They were clenched so tightly the skin was white. The ache in his knuckles felt right.

"Should I stop the adoption?" she asked as she leaned forward to try to make him look at her. "I will. I should have asked you or..."

Cole breathed in carefully through his nose and exhaled slowly while he forced himself to think. If he said no, Freddie would be spending most of his time in a kennel. Yes, he was safe and well fed and popular at the shelter, so he had lots of company.

But that wasn't a home. That wasn't freedom and a family all to himself.

He should have expected something like this to remind him how life worked.

Instead of spewing any of that frustration or anger onto Rebecca, Cole shrugged. "No. That's why we do what we do." He stepped back. "I better go make sure the van's ready to be loaded. I'll be back for the tubs later. Just leave them…"

Without pausing, Cole marched around the table. If he waited for half a second, the sympathy in her eyes would break whatever force field he'd managed to build over the years. Emotions were a liability.

This friendliness had opened him up to pain.

He'd had to learn early to shove the sadness and worry down. That had been insufficient but valuable training for living behind bars. There, without one second to call his own, he'd had to learn to shove everything down. Stitch had been fine as far as cell mates went, but touchy-feely emotions would have been blood in the water.

Now he could get the space he needed.

Escaping to the van took him right by the adoption table and Freddie.

As he approached, the little beagle spotted him and the lolling tongue seemed to be a grin of complete satisfaction. He wasn't worried about his current state. There was no reason Cole should be worried, either.

Sarah was a pro at this. She'd been running the adoptions at Paws for Love for months. Shelly and Les had been doing it even longer. They had a long list of questions that each prospective owner had to answer. He'd seen the forms himself. Did they have other pets? A commitment to exercising the dog as needed? Every person who took a dog or cat from Paws for Love had to sign that he or she would continue immunizations and routine health care. Sarah would follow up to make sure all those things were happening, too.

None of that mattered as Cole knelt down beside the happy dog. No one would take as good care of Freddie as Cole would.

"Hey, man, congrats. You made it out. You're going home." Freddie licked his hand. "Be a good boy." Cole noticed how the older woman sniffed and stepped away from him. Apparently, she knew his story. Was there no one in Holly Heights who couldn't point out the convict in the crowd?

The small surge of anger helped. Cole pulled the camera out of his pocket and handed it to her. "Here. Take a picture of us." He didn't give her a chance to argue but pulled Freddie closer. The dog immediately put his paws on Cole's leg and left happy kisses all over his face. He saw the camera flash twice before he slipped the beagle a final treat. "Call me if you need bail money, buddy."

After one final scratch of Freddie's ears, he forced down the emotion, slipped on the neutral mask and stood. Sarah was watching him with the same kind of eyes Rebecca had. Between the two of them, he was living on borrowed time. One or the other of them would corner him, make him talk. He wondered if he pulled Sarah aside and explained that he couldn't give Freddie up, would she cancel the adoption? Or kindly point out all the ways Freddie would be better off with this couple instead of a single guy who lived in a trailer with no yard and no air-conditioning? He wasn't good adoption material. "Headed for the van. I'll have the volunteers load up."

Sarah nodded. "Great work today, Cole. You've worked so hard this week. You must be exhausted. Drive the van home when you're done. We'll come get it if we need it, and I don't want to see you around until Tuesday. Take two days off."

Les clapped a hand on Cole's shoulder. "When the crowd thinned, I sent EW on home. I'll follow you and Eric to the shelter, help with the unloading."

Happy to have his orders, Cole tipped his chin at the man and then turned on his heel and walked away.

He wouldn't look back. He couldn't. If Freddie's grin had transformed to a worried frown, they'd both be making a run for the county line.

And at some point, if he was going to keep this job, he'd have to get a handle on these emotions.

"Hey, man, you ready to get out of here?" Eric asked. He and Mike were huddled in the shade of the van. Cole was surprised to see them there. In the old days, he'd have ducked out on his obligation as soon as the people in charge credited him for attending.

"Yep, let's start with the cat kennels in the front. We'll leave any empties here and get them on the next run. If we can get all the animals in one trip, let's do that." They'd all need to be fed and watered. There was going to be so much work to do. That was a good thing.

As soon as they had the van rocking with more than a dozen barking and meowing passengers, Cole, Eric and Mike made the quick trip to the shelter.

"How many animals were adopted?" Eric asked. "Think there'll still be work to do next week?" He glanced at the shelter's much smaller population.

"Got a waiting list of animals that need

a place. Then there's the fostered animals." Hearing his own worry coming out of Eric's mouth was reassuring. Paws for Love was a good place. They both liked working there. And there would always be more animals who needed him.

Cole shoved the air-conditioner setting to high. Something about choking down the lump in his throat made it hard to get comfortable. "There's always going to be work to do."

He looked over at the kid, who seemed to be relieved at his answer. "You and Les, you're getting along, huh?"

Eric tipped his chin up and stared hard out the window. The faint snort from the backseat made Mike's opinion clear.

"Got him dreaming big things. This week, he even studied for the science test. Like a stupid grade matters."

Cole could understand exactly what Mike meant. In his life, all that mattered was hard work. With or without a diploma, Mike and Eric would be working low-paying jobs, sometimes more than one. Or they could enlist, learn a skill.

Or…they could put their trust in a crazy

optimistic guidance counselor who had no idea how the real world worked.

He wasn't sure anymore what the best choice for these boys was.

He did know that Eric had impressed him.

"You did a great job today," Cole said as he parked in front of the shelter. "We needed both of you there, working, so I appreciate it." He pointed at the mangled cake that had taken a beating during his emotional walk to the van. "Take that with my thanks."

"A bet's a bet," Eric muttered as he slid out of the passenger seat.

Cole would have muttered something in return, but the small smile on the kid's lips convinced him that he was playing it cool. That's what guys did, but at eighteen, cool was pretty important. "Grab the leashes. We'll get the big ones first."

The smaller dogs could be carried in the kennels. Cole pulled out his key ring and unlocked the front door as Les and Shelly drove up. With their help, the four largest dogs were soon cooling off in their freshly wiped down pens and the remaining animals were swiftly unloaded. Shelly and Les moved into the cat room to put out fresh food and water for the felines. Settling them down again would take some time.

Most of the dogs were so tired they'd already curled up and fallen asleep.

Freddie's empty spot would tear him down if he stayed there too long.

He motioned for Eric and Mike to follow him. "I'll drop you off at home on the way to town." They could walk it like he usually did, but they deserved a lift. They stopped in the lobby so that Cole could lock the door. The shelter was closed for the day. They'd begin again on Monday, call people on the waiting list with strays that had been living on borrowed time.

Mike pointed at Sarah's office door. It was standing open, as usual, but all the lights were off. "Y'all closed tomorrow, too?"

Cole shook his head. "Yeah, but Sarah will be here during the day. Open or closed, she can't let a day pass without working. Too much she wants to do." It was an admirable trait. He worked to push the memories and worries as far away as he could.

Sarah worked because she believed in something.

"Surprised you have your own key," Eric said. Cole didn't answer as they slid inside the van. He started the engine and backed out of the parking lot.

"Because of my record?" Cole said as he pulled onto the highway. "Couldn't very well open the place without a key." And now that they trusted him to be there with the sunrise, Sarah and Shelly had both relaxed, sometimes arriving after eight o'clock.

"Yeah, but ain't there—" Mike picked at a loose thread "—I don't know, drugs and stuff in there?" He studied the trees along the side of the road.

"Well, they're dog drugs," Eric drawled. "You want to get rid of your fleas or something?"

Cole didn't laugh as Mike punched the back of Eric's headrest, but he was starting to like the kid. At some point, he'd given up on impressing Eric with how terrible his life could be and scaring the kid straight.

It had been a stupid impulse anyway. There was no need to explain to Eric how bad things could get. Even if he hadn't lived it already, he'd seen it close enough to know.

"Hope you're right about the work," Eric said as he picked up the mangled cake. "Need those hours or Debbie will skin me."

"No worries." Cole propped his arm on the

steering wheel. "You can count on hard work, even if the rest of life lets you down."

"That is seriously depressing, man." Eric shook his head.

"Guess I'll have to give up my dream of writing greeting cards," Cole drawled and then offered the kid his fist for a bump.

Eric huffed out a breath as he returned it. "Yeah, stick to what you're good at. Know a lady who'll help you figure that out." Then he slid out of the van and slammed the door. "Pretty, too, but a little intense."

"See you Monday." Cole raised a finger at Eric as the boys walked in front of the van. It was too bad Mike didn't have the same community-service sentence Eric had. With enough exposure, Rebecca might be able to fix him for the better, too.

Cole was still shaking his head when he rolled to a stop in front of Sue Lynn's diner. Brenda was gone; so were all the cakes and cookies.

Only Rebecca remained.

He'd much rather have kept suspicious Brenda than sunny Rebecca, but he didn't get to make decisions like that. Apparently, she was going to have her chance to talk to him about Freddie. She wouldn't be denied.

"So…" She didn't say anything else but raised her eyebrows.

"So." Cole eased around her. "Want me to drop these off at your house on the way to the shelter?" He did not want to do that, but Sarah would ask him to do it anyway, so he might as well swallow his medicine and get it all over with.

"No, I drove. All stacked like this, they'll fit in the backseat." She peered at him through her eyelashes. "What do you think?"

He thought she was crazy and a terrible judge of space.

Eric was right. Pretty and sometimes too intense for comfort.

"Let's see." He picked up the stack, waited for her to grab the other and then followed her to her car. How much different would his life be if he were any regular guy helping a pretty girl? He could be a boyfriend who'd been roped in to work on his day off from… What kind of job could he possibly have that would work in this scenario?

His imagination failed him.

She stopped next to a beige sedan and popped the trunk. "Some of them might fit here."

It took some ingenious cramming, shoving

and stacking, but between the trunk, back-seat and passenger seat, they managed to get everything inside.

"Are you going to be able to drive this way?" Cole asked. He wasn't sure she could see out the passenger-side window. "I don't mind stopping by your house." He *did*. If he lost his mind and all impulse control, he would kiss her again. And better this time. Knowing full well there was no way anything between the town criminal and the girl one step away from sainthood could work, he'd still kiss her.

Because he wanted to.

All this emotional upheaval? Getting tangled up with Eric and worrying over the dog. Yeah, it's her fault. Step away for your own good. No people, no trouble.

"You should have seen the way I packed for college. My parents couldn't move me, they were hosting a fund-raiser for earthquake victims in South America, and Daniel was already too busy with school, so I drove to Baylor with a three-foot-square clearance right in front of my face. It was dumb, but I managed." She sighed. "This is a piece of cake."

Cole frowned as he studied her face. Was she teasing him?

"Piece of cake. Get it?" Rebecca winked.

Yeah, he got it. He grunted a reluctant laugh.

"I wouldn't have guessed you were into puns." Rebecca blew on her knuckles and brushed them against her shirt.

"I'm so not into puns." Cole was pleased with his dry tone. He was going to make it out of there without rehashing all the emotion.

"Sorry about Freddie." Rebecca squeezed his fingers. It wasn't a kiss, but it was nice that she wasn't afraid to step close to him anymore. "He was your friend. That has to hurt."

Cole crossed his arms over his chest. "A little. The emotions surprised me. I don't like it."

Rebecca nodded. "I get that, but you still seem to be in control. It's okay to be sad. This adoption thing is always going to be bittersweet for us."

Hearing her lump them together, as if they were on the same team in this, was nice. Sweet. If he was included on her team, that had to say something good about who he was.

Then he realized this was how she got him. She sneaked past his defenses by pretending to care about him. When she found another project and moved on, it would be saying goodbye to Freddie all over again.

She could keep her encouragement. He didn't need anyone else.

Except for EW, the man who'd saved his sanity more than once.

And Sarah, who'd taken a chance on him when it seemed like a bad idea to everyone else.

Getting attached to Rebecca with the bright blue eyes, watching him, waiting for him to do the right thing, was not a part of his promise. She'd force him to get involved, to take on other people's problems.

Kissing her might make it worth the trouble.

"About the kiss..." Rebecca swallowed hard.

To save her the embarrassment, Cole said, "Yeah. It was a crazy second. I shouldn't have done that. I won't do it again."

She shrugged. "Not so crazy, but—"

"Hey, Rebecca, wait up!"

The shout came from across the street. Cole was anxious to hear how Rebecca finished her thought, but she'd already focused her attention on the interruption. A woman in a tie-dyed T-shirt was waving a notepad with one hand and clasping a large straw hat to her head with the other. Without a single glance either direction, she charged across the street, her grin Texas big.

"Hayley Michener, from the newspaper," Rebecca murmured. "Be nice."

The reporter brushed long black curls away from her face and blew out a gusty breath. "I'm so glad you're still here. I got some quotes from Sarah for the paper, but I wanted to meet this guy."

Cole had been doing his best to blend into the brickwork next to the diner window. He did not want to tangle with a journalist. There was no way he'd say the right thing, and the shelter was too important to mess up.

"Yeah, not a good idea." Cole pointed at the van. "I need to get that to the shelter. Just came to help pack up." He craned his neck both directions, but the volunteers had been ruthlessly thorough. The streets were cleaner than any other time he'd been through town.

"Sarah says you're working wonders with the dogs at the shelter." Hayley poised her pen over her notebook. "What's the secret to your success?"

Desperate for a way out, Cole glanced at

Rebecca. She made a "go on" gesture with her right hand.

"Patience." Cole cleared his throat. "In Prison Partners, we learned that all dogs want to learn and they all deserve a second chance. When you understand that mistakes don't last forever, it's easy to brush off a missed command and try again." He frowned, hoping that would be enough to send this woman on her way. "Also, treats work."

Hayley laughed and brushed a hand over his forearm, confusing Cole further. "Of course they do. Treats are power."

Was she flirting with him? No way.

He glanced at Rebecca. The tiny wrinkle in the center of her forehead suggested she was having the same conversation in her own mind.

And she didn't seem too happy about it.

"Okay, so that's a great angle for this story. Tell me more about the prison program." Hayley batted her eyelashes. "You're going to get me the front page."

Instead of chasing away the reporter as he was begging her to do with his eyes, Rebecca raised a hand. "Good work today, Cole. Next week, we'll finalize our plan for that prison visit." She didn't meet his eyes again, but when she slipped inside her car, she ruffled her curls and hesitated a minute before pulling away.

At that moment, Cole wished his team, the one he hadn't wanted but had collected somehow anyway, was here to run interference. On his own, this could be a disaster.

CHAPTER FOURTEEN

REBECCA'S OPTIMISM AS she dialed the admissions director of Southeast Texas Community College Monday morning was almost too much even for her to stand. The sun was shining. Fall was in the air. Eric had gotten a nearly perfect grade on his latest biology test, as she learned from her first email of the day. Good things were happening.

The only gray cloud in her life was the unpredictable waves of sadness that hit every now and then when she thought about Cole and Freddie. Cole had been devastated, and when she thought about never hearing Freddie and his joyous, sometimes obnoxious voice, she got a lump in her throat.

Had she spent entirely too many hours considering how Cole's conversation with the reporter had gone and whether they'd actually been flirting? Yes. Had she made any decision on what she'd planned to say to Cole about the kiss when Hayley interrupted? No.

Did she wish he'd kissed her again instead of being so apologetic about the whole thing?

"Admissions. Diane Clark speaking."

Instant relief washed over Rebecca. She was so tired of thinking about Cole Ferguson and that brief kiss.

One of the things she'd learned about Diane through the years was that she didn't waste anyone's time, or her own.

"Hey, Diane, this is Rebecca Lincoln from Holly Heights. How are you?" Rebecca made sure the smile on her face was reflected in her voice. That worked wonders and she was going to ask for big favors from Diane eventually.

"Busy, which is a good thing," Diane said. "You have a new batch of kids to send our way next year?"

Rebecca could hear the rustle of paper. Was she multitasking or getting ready to jot down names?

"You bet, but I've got a special case that I wanted to talk to you about," Rebecca said carefully. "STCC has a vet tech program, right?" Of course the school did. She was looking at the current year's class catalogue, but it was easier to start with a question than a demand.

"You bet. Highest job placement stats in the state of Texas." The satisfaction in Diane's voice amused Rebecca. "I'll send you some info."

"Great. And could you confirm your deadlines for financial assistance applications? I also need any updated grants or scholarships for next year. You know, when you have all that." Rebecca twiddled her pen.

"Sure, but you know as long as the kid's got the stuff, I'll make it happen. That's part of the mission here at the college. You send me the kids with the grades, I'll get them tuition." Diane click-clacked as she spoke. Rebecca knew she'd have an email rehashing their phone conversation two seconds after she hung up and the printed materials would be in her hands tomorrow. Diane did not hesitate.

"Well...here's the thing." Rebecca pondered the best way to say what she needed to say. "We're working on his grades."

"In his senior year?" Diane's voice was quiet. "How bad are they?"

"Not good enough to move mountains to get him financial aid, but he's volunteering at our animal shelter three days a week. He made a ninety-eight percent on a biology test.

And he lights up around the animals." Sure, it was the first week of Eric's new commitment at school, but if he kept this up, he deserved to have a chance. It took some kids longer than others to find their way.

"Hmm." Diane sighed. "That's less exciting, but you do have some time. If he turns it around, I'll figure it out. I always do. Any other programs this kid might be interested in? Automotive or even accounting? Those are our most popular, successful programs. Good chance he'll be hired right out of the two-year program."

Thinking of her conversation with Debbie and Eric's halfhearted suggestion that he'd enlist, Rebecca said, "Yes, please send them. I'll pass them along. I'm also going to have the army recruiter meet with Eric, because he mentioned it, but his sister will not be pleased."

Diane sighed. "Yeah, but he's got a lifetime to work. He needs to find what he loves."

Diane might be hard-nosed about her time and the wasting of it, but her heart was in the right place. She did what it took to help kids. Those were the kinds of people Rebecca wanted to work with.

"You bet." Rebecca turned up the chipper

in her voice again. "I know we can do this, Diane. Thanks for your help."

"Sure, but find me some good candidates for the early childhood education program or even the culinary arts. Those are the focus areas for the year, and kids don't know what the possibilities are. Either one of those certificates means a good chance of landing a job immediately after graduation, and the pay's not bad. Plus, there's room to move on. You know how many kids start here and transfer their hours to a state college. Teachers, Rebecca. You know how badly Texas needs more teachers, but our kids, the ones we work with, they can't see a way into the degree required. We're missing out, and those kids who might someday lead the next generation are lost and I hate it." Diane took a breath. "I'm sorry. I got wound up."

"I love it," Rebecca said passionately. "Don't you ever change. You want someday teachers? I will find them. Send me some printed material. I'll start hunting."

Diane laughed. "I'll hire a truck, make a special delivery."

"Not *that* much printed material, but I'm serious. Let's set up meetings, Diane. We haven't done that in three years. I'll pull together twenty or thirty kids, break them down into groups. You can present your programs."

Rebecca had already started a list with Eric's name at the top. This was what she'd been missing with her focus on the kids who were aiming for academic scholarships at universities and colleges. Not every kid had the grades or even the desire for those schools, but every kid had talent and dreams. Diane was the help she needed to reach the kids that were slipping through the cracks. Rebecca slowly crossed out Eric's name. They needed to start younger. Sophomores. But Eric was going to have his own meeting.

"Perfect. Let's do it. How soon?" The clicking and clacking convinced Rebecca that Diane was pulling up her calendar. After they considered and discarded a few different days, she and Diane settled on late November.

"I'm glad you called, Rebecca, even if that means I'm going to break my back to help out," Diane said. "If only everyone I work with could be as determined."

"I know what you mean." Rebecca glanced down at the list of things necessary to make this work and was already exhausted, but it would happen. Or else. "As soon as I have a chance to sit down with Eric, I'll show him the info. I could bring him and his sister down to see the campus and meet you." She'd never done that with any other student. Why hadn't she? The uncomfortable answer was that she usually picked much less challenging candidates than Eric.

"Good idea. Campus visits make it easier to imagine STCC as a possibility," Diane said politely, but Rebecca could tell she'd already moved on to the next item on her mental list, so she cut short the chitchat and hung up.

Then, as expected, the quiet beep of her email notified her that Diane had sent the summary with the November date in the subject line. So efficient.

Before she could move down the pile in her email inbox, her cell rang. She frowned as she dug around in her tote bag to pull it from the depths. Everyone knew she was at work. Who would be calling on her cell? When the shelter's number showed on the screen, Rebecca laughed. Sarah must have forgotten what day it was. Maybe she had an adoption event hangover.

"Hey, I'm working." Rebecca clicked on the first email and settled in her chair.

"Yeah, but I wasn't sure who else to call,"

Sarah said in a shaky voice. "I mean, the police, obviously. They're on the way. Shelly's already here. And Jen's in class." Sarah sniffed so loudly into the phone that Rebecca pulled it away from her ear. Was she crying?

"What's happened? Is it Will? Or one of the dogs?" What could rattle Sarah like this? She'd lived through being deserted by her father and losing everything without losing her cool.

"We had a break-in last night." Sarah sniffed again. "I wasn't sure when I got here, but I think the door was unlocked. The bake sale money and the donations, all gone." Her voice was choked. "Some of the small electronics. I need as many eyes down here as I can get. Can you come?"

"You bet. I'm on the way." Rebecca opened a new email message as she ended the call and fired off a short message to the principal. She didn't have any meetings scheduled that morning, so no one would miss her. On her way down the hallway, right past the dark corner she'd been certain would bother her every day but now no longer even registered, she typed out a quick text to Jen. Then she ran for the car.

Driving sedately through Holly Heights was

an easy task most days. Pedestrians treated traffic in the streets with a small-town indifference, so it was important to be on the lookout for the unwary, but today the streets were nearly empty. As she raced past the trailer park, she noticed the shelter's van and wondered what Cole was doing. Shouldn't he be at work?

Two policemen were getting out of a Holly Heights Police Department cruiser when she slammed to a stop in the parking spot closest to the door. Instead of waiting to make pleasant conversation as she would have every other day of every other year, Rebecca left her bag in the front seat and ran for the open front door. "Sarah?" she called as she stopped in the lobby. She'd expected a crowd to greet her, but the lobby was empty.

"In here. Putting my face on," Sarah said quietly. "While trying not to touch anything important." She poked her head around the doorframe of the tiny bathroom in the lobby and waved. Her eyes were puffy, but she was still so beautiful it was unfair. Even in a ragged T-shirt and jeans and with tearstained cheeks, Sarah Hillman had style.

Rebecca held out her arms. "I'm sorry." Sarah was nodding as she leaned against Rebecca. "But the dogs are okay? And the cats are fine?" Rebecca squeezed Sarah's shoulders hard. "Whoever was here was already gone by the time Cole got here?"

"We're all fine. Cole's off today, so I opened. I fed and watered and had the itch along the back of my neck that something was off. Then I went in my office." Sarah rubbed her eyes. "The filing cabinet drawers were all open. My laptop's gone. It's just… They took what they could carry."

"But why search the filing cabinet," Rebecca asked, "unless they knew that's where you kept the money?"

"I should have taken it home with me, but I thought it was safe." Sarah shook her head. "I'm so sorry. Whoever was here knew about the event. It's the *only* time of the year when this place has anything worth taking."

Rebecca wrapped her arms around Sarah again and squeezed as hard as she could. "Don't beat yourself up. You didn't do this. The police are here. We'll talk to them and then we'll…move on. That's it." She brushed her hands up and down Sarah's chilly arms. "Where's Will?"

"On his way. Chloe wanted to spend the night and have him take her to school this morning, so he's coming from Austin." Sarah sniffed. "That's why I was putting mascara on." Her watery laugh was sweet and heart-breaking.

When the two policemen entered the lobby, she and Sarah turned to greet them. Immediately, Sarah stiffened. "You. What are you doing here?" She shook her head. "No way. There's no way you're working in Holly Heights now."

The older cop held out a hand. "Now, Miss Hillman, I'm not sure what you mean, but…"

"I mean Hollister here." She pointed at the second man, a guy who might be handsome if he weren't so grim. "He harassed me at my home until I lost it. Then he followed me to my place of work and told my boss and boy-friend to fire me. Even after I helped him find my father, he refused to return my phone calls with any updates." Then she frowned. "Be-cause he doesn't work for the Austin police anymore, I guess." Her shoulders slumped. "You cannot be working here. Please."

"First week." Hollister ran a hand down his nape. "And everything I did was part of the job. If you aren't getting information about your father, it's because there's not any. That's it."

Rebecca was worried because Sarah stood

there, frozen, her mouth hanging open for so long that she started to wonder if something else was happening and they needed to call for an ambulance. Eventually, Sarah dragged in a ragged breath. Every bit of color in her face was gone. "I need Will."

Rebecca grabbed Sarah's hand and squeezed. "He's coming. Right now we'll help with the investigation. Then the officers will go, and you can tell me why I hate this man." She blinked at Hollister and shrugged as if to say it wasn't personal. Best friends hated people for no good reason all the time, just because. That's the way it worked.

The fact that he was a cop and possibly the most eligible bachelor around might have caused her to hesitate for a second, but Sarah's grip on her hand was starting to hurt.

"Walk us through the morning," the older policeman said. "Officer Adams." He offered his hand and Rebecca rolled her eyes.

"Yeah, Davy. We know you." Rebecca waved her hand. "You were the one who gave all the safety lectures at school. And you know us. No introduction needed."

"Give us the facts," Hollister said, and shifted easily out of the way when Sarah would have elbowed him to pass by.

"I used my key to enter. Now that I think about it, the door might have been unlocked, but I'm not sure." Sarah motioned them to follow. "Inside, I locked the door and dropped my tote on the counter here. Then I moved straight into the dog room and let out the first group of dogs. I cleaned kennels and refilled food and water until it was time to switch out the groups. I did that until all the dogs had been fed, watered and exercised. I gave every animal that needed it medication. Then about eight o'clock, I went into my office to check the email, hoping for more offers of adoption after the weekend."

Each step Sarah took was precise, an angry march that might have been different without Hollister in the parade following her. Rebecca was dying to know more about what had happened between them.

"When I stepped in my office and flipped on the light, I noticed the filing cabinet." She pointed. All the drawers were open. The top drawer was misshapen as if someone had yanked and shoved it to break the lock. "That's where I'd put the money from this weekend."

"How much money?" Hollister asked, his pen poised to make a note.

Sarah tipped her chin up. "Almost fifteen hundred dollars in cash. Some checks. I'll show you the receipts." She didn't glance in Hollister's direction. "All the desk drawers are the same. I don't even know why I lock them except I have files with addresses on them." She raised both eyebrows. "And they sure don't lock now." Every drawer in the metal desk was off-kilter like the ones in the filing cabinet.

"So you touched the door and the phone. Anything else?" Hollister asked. "In here, specifically."

"No. Once I realized what had happened, I got out." Sarah wrapped her arms tightly over her chest.

"Adams, dust for fingerprints. I'll check the doors and windows," Hollister said.

Davy Adams shifted, almost as if he wanted to argue, before motioning toward the hallway. "Ladies, if you'll—"

"We'll be outside in the play yard when you have more questions," Rebecca said, and towed Sarah by the hand down the hallway and out into the chilly morning air. There, it was easier to think. Some of the color returned to Sarah's cheeks.

"Want to tell me about it?" Rebecca asked

as Sarah dropped down on the bench. "Hollister?"

Sarah brushed her hair back. "He's the detective working on my father's case. *Was* the detective, I guess. Does he live here, do you think?" She shook her head. "I can't even imagine running into him in the produce section." She closed her eyes. "He can't live here."

Thinking that a man who worked in Holly Heights would be a fool not to live there, too, Rebecca patted Sarah's back and stared out over the yard without answering.

"His first week, we have a break-in and I have to call the police. Life is too much sometimes." Sarah pinched a pleat in her jeans. "I've come to terms with having my dad in jail. Really, I have. I want him close, so that I know he's okay. Hollister suggested my father might be dying alone somewhere and I can't get that out of my head. Here, I can see him again. He's a thief, but he's my dad." She sighed. "You think I'm crazy."

Rebecca eased down beside Sarah and tried to put herself in her friend's shoes. Family was important and Big Bobby Hillman was all Sarah had. Rebecca didn't want to imagine living her life without parents who'd encouraged her to be better, always to be better. Her brother, Daniel, had been an arrogant snot, but even when he'd destroyed his own reputation at Holly Heights Hospital, she'd wanted to help him, protect him, save him. That's what family was for. People without that lifeline, like Cole and Sarah, had no support. If she lost that, she might never recover.

But the fact that her parents and her brother had left Holly Heights did make living there much easier most days. Family was important, but Rebecca didn't mind the breathing room.

"You love him," Rebecca finally said. "Whatever he did, you can still love him. It's okay. Who cares what anyone thinks of that? But I'm sorry you've had such a hard time getting answers. That's not right."

"It's not." Sarah sighed. "Everyone thought I knew where he'd taken the money and I was guilty by association. Hollister wasn't alone in that. The whole town thought it." She waved a hand. "But you know that. The letters to the editor made it pretty hard to miss, but I didn't know he was stealing or leaving or where he went. And then, as soon as I had a clue, I sent it to Hollister, the jerk who was doing his best to wear me down so that I'd... confess, maybe."

Rebecca crossed her legs and struggled to find the right thing to say, but this was not a situation where any of her usual words worked. The guilt that edged into her brain was hard to ignore. What had she done to stop the gleeful whispers? Not enough. Rebecca pressed one hand to her stomach, the knot there upsetting.

If she'd been in Sarah's place, would she have been able to stand tall and fight for what she wanted? And would she ever have been as gracious as Sarah or would holding a grudge and getting even have been her priority?

Rebecca didn't know the answer. That was crushing.

"If Hollister can get me answers now, I guess that's something," Sarah said quietly. "But if I have to stand in line behind him at the grocery store, I could lose my cool. No one wants me to lose my cool."

Rebecca bumped her shoulder. "As long as the fallout's not aimed at me, I might enjoy that. I could sell tickets and popcorn." At Sarah's snort, Rebecca waggled her eyebrows. "We could make a fortune. *Another* fortune."

Sarah clapped her hands over her face. "The money. I'd almost forgotten about all that beautiful, sugar-driven money. Now what are we going to do? I was planning big with that cash. It wasn't in the operating budget. We could have spruced this place up."

"Don't worry about that, Sarah. We'll figure it out. The place already looks so much better. We'll just—" Rebecca pointed "—give Cole a hammer and a paintbrush and stand back. He'll put on a second story before we turn around."

Sarah tilted her chin down. "That's quite a change in tone about Cole."

Rebecca willed away the hot wash of color she could feel building on her neck.

Sarah's eyes grew. "What are you not telling me?" She scooted closer. "I've had a tough morning. It's your job as my best friend to make that better. Tell me."

"Best friend?" Rebecca asked.

"It's a small pool." Sarah wagged her finger. "And I'm not letting this go."

"It's nothing. When he came over to get the cookies…" Was she going to tell Sarah this?

Before she could decide, the door opened and the police stepped outside, followed closely by Will Barnes. He didn't look left or right, but zeroed in on Sarah and closed the gap between them in a flash. "I got here as fast as I could." He wrapped his arms around her and ran his hands over her back and arms. "You're okay?"

"Yes, I didn't stop the robber single-handedly. I told you they were already gone." Sarah shifted closer and clutched Will tightly with white-knuckled fists, wrinkling a nicely pressed white shirt.

Rebecca wondered how it must feel to have someone like that, a man who would come running at the first sign of trouble. Will wasn't focused on anything but Sarah's safety at that minute, but it was easy to see the second he remembered the other upsetting part of the whole day.

"Hollister."

His grim tone convinced Rebecca that if he thought he could get away with it, Hollister would be bleeding from his nose while Will shook an aching hand.

"Yeah. Hollister." Sarah locked eyes with him and whatever they said to each other, it was enough. She straightened her shoulders. "It's time to get some answers."

"Davy, do you have more questions or an update?" Rebecca asked, afraid of what would happen to Hollister when Sarah and Will teamed up.

"I don't see any signs of entry on the front

door. No scratches on the lock to show that someone picked it." Hollister tapped his notebook. "Are all your key holders here? We'd like to talk to them, rule out an inside job."

Sarah's jaw dropped and she had the frozen look again.

Will wrapped his arm around her. "It's not an inside job." Every word was bitten off like it was fired from a gun.

"You think I stole this money, too?" Sarah asked, her voice weak but getting stronger. "I love this place. You must be the worst cop in the history of cops." She snapped her fingers. "Someone bring me my phone. I will call in every single favor I have left in this town to get you fired. You watch me."

Davy Adams held up a hand. "No one thought it was you, Sarah. Are you the only one with a key?"

"No, Shelly and Les, who've been running this place since before we could stand to pay the light bill, have keys. I have one employee, Cole Ferguson, who also has a key." Sarah tapped her foot on the concrete. "Only an idiot would suspect Cole." She narrowed her eyes at Hollister, the man who had moved right to the top of Sarah's idiot list.

"He's a person of interest. If he's innocent,

all it'll take is a conversation to clear things up. Give me other potential suspects." He slowly turned from person to person, waiting for suggestions.

Fear froze Rebecca in her spot. What would the police do? Would they lock Cole up? How could he stand that again? And was this going to be Cole's life, immediately the prime suspect for any crime in Holly Heights? If so, he couldn't stay here. He deserved better.

And anyone who loved him deserved to live a life without the suspicion hanging over her head.

But what if he's guilty? As soon as the thought formed, Rebecca's stomach cramped. He wouldn't. He loved Paws for Love.

Sarah's grim lips matched her tone when she said, "He's in the trailer park. Down the road."

"The shelter van is parked in front of his trailer," Rebecca added as she moved closer to Sarah.

"We'll bring him here to talk to him," Hollister said quietly. "No need for a parade to talk to a suspect. While we're gone, put together a list of the volunteers, people who might have known about how much money you had on hand after the event."

When Sarah nodded, he turned to leave. On his way inside, he stopped and studied the lock carefully. Then he surveyed the fences and the windows. "Any reason this window has no screen?" He pointed with his pen and then motioned at the window on the opposite side. Only one had a ragged screen.

"Has it always been like that?" Rebecca asked as she studied the windows.

"I don't think so." Sarah marched over and did her best to lift the window. When it slid up easily, Rebecca realized she was holding her breath.

"Possible entry point." Hollister made a note and stepped inside.

"We've got so many fingerprints it'd be hard to narrow them down, but I'll check when we get back." Davy Adams leaned closer to Sarah. "Guy's got a real personality disorder, if you know what I mean, but he's good at his job. Impressive career. We'll solve this." Then he ducked his head and followed Hollister inside.

Sarah glanced up as Will wrapped his hand over her shoulder. "I wish…"

"I know. It's not a good situation, but we'll have to wait and see." Will shook his head.

"Should I call Doug Grant? He's the best lawyer I know in town."

And married to Cece, Sarah's archrival and a woman Rebecca knew would delight in having her words of doom confirmed so quickly.

"That's Cole's decision," Rebecca said. "Let's wait and see what he says." Her heart was racing with fear. How would Cole react to being questioned by the police?

Sarah and Will nodded and all three of them stared at the play yard as they waited for the police to return.

CHAPTER FIFTEEN

"YOU AIN'T GOT the hang of this vacation day business yet," EW muttered as he hammered the new railing in. "Supposed to be about sleeping late, watching television, some fishing, definitely junk food. Not work." He pushed hard to test the railing and grunted his satisfaction. "Best get a start on that now that this project is finished."

Cole gathered the few tools EW had brought over after Cole had knocked on his trailer door that morning with a cake in one hand and a project in mind. Fixing the loose railing had been one of those things on his list of things to do, mainly because he could picture Mimi's disappointed face. She'd worked hard to keep the place up. A loose railing wasn't just a danger; the whole world could *see* it.

He might not have much, either, but he was going to take good care of what belonged to him.

"I knew it wouldn't take long." Cole straightened in time to see a Holly Heights cop car rolling to a stop behind the shelter van. Had someone reported the van stolen? What would it take to convince the police that he had permission to borrow it? He should have refused Sarah's offer. He should have demanded a signed note or something.

The urge to hide flitted through his mind until he reminded himself he'd done nothing wrong. Even the police could be reasonable. There was no need for the panic itching across his nerves to bloom.

"Good morning, Officers," Cole said as he carefully held both hands out at his sides. "What can I help you with?" He recognized the older cop as one he may have run into in his early days.

The new guy studied the trailer and EW carefully before he said, "We're here to ask you a few questions. Can you tell us your schedule this weekend? Yesterday afternoon and evening in particular."

Cole glanced at EW. "Fished yesterday afternoon. Last night, played a pickup game." He pointed at the goal. "Today's my day off from work. EW and I have been looking after some repairs. What's this about?"

The younger cop, Hollister was his name, said, "We're going to search inside the trailer."

"With your *permission*," snapped the older cop, Davy Adams. The look he sent his partner was a mix of exasperation and strained patience.

"What's this about, Davy?" EW asked slowly.

"Shelter was robbed last night. We're going to talk to everyone with a key." Davy waved a hand. "If it's all right, we'll take a quick look inside and get you to come down to the shelter."

Was he the most likely suspect? "Go ahead. Look around." Cole waved a hand. "Won't take but a minute."

After the cops disappeared inside his trailer, he and EW stood quietly because there was nothing to say. Frustration, anger and something that tasted terribly like hurt tumbled in his stomach.

Then he realized it had been a while since he'd felt this particular mix of emotions.

Hollister paused in the doorway, Cole's work apron in one hand and the shelter's digital camera in the other. "Want to tell me about this?" His face was unreadable, but at least there was no satisfaction there. Maybe the cop was keeping an open mind.

"Shelter had an adoption drive in the town square. Rebecca was taking pictures and she asked me to hold on to the camera because Sarah was busy. I put it in my pocket and forgot about it. I would have returned it tomorrow when I went into work." But he should have placed it on Sarah's desk when he left the shelter on Saturday. Why hadn't he done that?

Hollister nodded.

"Nothing here," Adams said. "Let's head back."

Cole waited patiently for the cops to cuff him or tell him what they wanted, but they walked to the car. When he didn't move, Hollister said, "Follow us. I'm already on thin ice with Sarah Hillman. Anything happens to you before she sees you again and I'll spend the rest of my life looking over my shoulder." He braced both hands on the car and shook his head.

"Follow you? In the van?" Not as a suspect in the back of the cop car?

"You can ride with us, man, but we aren't running a limo service." Adams slid into the driver's seat. Hollister met Cole's stare over the light bar on top of the car. Whatever this guy knew about his past, he wasn't jumping to conclusions.

"Let me grab the keys." Cole trotted up the steps, snatched the keys off the tiny hook he'd found in the junk drawer and installed beside the refrigerator and stepped outside. "You coming?"

EW rubbed his hand over his mouth. "Think you oughta call a lawyer?"

Cole studied the van. The cops had already pulled out. They believed he was going to keep his word and follow them. "No. I think it's going to be okay." Why he felt that way was unclear. He'd never have expected Sarah and Rebecca to list him as a suspect, but he had nothing to hide. Really. It would be obvious soon enough that he had no access to cash like what the adoption event had brought in. "Can't afford a good one anyway."

When they walked into Paws for Love, everyone was crammed into Sarah's small office. And they were arguing. Loudly. "There's no way the volunteers did this, either," Sarah snapped. "Talking to Cole was a waste of time, like I told you it would be, so listen to me on this. The thief is not someone who works here." She slapped a hand on the desk, the color high in her cheeks, ready to throw down in defense of her people.

Hearing her say that about him instantly erased the dread building inside. Sarah hadn't made him a suspect. The police had.

But what did Rebecca believe? When she noticed him standing in the doorway, Rebecca immediately skirted the desk to reach for his hand. "Are you okay?" Her eyes searched his face.

Was she afraid of police brutality or hurt feelings or what? These Holly Heights police seemed cool as cucumbers. He couldn't imagine either Adams or Hollister losing his temper. "Fine. I forgot I had the camera. But that's all they found." Cole wasn't sure what was going on with his voice, but it was rougher than usual.

Rebecca's eyes narrowed, and she spun around. "I asked him to hold on to that camera. That's why he had it. He put it in his apron while he was working. That's it. That's all. What sort of fortune do you think he's looking for in a camera like that?" Disgust dripped from her words.

Uneasy with her over-the-top defense, Cole said, "Take it down a notch, okay? That's what I told them, and they believed me."

She didn't deign to respond to that but stepped closer to him. "Do you want us to call a lawyer? We will. Don't worry about the bill. I'll cover it."

EW's suggestion he could understand. His friend had had his own encounters with justice. But Rebecca's? If she thought he was innocent, would she be ready to lawyer up?

"There's no need for a lawyer," Hollister said calmly. "Nobody's under arrest. Ferguson here was as cooperative as a person could be. At this point, we will ascertain if any of you have any bits of info that might help us find actual suspects. Dust around the window in the back. Look around to see if the missing screen's been discarded around here." He held up both hands, noticed the camera he still held and set it carefully on the desk. "That's all we're doing here."

"So," Cole murmured in Rebecca's ear, "stand down." She shot him an irritated glare but nodded once, sharply. Whatever happened, it was almost worth it to see her this mad on his behalf.

She would be an awesome advocate for Eric and the rest of her kids.

"This Eric Jordan." Davy Adams tapped the list Sarah had handed him. "He there on

Saturday?" Over his shoulder, he said, "Kid's a minor league troublemaker, but..." Hollister nodded.

The realization that he should have already realized Eric would be the next target smacked Cole in the gut. Of course.

And it was disturbing that he couldn't immediately rule Eric out, either. That much money would be a treasure for the kid and his sister.

But they'd played a fierce one-on-one game last night and not once had the kid looked guilty. Was he that good?

"We'll give you a call with any news," Davy said, and waved the list. "Shouldn't take too long to track everyone down." He pointed at Shelly and Les, who were crammed together on the sofa under Bub. "Talk to the two of you outside?" When they nodded, he maneuvered through the crowd in the tiny office. With worried looks at Sarah, Shelly and Les followed.

The solemn atmosphere in the office made Cole uneasy. "Nice weather we're having." It was such a lame attempt at lightening the mood that everyone turned to stare at him. "What? That seemed like vacation day conversation."

Rebecca's lips were twitching. He was unstoppable. "You should be mad."

"Mad?" Cole remembered feeling that way on the drive over. Now he was resigned, deflated. "Relieved. Glad to know you aren't going to fire me." He glanced at Sarah. "You aren't, are you? I did forget to leave the camera here on Saturday."

Sarah covered her face with both hands. "Because you were exhausted. Which is why I didn't take that money directly to the bank. If you're going, I am, too."

"Well, I'm not staying here without the two of you," Rebecca said as she flopped down in her chair. "This place is a lot of work. I'm too soft for this. And I work in a *high school*."

For a long second, everyone thought about that. Sarah and Will both laughed and even EW had a silent chuckle. When Rebecca checked on Cole's reaction, he smiled. He couldn't help it.

"And, if the crisis is managed, I'll go *back* to school." Rebecca stood slowly. To Sarah, she said, "I'll text Jen and Steph, keep them in the loop. Go have a good lunch after the cops leave." She pointed at Will. "Make this happen."

Sarah saluted. "Cole is having his vacation day or else." She pointed at the window. "Is that the van in the parking lot? You and EW take it home. Bring it in tomorrow." She waved a hand. "Get."

Cole waited for Rebecca to pass, trailing lemons and sweet warmth, before he and EW fell in line behind her. When they were outside, he tossed the van keys to EW. "I need a minute."

EW whistled tunelessly and slid into the van. He closed his eyes, dropped his head back and pretended to sleep. Privacy. He understood the importance of privacy.

Before Rebecca could get into her car, he put a hand on her back, relieved some of the tension that had made her seem so brittle she could break had disappeared. "Before you go…"

Rebecca turned to face him, her hands tightly knotted together. "We didn't tell them to come talk to you. You know that, right?"

Cole nodded. "Sure, but I get the feeling you weren't as convinced of my innocence, not at the beginning anyway."

She sagged against the car. "I'm not sure what to say."

He wagged his head. "Guess it's good I know where I stand." Even he could hear the bitter resignation in his voice. "Glad you're getting smarter. Blind trust of the criminal in the neighborhood would be pretty dumb."

"I was so worried about you and those cops. 'What if he's guilty?' was just this fleeting thought, one I couldn't chase away fast enough," she whispered. "Let me know where this sits on the dumb scale."

She wrapped her arms around his neck and pressed her lips to his. No matter how irritated he was at her doubts about his innocence, he wasn't going to waste another shot at a good kiss. Nothing could stop him this time. Not the dusty gravel parking lot's lack of romance, the threat of an audience or interruption by the cops. He slanted his lips against hers, and every bit of the sweetness he'd been searching for burst on his tongue.

Then she wiggled her arms between his to pull him closer, and the whole world fell away. Until he stepped back, gasping for air, he forgot every worry that plagued him.

"You know, even if you had robbed the shelter, I would help you," Rebecca said as she stepped back. "For better or worse, I can't not help you."

The way she studied his face made him think she wanted to convince him she was telling the truth. Of that, he was certain, but in this case, a little less truth would have gone a long way.

He didn't want to *know* about her doubts. If she insisted on telling the truth, he couldn't pretend it didn't hurt. So much for staying out of trouble. She was full of it.

Cole stared hard at the ground while he tried to order his thoughts. "But I didn't rob the place. What would it take for you to believe that instead of planning a defense?" He shook his head. "This is why I wanted you to stay away. Even though I'm trying to do the right thing, to support your project with Eric, you punch me in the gut. You don't even have to try hard to tear me down. This is why people are overrated. Even the good ones will break you."

He watched her struggle to come up with the right words. She was supposed to be the solid one, the good one who made the right decisions. This good man, baking him special cookies, but not quite trusting him while she threw herself in his arms? He didn't need that.

"What was the kiss about?" Cole demanded. "You have to decide whether you're in or out, Rebecca. Trust me or don't, that's your decision. I get the doubt, believe me, but I can't…

get any closer to you like this. Kissing me is…too much. You don't trust me. You don't need me. You can find another man to save, no doubt. Move on."

Rebecca rubbed a hand over her forehead. "I just… I had to. I was so worried about you and I needed you. I had to." She closed her eyes. "You aren't a project to me, Cole. Maybe I need some time to…"

"You need to get to work." Cole stepped back. Her face perfectly reflected his own confusion and hurt. They were no good together.

Even if her kiss made the rest of the world fade.

He didn't move until she managed to put the key in the ignition, start the car and back slowly out of the parking space. After she safely made the turn out onto the highway, he forced himself to walk sedately to the van and climb inside.

EW's eyes were still closed, but his lips were curved at the corners. Cole gripped the steering wheel. *This feels like the end of the world, but it isn't. Get a grip.*

"You enjoy the show?" Cole grumbled as he followed Rebecca out of the parking lot.

"Best I've seen in a long time, young fella."

EW rubbed a hand down his face. "Didn't think you had it in you anymore. Kissing's about living, not existing."

"Yeah." Cole shook his head as he drove. "What's that all about?" Too bad she'd ripped out his heart and stomped on it, too. He squeezed the steering wheel. *Won't be your last kiss.*

Might be the last one with *her.*

Just keep putting one foot in front of the other. Focus on what you want.

When had he changed his mind about what his life was going to be? As he'd walked out of Travis, surviving was the only goal. EW was right. Thinking of business ideas and kissing beautiful women were new developments. Losing them might crush him.

"Your grandma would have been pleased. Oh, not about the PDA." EW shook his head.

"How do you figure? I promised to stay out of trouble. Police at my door is about as much trouble as I can handle." The fact that he'd been nearly certain he was okay the whole time Hollister and Adams were there surprised him.

"Sure, but you got real friends to watch your back this time." EW cleared his throat. "You ain't on your own."

He said it as an encouragement. All Cole could think of was how easy it would be to lose all that.

As the road into the trailer park came up, Cole said, "Want to go to the grocery store?" He needed to get back to normal, day-off stuff. He needed to stay busy.

"Beer?" EW raised an eyebrow. "Been a while since I had a good beer."

Cole couldn't tell if he was happy about that or not. The small frown on EW's brow suggested he might not have even realized it.

"No, but for you, I'll get a six-pack, too," Cole said, disappointed that whatever streak EW was on was coming to an end.

EW pursed his lips. "Brownies. Think you could make some of them? I've had a craving. That cake you brought over tasted healthy." His tone made it clear healthy cake was a lie.

"If I remember right, brownie mixes come in boxes. Anybody can do that," Cole said as he pressed the accelerator.

EW rolled down his window and hung his arm out the side. Driving through town with his best friend in the world, an elderly black man, in a van decorated with cartoon dogs and cats was satisfying. It was a beautiful day. He didn't have to do a thing but whatever he wanted. He had a bit of money to spend. He'd learned a good lesson today.

Instead of shutting everyone out of his life, he should be careful who he let in. The one person who had the biggest potential to hurt him had to go. He and Rebecca were never going to be on the same page. Getting that through his head wouldn't be easy, but he'd done harder things.

CHAPTER SIXTEEN

"Not again," Rebecca muttered as she dropped her keys in the hallway on Thursday morning. It had been a week of dropping things, running into things, and generally losing track of her own thoughts. Misery had that effect on her. There was only one person to blame for that.

Cole Ferguson had hijacked her good sense with the best kiss she could remember before crushing her by making her see how unfair she'd been to him. Sarah had been able to reject the idea of Cole as the thief immediately.

Seeing Cole's bitterness and complete lack of surprise that she hadn't been able to do the same had kept her awake.

To top it off, she wasn't sure what to do about the situation. Except avoid the shelter and Cole. Until she got her head on straight, they'd both be better off with some distance. Missing him had come as a big surprise. She'd grown accustomed to the sizzle of awareness she felt when he was around and the happy jolt she got whenever a little more of his grim shell cracked.

She bent to pick up her keys and then shook her head. What a mess she was. Poor guy. He'd had the right idea to chase her away that first night.

"Rebecca, when you have a minute, I need to speak with you in my office." Principal Arturo Sepulveda was standing in the doorway of the administration offices. Instead of a cheerful grin, his usual greeting, Art's expression was grim. Did he have bad news? Was she in trouble somehow? Impossible.

She pointed at her office. "Let me drop off my things and I'll be right there. What should I bring?" Did they have a meeting she'd forgotten about? Again, impossible.

Art waved a hand. "Nothing. Just come." He was normally an easygoing guy with a fun connection to his students. Whatever was going on was serious.

Nerves made it difficult to unlock her door, but as soon as she stepped across the threshold, Rebecca breathed in slowly and stared hard at her bulletin board, the one covered with thank-you notes and newspaper clippings about student successes and a million other small victories she'd won over her years at Holly Heights. No matter what Art wanted to talk to her about, it had nothing to do with her job performance. She was good at what she did.

Then she remembered Eric and how close they'd come to losing him and the other marginalized students she might have neglected. Had a parent complained?

Stop guessing and get to his office.

Rebecca dropped her purse in her desk drawer and then wiggled her mouse to wake up her computer. "Just a minute to put in my password and see what the inbox situation is." Rebecca typed and dug around her desk for the printed outline of her conversation with Diane at the community college. If there was a problem, it wouldn't hurt to have a proactive plan already in motion.

As soon as her email inbox came up, Rebecca gasped. "Twenty messages. In one night?" She quickly scanned the subject lines. Some were hard to interpret, but at least two of them left nothing to the imagination. "Pulling Madison from the shelter volunteer program?" Breathing became a challenge and it was almost impossible to stand and leave without opening that email.

But the principal was waiting. In her whole career, she'd never had a morning like this.

It took twice as long to walk to Art's office as it had to come in that morning because her feet wouldn't move any faster. When Rebecca went into the principal's office, even as a student herself, it had been for commendations or thanks for some project she'd taken on.

Nothing like this.

She paused in the doorway as she caught sight of the five other people in Art's office. School board members. Whatever it was, this was big. Art motioned at the chair in front of his desk. "Have a seat, but close the door first."

Rebecca eased the door shut, hoping to avoid the attention of the people outside Art's office, and perched on the edge of the chair. When she noticed the way she was clutching the single paper she'd brought along for her defense, Rebecca smoothed the paper against one leg.

Cece Grant cleared her throat, but when Rebecca glanced her way, the woman was picking lint off her perfectly tailored slacks.

"Have you seen the newspaper this morning?" Art asked as he spread it across the desk. "You and your shelter are front-page news."

"Because of the robbery?" Rebecca asked as she scanned the headlines. The largest one above the fold was about the adoption event with the headline Prison Training Gives Pups a Second Life, but it made no sense that this would cause trouble for her or Art.

"No, the adoption event in the town square. You knew about that," Cece said as she looked up and raised both eyebrows.

He nodded once. "Check the bottom of the page."

Rebecca read slowly, "Robbery at shelter. Police interview Cole Ferguson."

Rebecca quickly scanned the snippet that fell conveniently under a small photo of her and Cole at the adoption event. He had his hands on her shoulders. How was that even possible?

Then she remembered Cole's grief at watching Freddie's adoption and her attempt to help him through it. They had stood that close, but this picture conveyed something more.

The bare details of the robbery were listed, including the amount stolen and the police phone number for any tips. "So, the newspaper wants to go ahead and sentence Cole.

Skip the trial altogether. He's the only suspect listed, but he's already been cleared."

Art didn't say anything as she carefully folded the paper and leaned back in her chair.

"That almost explains all the angry emails in my inbox, but I'm not quite sure I see the connection." Rebecca crossed her arms over her chest, unfamiliar with this avalanche of fear and frustration. "Or the reason for the impromptu school board meeting."

"Those emails are from concerned parents. I've had phone calls from parents of all of our kids who are part of your volunteer program. They're upset." Art shook his head. "And most of them aren't even working at the shelter."

"I can understand that all those phone calls are a problem," Rebecca said as she glanced from one face to the next, "but no one wants to end the program." She licked dry lips. "Do they?"

This was her thing, her chance to make a mark on the world, to be a full-fledged Lincoln. They couldn't shut it down.

"Perhaps if you pull kids from the shelter," Cece said smoothly from her spot in the corner.

"I don't think it matters. The whole high

school program..." Art sighed. "I'm getting phone calls from parents of kids in other volunteer positions, like Faith Watkins, who's working at the hospital. Her mother is demanding to know what sort of background checks are performed on the employees *there*. At the hospital." He shook his head. "I mean..."

Rebecca studied his face as she tried to figure out what he was telling her.

"Are you saying that all it's taken to derail this program that I've spent years building is one man?" Rebecca shook her head. "And he's not even the villain here. Cole Ferguson has worked wonders at the shelter." She snorted. "I mean with the dogs, with the yard Sarah needs to keep the place open..." She waved her hands. "With the kids, Art. Did you know that Eric Jordan had stopped coming to school completely after his suspension for fighting?"

Rebecca stood to pace. If she didn't move, she might explode.

"That kid made a stellar grade on his science test and you want to know why? He's figured out what he wants in life." Rebecca leaned over Art's desk. "And do you know how that happened? Cole challenged him to a basketball game, won it and demanded the kid come in to help out at the shelter. There he found our veterinarian, and the rest is going to be history someday when he's a successful adult. Because of Cole Ferguson and the shelter." She tapped her finger hard on Cole's photo.

Aware she was pushing her luck, Rebecca straightened. "This uproar will die down. I'll move any kid who requests it until then."

When no one agreed with her plan, Rebecca held both hands out. What would she do if she couldn't convince them? "If you could see those kids at the shelter, Art." She closed her eyes, feeling her program slipping away. "What do you want?"

Art exhaled a long, slow breath. "For now, put the program on hold. The whole thing. We'll have a meeting with concerned parents, but this upset… We have to make a change, Rebecca." He didn't say he was sorry, but it was there in his eyes.

Dizzy all of a sudden, Rebecca held the chair for balance. "What if I refuse?" she heard herself ask, but she'd had no intention of saying those words. She wasn't an employee who refused the boss's orders. She wasn't a person who said no if there was any way to say yes.

"Then we'll have to…" Art shook his head. "Listen, you do a great job here. But I will shut the program down myself if I have to. You'll hand over your files."

"But the hospital, the thrift store, the offices around town…" Rebecca pointed as if they could see the places she named off. "Cole's not in any of those places." They'd be better off if he was.

"At this point, it's not Cole, Rebecca." Art winced. "It's *you* and Cole."

Rebecca's mouth dropped open as she tried to wrap her brain around what he was saying. She was the problem? Rebecca Lincoln was the problem? Of the Holly Heights Lincolns? The ones who'd supported every charity and good cause and underdog for a lifetime? What was happening?

"One mistake is all it takes with parents and their kids," Cece said softly.

"I haven't made a mistake." Rebecca pressed her hand over the ache in her chest. "This is no mistake." It was stupid and close-minded and hard-hearted and *stupid*. That was all this was.

"I'm good at my job." Rebecca waved her crumpled piece of paper. "Here's a plan I've developed with STCC to help more kids like Eric, the ones we're missing every single year, and what happens to them?" Some of them turned out like Cole, kids who had no better options.

"I'm not saying you're not good at your job, Rebecca. You care about these kids." Art stood up. "But you have to understand that these parents do, too. There's some overreaction going on, but you can't blame them for trying to protect their children. Close the program temporarily. Call all the employers you've got lined up and let them know we'll be suspending the program for…a month. That should be enough time to schedule a meeting."

Rebecca nodded and put her hand on the doorknob. Whatever she decided to do, Art wasn't going to change his mind.

Distracted by the shock of being on the receiving end of such disapproval, she waded out into the crowded hallway in a fog. When the first student bumped her in a rush to beat the tardy bell, she had to catch her balance against a row of lockers. The cold metal under her hand brought a flash of the time Eric had pinned her.

"You okay, Miss Lincoln?" Eric Jordan was

frozen two feet away, his hand held out as if he was tempted to help but unsure of his next step.

"Sure, Eric, I'm fine." She blinked slowly and then said, "What class are you headed to?"

"English," Eric said with a grimace. "Paper due on *Grapes of Wrath* today."

"And...did you write it?" she asked, grateful to fall into her usual pattern.

"I did." He shook his head. "But doing homework isn't as much fun as you'd think." He rolled his eyes.

"And you read the book? Because watching the movie is cheating."

"There's a movie?" The horror on his face teased a chuckle from Rebecca. Whatever else changed, kids never did.

"It's black and white, and the book is always better than the movie." She lightly touched his arm. "Better get to class. I wouldn't want to get you into trouble."

"No. Don't need any trouble." He shifted his backpack. "Are you sure you're okay? Your face is pretty pale."

Rebecca swallowed hard and lifted one hand to her cheek. "I'm a little under the weather."

Eric pointed at her. "I wondered where you've been. Missed you at the shelter."

"Yeah, it's been a crazy week." Rebecca sniffed. "But I had a chance to call about the vet tech program. You and your sister and I should tour the campus."

He wrinkled his nose. "What for? Can't afford it." He took a step back. "Don't get my sister's hopes up. Only way for me to help out is to get out of her way. Army will do that, and Debbie can see about her own life. She needs to do that. I can handle basic training, no sweat." He looked so young as he said it that Rebecca could imagine how Debbie would feel saying goodbye.

Rebecca shook her head. "You're her family. She needs you, Eric. Give me a shot. I have friends at STCC who will move mountains."

"I'll think about it," he said as the bell rang. He raised a hand and trotted down the hall. "See you at the shelter!"

The reminder that her program was going to be shut down was another punch in the stomach.

"It's only temporary," Rebecca muttered as she dropped into her desk chair and pulled out her list of volunteer spots. She'd have to call every contact and pretend to be cool, calm and collected, or the story about how upset she was would spread through town by the end of the day.

The frustration and outrage rolled over her again. A lifetime of doing nothing but good for this town and they couldn't trust her judgment any further than this? Whatever happened, the program she'd been building was in danger and it was so unfair.

Lincolns didn't complain when things were unfair, though. Not outwardly. They saved that for trusted friends. Rebecca picked up her cell to text Sarah. Have you seen the paper?

It was an indication of how bad things were that Sarah immediately answered. No, but the paper's Facebook page has posted links and tagged us so I've read the front-page stories. How bad is it?

Parents complaining. School board alarmed. Criminals lurking. I'm a bad judge of character. Rebecca rested her head against the chair and studied the small water stain on the ceiling tile.

The ding of another text got her attention. This will blow over.

Sarah was right. Eventually, it would, but

not today, and Sarah deserved fair warning. Your volunteers won't be in today. Sorry.

She hadn't put her phone down before Sarah answered. I've been through worse, but as always, DON'T READ THE COMMENTS.

For a split second, the urge to log on to Facebook to find out the true extent of the storm was overpowering, but her cell rang. Mom was on the display. There could only be one reason for her mother to be picking up the phone to make a call.

"Everything's fine, Mom," Rebecca said as she answered the call. "Art and I met to make a plan and it'll all blow over by next week."

"Hello. I'm fine. Yes, the weather here is lovely." Her mother's exasperated sigh was crystal clear. Cell reception was good wherever she was golfing. "Didn't anyone ever teach you how to answer the phone?"

Annoyance wasn't a new thing when Rebecca talked to her mother, but allowing herself to feel it was. "You're busy. I'm drowning. Who called you?" There was no way the Holly Heights newspaper had made it to Florida by mail today.

"Dinah called. I knew it was bad news. That's the only time she pulls me back into the loop. I swear, she loves gossip so much she's forgotten how little she liked me when we were neighbors," her mother said. Dinah had taught her daughter, Cece, everything she knew, so the next generation of Holly Heights could continue the tradition.

Rebecca bit her tongue to swallow her immediate answer but decided to go with it. "Then why are you paying any attention to her?"

"I don't, not unless it includes my children." Her mother drew out the word. "What have you done? Started an affair with a robber or something?"

Rebecca closed her eyes and considered hanging up the phone. She didn't have the energy for this.

"I did what you taught me to do, Mom. I gave a man the help he needed." Never mind that her friends had to force her to do that much. The outcome was the same. "He's doing a great job."

"Well, then, keep up the important work," her mother replied.

"Even if my boss is telling me not to and the town's in an uproar?" Rebecca frowned at the phone. Was her mother encouraging her to go against the town, to stand with Cole? No way.

"You have a good brain and a better heart. Your father and I worked hard to make sure of that." Her mother cleared her throat. "We worried so much about Daniel and look at him now. He's found his calling. We miss him, but we wouldn't change his life, even though we were sure he'd made the worst mistake there was, burning bridges at the hospital."

Rebecca traced a finger in the dust on the bookshelf beside her desk as she tried to follow her mother's train of thought.

"This time, with you, we're going to trust *you*."

Rebecca squeezed her eyes shut. Of course. This time she wanted her mother to lay out the proper plan of attack, one that would make everyone happy. And this time her mother let go.

"Even if that means this...man changes everything."

Rebecca could hear the worry in her mother's voice.

"We know who you are. If you say he's worth the trust, then..."

Her mother's long sigh was so familiar Rebecca sighed too.

"I can't wait to see you."

That last part was heartfelt, even if the

rest of it might have been uttered through clenched teeth.

"Me, too, Mom." Rebecca would give almost anything to have her mother close even though she'd celebrated the fact that Florida was so far away. That was how it went.

"Okay, get back to work. Love you, Bex." Her mother ended the call and Rebecca set the phone down slowly.

At this point, she had a decision. She could follow Arturo's orders and lie low until everything calmed down. Or... Rebecca picked up the phone, ready to dial the first parent on her list. One quick flash of Cole's face when he'd explained how her suspicions about him and the robbery had only confirmed his opinion of people, including her, was all it took to hang up the phone.

Her other option? Sticking her neck out for what she knew was right.

Rebecca studied her file of volunteer applications and assignments and closed the cover. This time, she couldn't write a check or smooth things over. There was no doubt in her mind that everyone else was wrong.

Instead of a bad day calling parents and pretending she understood, she was going to hand over her file to Art, come back to her office and do the rest of her job as well as she could. The principal's day would get a bit worse, but she wasn't going to give in this time. Thanks to Cole, she'd learned that real caring led to hard decisions. Luckily, the right thing was easy to determine this time.

The only question was what her next step *would* be in the fight to save her program.

THE FIRST CLUE Cole had that something was wrong came Thursday afternoon when he walked inside after cleaning the play yard. Since the weather was beautiful, he'd done his best to spend as much time as he could outside working on the pens he was building for Les. Winter in southeast Texas was unpredictable. The cool temperatures could hold for months, summer could return with a vengeance or a freak snowstorm could bury the place.

The complete silence in the dog room was unusual. At this time of day, there should be at least three volunteers giggling over one dog or another while they brushed or fed or worked on basic commands. It had taken a few weeks to get the pattern down, but Thursday was always a busy day around here for Rebecca's students.

But today, nothing. Not even a chirpy hum from Shelly, who was happier cleaning litter boxes than any human had a right to be.

The small trickle of unease that crept through his brain reminded him of other times when he'd felt the same. In prison, the premonition had more to do with keeping his guard up, but it was the same gut feeling that something he didn't like was lurking.

Don't be so melodramatic. If you can weather a break-in and police investigation, whatever this is can be fixed, too.

Eric hustled past on his way to the trash can.

"Sure is quiet today," Cole said as he washed his hands.

Eric didn't meet his eyes but shook his head. "Yeah. Soon as I finish with Les, I'll see if Shelly needs me to scoop outside or something."

Cole wasn't sure why he expected Eric to know any more than he did, but the unease was building. "Think I'm off tomorrow. You want a game?"

"Yeah, but after the shelter closes. Les says they'll be shorthanded. Asked me to make sure I was coming in. Like it's important or something."

Eric tried to pretend it wasn't that big a deal, but Cole imagined how he might have felt when he was a kid if someone he admired had asked him for a favor. His opinion of himself would have grown.

"Cool. I'll just…" He had no idea what he'd be doing in the morning. If he didn't find something, he'd obsess over the upcoming trip to Travis. He knew it was important for Sarah to see the training firsthand. He wasn't sure how he'd gotten roped in to returning to that place voluntarily.

Eric waited for him to fill in the blank. "You could come in. Sounds like the volunteer situation is not good." Eric frowned. "I mean, from what I've picked up. And when I saw Ms. Lincoln, she did not look well. Don't think she'll be in today, either."

"Sick? How?" Cole asked.

"Real pale." Eric shrugged.

Sarah would know what was wrong. He'd demand answers. First, he needed more info on whatever else was going on. Cole knew he shouldn't encourage the kid to eavesdrop. It was a bad habit that adults should discourage. In this case, he needed to know. "What have you heard? Where is everyone?"

"The volunteer program is on hold for a

month while they review the process," Eric explained. "That's what Sarah said, real slow and real loud like she meant it in a sarcastic way. Shelly and Les asked her to repeat it twice before she stormed off. No volunteers from the school."

Cole wiped his hands on a paper towel as he considered that. There was no way Rebecca would ever halt her program voluntarily. She was passionate about it, so much so that she'd forced him to get off his couch and do something to help the kids. What was going on?

"That's all I know, man. I gotta get in there. Les is removing stitches from the cat that came in last week." Eric hung his head. "Cats are the worst. It's the claws."

The chug of EW's truck trickled down the hallway, so Cole headed for the front, but he paused beside Sarah's office door. It was closed. That was unusual, too. He waved at EW through the window as he checked the parking lot for Will Barnes's truck. When he saw Rebecca's car, he knew who was in the office with Sarah.

Cole quickly tapped on the door, his ear pressed against the wood to see if he could hear anything.

"Come in," Sarah called. She was moving around the desk as if she'd been sitting next to Rebecca when he knocked.

"Are you gone for the weekend?" she asked brightly as she reached into her desk drawer to pull out his check. "I've got this ready, but I'm glad you stopped in to say goodbye for the day." She offered him the check.

Cole reluctantly took it and folded it once down the middle before he shoved it in his front pocket. He wasn't sure exactly how to get the conversation started, but one look at Rebecca's pale face convinced him that didn't matter.

"What's wrong? What's going on around here?" Was he about to get fired? What would he do if that was the case? And why would they fire him? Had the police turned up something else? Impossible.

"Oh, nothing for you to worry about. We're having a…setback with the high school's volunteer program, but Rebecca will straighten everything out. Until then, we'll all be doing a few more hours here and there." Sarah waved her hand breezily. "I warned Shelly she was getting soft. This will be good."

"Do you need me to come in tomorrow? I can work no charge." Cole scratched his temple and studied Rebecca's face again. She wasn't meeting his eyes. That was for the best.

He'd told her exactly what he'd thought about her doubts. Why should he be sad that she got the message loud and clear? Nothing made sense, but he hated the tight line of her mouth and the fact that she was avoiding him. He'd gotten used to her direct stare and the way she'd go toe-to-toe with him.

"No extra hours." Sarah sat down and picked up a pen. "We'll cover this weekend. I may add a few hours next week if that's all right." She tapped the calendar. "And Tuesday, when we head to Austin to visit the prison, Shelly will have her hands full." Sarah bit her lips. "Will could stop in that day…" She scribbled a note and seemed to forget he was still standing there.

Cole opened his mouth to make a reasonable argument about why it was better for him to work at the shelter instead of visiting the prison program. "Shelly could—"

"You're going. You're on the list. Shelly is not." Sarah pointed at him. "That's final."

Cole decided to take her at her word and go, but Rebecca's silence was a worry. "What's happened with the volunteers?" He wanted to turn to face Rebecca directly, but more than that, he wanted to be let in on the problem without insisting. Like a real member of the shelter team. "I can handle the truth, whatever it is."

Neither one of them answered, but Sarah fiddled with the edge of a folded newspaper. Cole eased forward to pick it up. "So it's the interview. With the reporter. I told you it was a bad idea," he muttered, and shot an irritated look at Rebecca. Instead of firing back at him as he hoped, she folded her hands together in a tight knot.

Uneasy, Cole scanned the front page. At first, he thought it was an okay story about the adoption event. A bit light on all the feel-good aspects like the fashion show, but the reporter had included the fund-raising amount and the number of animals that now had homes. Then he unfolded the paper.

"Guess they need an inside source at the police department, since I've already been cleared of this." Cole folded the paper and dropped it on Sarah's desk. "Is that the problem with the volunteer program? I don't get it."

"I didn't get it, either," Sarah muttered.

"Lots of parents are upset that we've got

kids working here at the shelter and now they're questioning all my placements." Rebecca shrugged to try to convince him that she didn't care. He wasn't buying it. "The principal ordered me to suspend the program for the time being. I refused, so he did it himself. Long story short, no volunteers until this is sorted out."

"I've got one more person starting tomorrow who's been referred from Judge Overmeyer's office for court-ordered community service—" Sarah sighed loudly "—but it will be difficult to cover all the kids. And that may be more fuel on the fire." Then she clasped her hands and smiled brightly. "Luckily, I've worked here when the town of Holly Heights was convinced a devil was in charge of this place and stayed far away. The animals will never know and eventually the head bogeyman in charge will figure out Plan C or D or whatever we're on. Count on it. Until then, we'll postpone the plans to open the second wall of kennels and the play yard."

Rebecca pressed her hand to her forehead but didn't say anything. Cole wasn't sure what they expected from him, but he couldn't stay quiet. "You don't need to keep me on, then, do you? Without the expansion, I mean." The dread that hit him was unexpected, but without this job, he was going to be facing a long line of days. "I should give you my notice."

Both of them immediately straightened in their seats. "No." They spoke in unison, and it had the effect of a shout.

Cole held up both hands. "Listen, I don't want to cause the shelter any trouble. If that's what I'm doing, I need to go."

Sarah laughed wildly. "Are you kidding me? Have you seen this place since you got here? Everything is working better. I mean it, Cole. Not just the play yard or the dogs or even me. Shelly is happier. Les has found his protégé. And…we need you. This will blow over eventually. Things like this always do." Sarah reached over to take his hand. "Listen to me. You aren't going anywhere. That trial period? It's over. You're permanent. Don't you even try to wiggle out of my clever trap now."

Her certainty was nice, but he knew what he had to do. This was what he'd expected all along. The villagers had picked up their pitchforks, and what Paws for Love did for the animals was more important than his paycheck.

And if he had any idea where the next paycheck might come from, he'd already be out the door.

Rebecca touched his shoulder and it was impossible to move. "Cole, listen." She smiled, but her eyes didn't brighten. He'd spent a lot of time thinking about her real smile. This one, the encouraging but false one, was dissatisfying because it was for his benefit alone. "We need you. I know you hate that, but you've already made us depend on you."

Cole grunted. "That's low."

Rebecca wrinkled her nose. "I know. I play dirty when I have to." She squeezed his hand. "Promise me you won't let this derail you or the shelter."

He scrubbed his hands over his face. "I'm not making another promise, Rebecca. I'm losing faith in my ability to keep them. All I had to do was stay out of trouble, and I can't manage *that*."

"This is about me as much as you. People are disappointed with me or surprised or angry that I'm not acting like they want me to, but none of that matters here. I'll keep my distance. You'll keep the shelter doors open. We'll regroup when this is over." Rebecca straightened her shoulders. "It'll be like this week and we all made it through."

Disappointment crashed over Cole.

He wouldn't see her. He wouldn't have to anticipate her arrival in the afternoon, dawdling long enough for her to come in so that he could catch sight of her smile once before he left. They wouldn't be alone in the play yard or in her kitchen or even on a sidewalk in the middle of town.

Which was better for her. Without the eyewitness account of their moment in front of the diner, Cole was almost certain this story would have been a blip. Maybe the parents whose kids worked at the shelter would have been worried, but this amount of coverage in the newspaper would never have happened.

Something like grief stole his breath and the jumble of his thoughts tied his tongue. His only consolation was that she didn't seem any happier about the arrangement. If the shimmer in her eyes turned to tears, he'd... He wasn't sure what he'd do. What did trained bears do when their emotions overwhelmed them?

Hide. That was what all wounded animals did. He used to be good at that. Then she came along and he could see how caring and trying mattered. Watching Eric at this shelter had changed him. So had EW's help and

Sarah's support and it felt completely wrong to let this situation go down this way. There had to be something he could do to help.

Unfortunately, the person he'd look to for inspiration had wilted into the chair as if she was too tired to stand. Was she quitting? "No check or amount of money to smooth things over, huh? So you'll stand by instead of jumping in. Or worse, you walk away? Good people don't do that. Isn't that what you told me? I'm not your project, but this is and you just…" He was so mad he couldn't come up with the words.

Escape was the only answer. Breathing was easier when he stepped outside, but for once he wanted the searing heat of August, not the beauty of a cool September. He couldn't believe he'd lost control like that. He could not contain the disappointment. It felt a little like betrayal. She couldn't walk away the minute things got difficult.

Except she *could*. How nice for her.

"Eric's not coming today," Cole said as he slid in beside EW and slammed the door. "Too much work."

"Well, now, that means more fish for us," EW said calmly as he drove out of the parking lot. The silence stretched between them until Cole couldn't stand it any longer.

"I knew this would happen. I was right. This is how it feels to *dream*." At least his mouth was twisted in bitterness. That was a manly emotion. All the rest of them, they could stay stuffed down where they belonged.

A beleaguered sigh was EW's only response.

"What?" Cole snapped. "I was right."

"Young fella, you wear me out," EW said. "You got to learn there ain't nothing permanent here. Good times is good. Bad times is bad. Ain't neither one of them forever. Just a bunch of gossip that made it into the newspaper anyhow. Happens ever' week."

"This time, it's jeopardizing the shelter and my job." And making him want to do *something*.

"Well, now, here's the part you forgot." EW tilted his head down and waited for Cole to answer.

"What?"

"You want good? You go get it. It's on you to make the change." EW rolled his eyes. "Kids. Always thinkin' they so smart and forget the most important piece. Work."

The truck was rolling. That was a good thing. Cole wanted to slide out of the seat and slam the door so hard the thing might never open again.

None of his rage bubbled over to EW, though. His friend whistled a tune and said, "Sure is a pretty day today."

Cole leaned an elbow on the truck door and pressed his forehead against his clenched fist. Hard.

Eventually, the cool breeze and EW's odd whistled tune eased some of the tension until he could get his brain working again. Was he going to retreat into his cave, go back to the way things were? Could he stop caring now that she'd convinced him to start? Frustration and unwilling respect warred inside him. Whatever happened with Rebecca would happen. That had no effect on what he could do himself if he tried. He was still so angry with her that he could yell, but he had to admire how well she wiggled her way through defenses to improve who a person was on the inside.

Then he realized that instead of just being mad, he could take that emotion, control it, do something with it. That was the man he was going to be, one who did something instead of ducking his head to avoid trouble.

"I need to make a stop."

EW raised an eyebrow.

"At the newspaper." Cole squeezed his eyes shut and then nodded. "Because *you're* right. If I want good things, I'm going to have to work at them." He tipped his chin up. "And I'm not afraid of work."

EW tapped his fingers on the steering wheel. "Maybe I oughta know some more about this visit to the newspaper office. We've already established you don't have the mind for any criminal activity."

Cole couldn't stop the surprised laugh. No matter how bad his temper got, EW rolled along. And he didn't hold any grudges. Everybody should have a friend like him. "Since brownies have replaced beer as your favorite compensation, I'll owe you a whole pan."

EW tilted his head. "Still need to know what you're planning to do at the newspaper office."

Cole exhaled loudly. "I'm going to issue an invitation. And I'm going to put in the work to get what I want."

"Well, all right, then. Here we go." EW's whistles picked up in volume and cheer even

if they still didn't make a song. Cole closed
his eyes and offered his best, awkward wish
that his plan worked.

CHAPTER SEVENTEEN

"I'LL MAKE THE offer one last time. Let me stay here, help out." Cole opened the passenger door on the van early Tuesday and waited for Sarah to answer. He didn't want to return to Austin or Travis. He wanted to stay here where he was comfortable and knew what to expect. Sure, the place had lost a bit of its shine since he hadn't seen Rebecca in days, but there was still the fact that he could come and go as he liked. There were no guards, no fences, no rules that said he couldn't leave.

"In the seat, mister," Sarah muttered as she buckled her seat belt. "It's too early for me to be having this conversation. I've had no coffee. We will fix that on the way through town and then I will be much more cheerful. Until then, sit down and hold on." She started the van. "I need that coffee."

Cole followed directions without another word. Whatever he'd thought about Sarah Hillman on his first visit to Paws for Love, he'd come to respect her brain and her heart. And it was easiest to keep his mouth shut. She pulled into a fast-food drive-through, ordered large black coffees for them both, even though he didn't drink the stuff, paid and then hit the highway. About ten miles down the road, she stretched. "Okay. I will now make conversation like a normal human being. Good morning, Cole."

Cole was surprised at how quickly she could lift his mood. He'd dreaded this day for weeks, but sitting beside her, he believed it was all going to work out. Should he warn her about his surprise visitor?

Sarah drained her cup and then reached over to snatch the one he'd been holding. "Thanks. Beautiful weather, right?" He thought about warning her that too much caffeine would stunt her growth, but with every sip, Sarah brightened. There was no way the institutional walls of Travis would be able to dim her for long.

"Looks like this is it. There's Rebecca." Sarah pointed as she turned the steering wheel to take the parking spot next to Rebecca's.

There she is. The fact that his heart sped up was the worst kind of romantic cliché, but it was impossible to ignore. Then he remembered that the hurt and anger had simmered down but he was still irritated with her failure to fight.

Instead of the professional dress she chose for work, today Rebecca had gone for jeans and a Paws for Love T-shirt. It satisfied all the prison's dress code rules for visitors. And they were a team.

If she'd seemed like her sunny self, he might have said the right thing to start a fight. Instead, she was a pale copy of herself, but the determination in her eyes was familiar. He didn't want to fight. He wanted to wrap her in his arms and promise everything would work out.

"Are you sure that's a good idea?" Sarah asked as she waved a hand to indicate Rebecca's outfit.

Rebecca studied her clothes. "Why? Everything's covered the way it should be."

Cole knew immediately what Sarah meant. Wearing that shirt to school after their visit to Travis would be like waving the red flag, daring the principal to charge.

"Aren't you going into work after this?" Sarah pointed at Rebecca's car. "That's why you wanted to drive yourself, so you could

leave early if you have to. And what about the
school board meeting tonight?"

Rebecca ran a hand through her curls. "Oh,
well…" She shot a quick look at Cole. "I won't
be a part of the school board meeting, not *in*
the meeting, at least. They've asked any parents to air their concerns, but Art made it
clear my presence was not required." Rebecca
cleared her throat. "I thought I was late. We
should get inside."

"Okay," Sarah said, "let's do this." She motioned with her chin at the door, her eyebrows
raised in question at Cole.

Yes, that was the way in, but his tongue
was doing that thing again where it was frozen in place. All these jumbled feelings. Were
they a terrible or reassuring sign that he was
returning to life?

Cole yanked the door open.

They were silent through the check-in and
the old tension and certainty that someone
was watching him at all times settled over
Cole, the tingle across the nape of his neck
familiar. Breathing became something he had
to think about.

*Breathe in. Breathe out. No one is going
to try to stop you from leaving.*

Having a panic attack would kill him, so

he had to get control. He tried counting. Then he pictured himself calmly working in the yard at Paws for Love. That was where he was most comfortable.

Before he had a full handle on his emotions, a guard let them into the receiving room where all the graduation ceremonies for Prison Partners were held. It was big and open with harsh fluorescent lights and gray linoleum. There were enough chairs for all the visitors on the list. The inmates and their dogs lined the wall farthest away from the entrance.

"What is she doing here?" Sarah whispered as she pointed at the newspaper reporter. Hayley Michener had chosen a seat front and center. The camera she held in one hand suggested she was prepared to get the perfect shot to illustrate her story.

She'd better. After Cole had stopped in at the newspaper, he'd had to move mountains to get her name cleared in time for the ceremony. David Thomas, the program coordinator, was probably still irritated with him.

Not that it showed in David's wide grin as he crossed the room. "Cole Ferguson. I never thought I'd get a chance to say this again, but it's good to see you." He offered his hand and

Cole shook it as he introduced Sarah and Rebecca. David shook hands but said in a low voice, "There's your friend, in the front row. If I wasn't happy to have the publicity, any publicity, you'd owe me big-time for that."

Sarah and Rebecca stared hard at him before they took the chairs David pointed them toward. "Have a seat. We're about to start."

There was no stage. No podium. No officials in fancy dress, just sixteen inmates holding leashes for sixteen well-mannered dogs who either sat or lounged at their feet. There was no music. No fanfare. And when the ceremony was over, the inmates would go back inside. They would say goodbye to the dogs they'd shaped and return to their bunks.

Cole couldn't catch his breath. Before the thing even started, he was going to pass out. Rebecca stood up, took his arm and shoved him down in her chair. Had he been gasping for air? He had to get out. Rebecca's hand came down to clamp hard on his shoulder. To move, he'd have to shake it off.

"I want to thank you all for coming today. It's always bittersweet to say goodbye to a class of dogs here at Travis County." David Thomas gestured at the line of inmates and dogs. "We've spent a lot of time getting to know each other, so it's like telling a friend goodbye forever." David was solemn as he addressed the crowd. "But we know they're headed for wonderful things. To the families who are lucky enough to be taking these dogs home today, we'd like to say thank you. Rescues most often end up here only because of bad luck. We believe each of you can turn that around for these animals. And Prison Partners depends on families like yours for support, donations and word-of-mouth publicity. We believe in what we're doing here and rely on your help, so thank you."

David studied the line of inmates. "Antonio. Let's start with you." A young man stepped to the center of the room, a Lab mix walking sedately behind him. "Antonio's been here at Travis for three years. He's a good trainer who gets to work with dogs who learn so fast they can handle advanced lessons, dogs like Trixie. Tell us about Trixie."

"She's a Lab mix. Her favorite treat is cheese. When she sleeps, she likes to have her head covered and her tail wags when she dreams." Antonio opened the small book he carried. "We met in July, but Trixie already knew how to sit and stay. Now she can do this."

The laughs that trickled through the crowd

as Antonio gave commands and Trixie did things like roll over, shake hands and play dead in a very theatrical way made it easier for Cole to breathe. He could hear the reporter's camera snapping away. That was something he'd done; he brought that reporter here. If she did a follow-up story on the shelter or one on the positive things happening here, everything would be worthwhile.

When Rebecca let go of him to clap wildly for Trixie and Antonio, Cole had to force himself not to reach for her hand. That would be a mistake.

"And now let's talk to Jay and his dog Cherry." David Thomas waited for the new inmate to step forward. "Cherry's story is different. She was an emergency rescue from a kill shelter. She'd been abandoned along a highway and limped pretty badly when she arrived here. But Jay and Cherry have figured out how to work around that."

"Ch-Cherry has a leg that doesn't bend, s-so s-sitting is too hard." Jay bent and tapped the floor. Cherry slowly stretched out on the floor, her front paws and nose resting above the spot Jay had tapped. "Instead of s-speaking, we use hand s-signals." Jay continued to show exactly what Cherry could do. "We make a good team."

Whoever took her home would be dealing with medical issues for the rest of Cherry's life, but her beautiful brown eyes only showed gratitude with every step she took.

The loud sniffle coming from behind him startled him.

"Sorry," Rebecca whispered. "It's so sad and happy and…" She swallowed hard.

Sarah was wiping under her eyes as she nodded. "It really is. Get out your checkbook." Her voice broke on the last word and Cole couldn't help the smile that tickled around the edges of his mouth.

As each family accepted the dog's leash and the inmate's journal and posed for a picture with the Prison Partners photographer, Sarah had to choke back sobs. As usual, there wasn't a dry eye in the place when David Thomas thanked everyone for coming.

After the inmates filed out and all the other visitors left, only David and the reporter remained in the room with Cole, Sarah and Rebecca. Hayley Michener loudly blew her nose into a tissue David offered her, and the satisfaction Cole felt was immense. There was no way this story was going to be anything but positive for Prison Partners and, by extension, Paws for Love.

David offered tissues to both Sarah and Rebecca. "Sorry. I should have given you one earlier."

Sarah could do nothing but wave her hand helplessly.

Rebecca was in a little better shape. "I want to know what it will take to expand this program, David."

"I want my dogs in," Sarah managed to add.

David glanced at Cole and then said, "As always, we're hampered by resources. All the prisons currently involved are at capacity for every class, and we have a list of shelters waiting for spots."

"Is every prison in Texas involved?" Rebecca asked. "Do you have more dogs than you can adopt out?"

David shook his head. "No and no. But it's a hard sell, fund-raising for prisoners and dogs. People always tell us how many other good causes there are out there." He sighed. "And I get that, but when you see something like this, today, and the way it can change a man's outlook on his life as well as give a dog a future, I can't give up."

"You need a success story," Hayley Michener said from her seat. "A man who's successfully rehabilitated. You can find a hundred happy families with dogs from the program, I have no doubt. But you need someone to speak for the men here." She glanced at Cole.

"Yeah, wonder where we could find one of those. On the front page of the newspaper?" Rebecca turned her back on Hayley. Cole studied her irate expression and fought the urge to rub the ache right over his heart. Rebecca thought he'd already proven he was rehabilitated and she was ready to fight his enemies. If they ever figured out how to make anything between them work, her loyalty would be priceless. Unforgettable. Worth some trouble.

"Here's what you do, David. Put together a proposal. Send it to this guy. He's always looking for good places to spend our money." Rebecca offered him a card with Will Barnes's name on it. "We are going to help."

David took the card and tapped it against his hand. "Just like that? No trade required? Like, if I don't help the shelter, are you still committed?"

Sarah stopped sniffing and stood tall. "Hey, we're committed. My shelter is doing fine, even if I want this for my dogs. Do the proposal. I'll give you a list of everything you need to make sure Will says yes. I know him pretty well. Call the shelter."

David laughed. "Okay, I will." Then he turned to Cole. "Interested in being a spokesperson or something?"

Cole shook his head violently. There was no way he would be speaking on behalf of anyone.

"We'll work on him," Rebecca said as she offered David her hand. "This has been amazing."

Instead of a handshake, Sarah hugged David. "You call me. I can tell you how to get whatever you need from these softies. And Cole's in," she said as Rebecca dragged her toward the doorway.

When the door banged shut behind them, Cole said, "Seriously, man, find another spokesperson."

"I'll try," David said as he stacked the chairs, "but I'll guarantee I won't find anyone who can match you."

"You don't even know how it's going for me. Last week, I was a police suspect and am single-handedly destroying a woman's career." He shot a look at the reporter who was loitering by the door.

"But you also made friends with donors who could change the life of Prison Partners forever." David propped his hands on his hips. "You know how often we talked about expanding this, identifying new prisons and even programs in other states."

Cole rubbed his forehead, thinking of all the networks Sarah, Jen, Stephanie and Rebecca had established. "Yeah, they could help you out with that. Not with one check, but they have enough smarts and determination to change things."

David clapped his hand on Cole's shoulder. "So I gotta say thanks to you. For the connection. Then I've got to polish up the fundraising request I've been using since I took over Prison Partners. It could work this time."

Cole nodded. "Yeah, but you better call Sarah. She likes to help. You know where to find me if you need me."

"I'm going to set up some interviews, maybe TV. You'll be available?" The gleam in David's eyes was impossible to miss.

Cole could imagine the endless hours of conversation Sarah would commit to if he hesitated. "Let's do one, see how it goes. Gotta keep the boss happy."

When David chuckled, Cole tried to figure out when he'd become such a pushover. It had to do with the day he'd walked into Paws for Love, that much he knew. They shook hands and Cole headed for the door.

Hayley Michener seemed wrung out from all the emotion in the room. Her face matched his energy level, but she held out a hand to prevent him from opening the door. "Hey, thank you for getting me in. This story is going to be awesome." She tried an awkward thumbs-up.

"It better be." Cole waited for her to step aside and then pushed open the door.

Hayley made a beeline for David, her notebook raised. Outside, Cole braced his hands on his knees to catch his breath. Then he realized that he'd done it, the thing he'd been fearing ever since he left this place. He'd returned on his own terms. And he'd survived. Whatever happened next, he'd made the effort.

If someone had told him he'd actually agree to do something to help Travis the day he'd left this place, Cole would have assumed that person needed a psych evaluation.

There were only two women in the world

who could have forced him to do this, leaving him feeling as weak as a kitten and…

Cole straightened and walked toward Sarah and the van while he tested the word.

Proud.

Unwilling to study his feelings too closely, Cole asked, "Rebecca on her way to work?"

Sarah was collapsed against the side of the van as if she lacked the energy to climb inside. "Yeah. She's got a big day ahead." She held out her hand. "Here. You drive. I'm not up to it."

Cole waited for her to climb into the passenger seat before he closed the door behind her. She seemed as exhausted as he felt. He wanted to know what was going on with Rebecca.

Then he remembered he was going to keep his distance.

When they were on the highway headed home, Sarah took out her cell phone. The mystery of who she was calling didn't last long. "Hey, I need you to call David Thomas today, make sure he's working on a proposal for Rebecca." There was a brief pause. "Then put a note on every other day in your calendar to check in with him."

Will must have thought that schedule was

excessive, because Sarah frowned. "This is important to me." She straightened in her seat. "Yeah, it was amazing. You and I, we're going to brainstorm some ideas tonight. Prison Partners will be expanding." She said it with certainty. Then she grinned. "I knew I could count on you, baby. Call me later." Sarah ended the call with a happy grin.

Cole was about as uncomfortable as an employee could get while listening to his boss call someone "baby," but the reminder that the ball was rolling filled him with new energy. "Spokesperson. You think that will make a difference?" He knew he didn't sound convinced.

Sarah laughed. "Yeah, I do. Anonymous asks will fail most of the time." She turned to face him. "Add a name and a story and show how small contributions matter, and people have a hard time forgetting." She tilted her head. "Kinda like you and Eric. Every now and then for the rest of your life, you'll wonder how he turned out. That's human nature, to care about the people who come into our lives."

"Really?" Cole wondered if a scoff would be insubordination. "Human nature?"

"I hope so." Sarah pulled out a pen and an

old envelope. "Someday I'm going to remember to put a notebook in this purse. Today is not that day."

One quick glance showed that she was making a numbered to-do list.

"And someday, you are going to know what it feels like to make a difference to prisoners all over the state of Texas." Sarah waited for him to look her way again. "And that's going to be soon. How does that feel?"

"Like breaking a promise, but doing the right thing," Cole said quietly. Sarah's quickly indrawn breath sounded like a sniffle, but he refused to look her way. If she was crying again, he'd have to pull over so they could both recover.

"Oh, wow," she said, "that's a bad spot."

Cole shook his head. "All my Mimi wanted was for me to stay out of trouble. The last week has proven I'm failing at that." He gripped the steering wheel. "But I can't come up with one thing I should have done differently." That was a change. Always before, his regrets were numerous, but lately, they'd dwindled to only one: disappointing his grandmother, the one person who'd always been on his side. Caring exposed him to trouble, but it also meant he was never alone when that trouble arrived.

Rebecca, who cared more than one person should, was withdrawing. He'd tried that. He could tell her it wouldn't work.

"Inviting the reporter was brilliant." Sarah squeezed his shoulder.

"I wish I could think of something else to try," Cole murmured. "I can't believe Rebecca's quitting her program this way." He stared hard at the road through the windshield.

Sarah sighed. "If you think that, you've got it all wrong. Come to the school board meeting tonight. Make your voice heard."

Was Rebecca going to stand back and let others do her fighting for her? That was disappointing. She had said herself she wasn't going to the meeting.

Cole knew his disappointment was showing. Sarah rolled her eyes. "Man, you do not handle setbacks well. Gotta learn to get back up. Rebecca's going to have her program and help her kids, one way or another. Shutting her out? Yeah, that's an invitation for her to get creative." She narrowed her eyes at him. "This attitude of yours…it makes me think of a man who's disappointed in someone more important than a coworker." She tilted her head. "Something you want to tell me?"

"Nope." Cole focused on the road, a confused

jumble of thoughts about what Rebecca's next move might be distracting him. She needed the school to get to the kids. If the principal was going to shut the program down permanently, what kind of options did that leave her?

The rest of the trip to the shelter was filled with Sarah's quiet scribbling and Cole's deep thoughts. When he pulled in, only one car other than Shelly's was in the parking lot.

"Thought we were closed for visitors this morning."

Because they were shorthanded and mornings were slow during the workweek, Sarah had insisted Shelly put up a sign asking visitors to return in the afternoon.

"Yeah, there must be some kind of emergency." The quiet drive had restored some of Sarah's energy apparently, because she was out of the van and rushing for the door before Cole's feet hit the ground.

Then he heard it, the sad howl of a theatrical beagle.

Freddie was back.

CHAPTER EIGHTEEN

"HEY, BOSS," SHELLY said from behind the desk. "I'm so glad you're back. We've got a situation with the Scotts and Freddie."

Howling Freddie and his dismayed owners stood across from her. The way Mrs. Scott clapped her hands over her ears and flinched from the dog suggested things weren't going well with the adoption.

Freddie's howls changed to yips interspersed with hoarse coughs as Cole knelt down beside him. "What's up, Fred?" Cole scratched the dog's chin and tried to slip his finger under Freddie's collar. When it was impossible, his anger ticked up a notch. "Think this is too tight for you, boy." He quickly loosened the collar and ruffled Freddie's ears. "Now you can bark even louder." His scowl would have intimidated anyone.

"He pulls out of the collar unless it's that tight. I chased him all over the park on our first walk." Mr. Scott clutched the leash tightly. "I should have let him go."

The atmosphere in the room immediately cooled. Ice-cold. Cole was pretty sure it wasn't all coming from him.

"Let him go." Sarah repeated it carefully. "As in run away or abandon him in the park?"

"In less than a week, that dog has destroyed a dining room table, six pairs of shoes, four lamps and every single rug in the house," Mrs. Scott snapped. "You should have warned us he had behavior issues."

"He's wild. Just wild." Mr. Scott pointed at Freddie, who was now wildly happy. His back leg was thumping in time with Cole's scratching fingers.

"Freddie is still learning," Shelly said with a forced smile. "You could take some obedience classes together."

Cole could almost see the bright light of an idea appear in Sarah's brain. She muttered, "Make a note. Obedience classes. Puppy classes. You could charge a fee for training." Then she pasted on a patient expression. "Why are you here?"

Cole's lips were tight as he stood. He wasn't happy with the way the Scotts had treated

Freddie. He didn't want to let them walk out with his dog again.

Then he realized that was the kind of thinking that would make it impossible to get over Freddie.

"We're returning him." Mrs. Scott tipped her chin up. "We'll either take our adoption fee back or we'd be happy to try another dog, one with some manners." She sniffed and shook her head. "Do you have any of those?"

Sarah's chuckle wasn't friendly. "He's anxious, in a new place, after he's been bounced in and out of homes. He needs some time. I thought you knew something about dogs."

"We had *outside* dogs. We have a big yard. Freddie won't stay outside because he howls." Mr. Scott waved a hand. "But inside, he's destroying the place. There's no solution."

"Patience is the solution," Cole said, and scooped up Freddie in his arms. "We're going outside while you figure this out."

He was moving as quickly as he could, but not quite fast enough to escape the insult directed at him.

"Is he dangerous?" Mrs. Scott asked, one hand pressed to her chest. "He seems so angry. We didn't want to approach him *before* we knew about his record." She whispered the last word. "But now…"

Cole wanted to hear Sarah's answer, so he slowed his march.

"Of course not," Sarah snapped. "Sign this, and we'll take Freddie from you. We will not be refunding the adoption fee and you will not be taking another dog home." Sarah's tone was flat and brooked no argument.

Mr. Scott decided to bluster anyway. "Now, wait a minute. We paid you for a dog. This is not proper."

Sarah pointed. "Check your original contract. There will be no refunds of adoption fees. Those went to cover the costs of vaccinations."

"What about another dog, then?" Mr. Scott looked at his wife. "We promised the grandkids."

Mrs. Scott's voice dripped icicles. "This is our fault? You give us a wild dog and it's our fault we can't live with him."

Shelly didn't answer, but every bit of her body language screamed "yep."

Sarah held her hand out toward the door to suggest they might want to step through it. "Sign this surrender contract and you can be on your way."

Mr. Scott snorted. "We won't be signing

and this isn't the last you've heard from us. A place like this, what did we expect? Criminals in every corner." Mr. Scott put one hand on his wife's back and urged her out the door.

While Shelly and Sarah scribbled notes furiously on the unsigned contract, Cole made his escape outside.

"Looks like you're here for a while, Fred." He set the dog down, uncertain of how long Freddie had been inside, when he'd been fed or what sort of care he'd gotten. Instead of running away for a happy investigation of his old yard, Freddie jumped up and put his feet on Cole's knees. Relieved, Cole picked the dog up and held him close to his chest. "What a day."

All he'd dreamed of while he was in prison was control. Cole wanted to make decisions about his own life, what he'd do every day and how he felt about that. This day had been out of control in almost every way. He'd gone to Travis under orders from his boss, and his emotions were rioting from pride to fear to anger to relief. It was peaceful to sit there in the cool sunshine holding a happy dog.

For one single moment, he was exactly where he wanted to be, doing what he wanted to do, and he knew how he felt about it. "I'm happy to see you again, Fred."

The dog sighed as he rested his head on Cole's chest, so he took that as Freddie's agreement.

He lost track of time while they sat there. When Sarah sat next to them with a delicate thump, he remembered he was supposed to be working. "Guess I'll need to set a spot for Freddie. Want new photos?" He wasn't going to let himself worry about what would happen when the next family wanted to take Freddie home. This was the job. For now, he'd be happy.

"Yeah, I guess so," Sarah said as she ran a hand over Freddie's head, dodging his pink tongue. "I wish you could take him."

Cole bent to let the dog down on the grass. This time, Freddie took off for the fence line like a shot, ready to patrol. "Yeah, well...I can't." He couldn't. His trailer still wouldn't work for Freddie. The dog needed an owner who wasn't perched on the edge of disaster. Paying for everything Freddie needed would wipe him out. "But he's here now."

"We'll make sure it's the right fit the next time," Sarah promised.

Cole watched Freddie prancing and wondered how she could manage any optimism.

Sarah punched Cole's arm lightly. "Listen, don't you give up on...Freddie, or me, or anyone in this town, not yet. It's too soon. I know whereof I speak, mister. There are so many good people in this place. All you gotta do is find them." She held his stare and nodded slowly.

Cole didn't answer. There was work to do. He'd do it. And until the right people walked in the door, he'd work with Freddie, improve his manners. The next adoption would stick and he'd count it a happy ending. Rebecca would find her own way and he'd adjust. This was the point where lots of practice putting one foot in front of the other no matter what came in handy.

For the rest of the hours he spent at Paws for Love, Cole worked hard to make up for lost time. He and Shelly cleaned and washed dogs and cats, and by the time he gave Freddie his last afternoon treat, Cole was approaching normal.

A hard basketball game should screw his head on properly. He waved at Sarah, who was on the phone when he passed her office, and slid into EW's truck.

"Everything work out in Austin?" EW asked as he pulled out on the highway.

Cole had never mentioned his concerns about going back to the prison.

That didn't mean that EW couldn't read between the lines.

"Yeah, the women at the shelter are going to help spread the program to more prisons," Cole said.

EW pursed his lips. "'Bout the best outcome, then." He offered his hand for…a fist bump? Cole was shaking his head as he answered with his own fist. He would not ask about this new development.

"Things is working out," EW murmured, "like I knew they would."

"Yeah." Cole was fighting a smile, certain he'd turned a corner into some weird emotional amusement park, when EW pulled into the trailer park. There, Mike and Eric were hanging out under the basketball goal with the third kid, the owner of the beat-up car.

"Feel like a game?" Cole asked with a glance at EW.

EW raised his eyebrows. "Now, then, a young fella who wants to engage with at-risk youths… Wonders will never cease."

Cole grunted as he slammed the door. "Just back me up."

He didn't slow down until he was standing under the goal, the basketball in his hand. "I was hoping I'd catch you." He offered his hand to the third guy, a kid about the same age as Eric but with miles of hard living on his face. "Cole Ferguson. Want to play three-on-two? These two'll vouch I can handle it."

The kid didn't shake Cole's hand. "Nah, I'm out." He pointed at Eric and Mike and backed away toward his car. All of them watched him climb in and drive away.

"Didn't mean to send away your company. Nice kicks, though. Look expensive." Cole pointed in the direction the car had disappeared as he dribbled the ball with one hand. Neither Eric nor Mike seemed that comfortable. "What's his name? He go to Holly Heights?" Cole tossed the ball to EW, whose beautiful jump shot drained the net.

"No. He visits his girlfriend." Eric caught the bouncing ball and held it.

"Ain't in school," Mike added.

If Cole had to guess, Mike wished he could run away. Since he knew how to play rough, Mike's concern wasn't about the game.

"Same rules?" Cole asked. When Eric and

Mike nodded, Cole tossed the ball to EW and waded into battle. The game to ten was quick and dirty and exhausting, but so much fun that Cole was grinning even as he wiped blood off his lip. "You boys have been practicing."

Neither one of them said a thing, but the gasping for air Mike was doing satisfied Cole on a deep level. This time, EW managed to catch everyone off guard by stealing the ball and scoring the winning shot. EW caught the ball and dribbled it while he shook his head. "Not practicing quite enough."

Cole was happy to see both Eric and Mike were bent over, resting their hands on their knees as they panted. Just like he was.

The sun set earlier this late in September, so the shadows were already growing when he straightened. "Good thing we didn't bet anything this time."

Eric didn't smile, but he nodded. Cole studied his face. It seemed like the kid wanted to say something, but he hesitated. Cole offered him his hand. "Better luck next time."

Eric shook it but didn't meet his eyes. Cole turned to Mike. "Nice hook shot."

Mike quickly shook his hand and shuffled back, before he stopped. "Right. Uh, I'll see you tomorrow, Eric." He didn't look at them as he walked away.

Cole turned to EW, raising his eyebrows to ask if he knew what was going on.

"Where does Mike live?" Cole asked as he watched the darker shadow retreating. "This trailer park?"

"Yeah, in the back. Next to Red's girl. That's the guy who left. Red asks a lot of questions." Eric scuffed a line in the dirt and shoved his hands in his pockets. Whatever he wasn't saying weighed heavily. If Cole had to guess, Red was trouble.

"Questions? About what?" Cole asked as he bounced the basketball.

"School. The shelter. Things like that." Eric scrubbed a hand through his hair. "Spends too much time with Mike." Eric darted a glance his way before adding, "Guess I better get inside. I have homework."

Cole watched Eric until he climbed up on his porch, the thick greenery giving the whole place a nice appeal. An old Subaru was parked in front.

"Think I ought to go ask Eric about the money?" The cops had interviewed all the volunteers but didn't have much new information to go on. The few items that had been stolen had yet to turn up at the town's single pawnshop. Neither cop was surprised. Only the dumbest criminals would try pawning stolen goods here in Holly Heights.

"Cops already did." EW bounced the ball slowly. "What would you have said? At that age?"

Their eyes met in the growing darkness. He'd have lied to protect his gang. That was the code they'd all lived by. It had made them closer than family sometimes.

Until Ricky Martinez had broken that code to save his own neck.

"Know Mike's last name?" Cole asked.

EW pursed his lips. "Naw, but the police'll be able to figure that out."

Cole braced his hands on his hips as he tried to figure out what he was going to do. Informing on anyone pretty much went against his better judgment and his promise to keep out of trouble. In jail, if he'd even considered going to the guards with something he'd seen or heard, he'd have ended up in the infirmary or worse.

But he wasn't in prison anymore.

Was a suspicion that Eric and Mike had talked to Red about the money at the shelter even count as a tip? What if Mike had been involved? Or worse, Eric, the kid he'd been patting himself on the back for helping?

What if he didn't say a thing and the next thing Red talked Eric and Mike into trying was worse? Breaking and entering was bad enough, but there was no violence involved. Almost any other scheme would increase the danger to the kids' lives *and* freedom.

"Can I borrow your phone?" Cole asked as he started walking to EW's place. If Hollister or Adams happened to be at work, he'd mention what he'd seen. If they weren't, he'd sleep on it.

Or he wouldn't sleep so much as worry about it all night long, but he'd call again in the morning from the shelter. That was all he could do.

Paws for Love mattered to him. Then he remembered Sarah's certainty that human nature would make him worry about Eric and his future for the rest of his life.

Because of one woman's insistence and a basketball game, he and Eric were tangled together forever. If he'd refused her, this would be someone else's problem.

In this case, it would be Eric's burden. Cole had lived in his shoes. He couldn't turn his back if he had the power to help, not anymore.

EW's shuffle behind him was reassuring. He didn't argue, so this was the right thing to do. Had to be.

He wasn't convinced even as he picked up EW's cordless and dialed the number from the phone book. Then he remembered Eric's face, the uncertainty and the inability to meet Cole's stare head-on. Whatever the kid knew, he didn't want to be the one to tell the police.

So Cole would do it. He was an adult. He didn't stand to lose much if he was wrong or if he was right. But Eric would be able to let go of some of that worry.

That was enough to convince him.

As soon as an officer answered, Cole said, "I'd like to talk to Officer Hollister. I might have some information on a robbery."

CHAPTER NINETEEN

REBECCA NERVOUSLY CHECKED to make sure her T-shirt was still neatly tucked into her khakis. If this wasn't the quintessential teacher outfit, she didn't know what could top it. Maybe if it had a Holly Heights mascot on the pocket instead of the Paws for Love logo.

"What are you doing out here, Rebecca?" Arturo asked in his tried-and-true principal's voice. "As I mentioned when I told you about this meeting, there's no need for you to attend. We're gathering information at this point. I'll tell you how everything turns out in the morning."

When she reached down to grab the poster board sign she'd made, Rebecca did her best to calm her nerves. She'd never done anything like this. Protests, peaceful or otherwise, were nowhere near her comfort zone. But she wanted to be heard.

"Sorry, Art. I'm not going to wait for you to decide what's best for me and my program."

She held the sign up like a shield. "I'll be out here. Handing out information on my new project. It's called Mentor Me and it's for kids of all ages. I'll do it on my own time." She held out a copy she'd managed to sweet-talk Will into letting her make on his office machine. "Here's some info."

As she remembered Jen's angry insistence on a real protest, Rebecca added, "There might also be chanting and marching. We'll have to see." Stephanie and Jen were prepared to come out swinging to make sure Rebecca got what she wanted. That precious loyalty could only be explained by the bonding that surviving high school together would bring.

It had taken her most of the day to come up with something clever to yell, but she'd settled on "Volunteers, yes. Closed minds, no."

She should have asked Stephanie for help. Rhyming would be better, but it captured her feelings anyway. Since Jen, Stephanie, Sarah, Shelly and Les were all planning on joining her here, she'd exceeded her glitter quota on the signs. The chant might be lacking and the flyers she'd put together were rough, but the signs were on point.

"You can't do that here. This is school property," Art pointed. "Go down to the street if you insist on this…exhibition."

Before Rebecca could decide whether she was going to cooperate, her backup rolled out of the Paws for Love van. Jen picked up a sign. "We like it here." She linked her arm through Rebecca's and the rest of them followed suit. Their chain was long enough to block two of the three sets of doors.

"If you insist on being a nuisance, I will call the police." Art leaned forward. "Please don't make me call the police on you, Rebecca."

If she hadn't already lived through the storm of public opinion, Rebecca would have folded immediately. "Listen, Art, do what you have to do, but this is too important to me to back down."

"You're ruining any hope of letting this simmer down," Art said, his lips grim.

"Fine. Holly Heights needs to understand that this is wrong. These parents know me. I love this town and their kids. Either they trust me or they don't."

Saying it out loud was enough to make Rebecca understand that was exactly what Cole had meant in the parking lot at the shelter. In or out, the choice to trust Cole was up to her.

It was as easy as making up her mind to trust the good man she'd come to know.

And now, as soon as she settled this thing with Holly Heights, convincing Cole to trust *her* was first on her agenda.

Rebecca watched Eric, his sister and a few of the shelter volunteers walking through the parking lot. Were they here to listen to the school board meeting?

"What about your job?" Art asked. "An arrest? How will that look?"

She hadn't quite reconciled herself to losing her job, but she wasn't going to stop. "Go stare at my bulletin board of successes, Art. Then we can talk about my job." It was a gamble, but she'd have to take it.

When Eric stopped behind Art, the principal turned. "Go on in and have a seat."

Eric wiped a hand across his mouth. "Actually, we were wondering if you have any extra signs. I didn't get that memo." He shoved both hands in his pockets.

"Take mine. I don't do glitter," Jen said as she offered it. "Go on down to the end."

Art was shaking his head as he stalked away.

Rebecca turned to Sarah and Jen. "Kids? We don't want kids involved."

"It's their decision, Bex," Sarah said. "This directly affects them. If they want to be heard, let them." She patted Rebecca's shoulder.

Debbie Jordan held out her hand for the papers Rebecca was mangling. "Better give me those. I'll hand them out." She quickly scanned the flyer. "A mentoring program for kids of all ages. Free after-school programs. Spring break camps. Summer day camps." She whistled. "You turned up the heat, didn't you?" Debbie nodded. "Good for you."

Rebecca stared hard at the line of kids and grabbed Debbie's wrist before she could pursue the group of parents crossing the parking lot. "Hey, this week I'm going to stop by the Shop-on-In. That okay?"

"What did he do now?" Debbie drawled as she glared at her brother. "We were doing so well."

Rebecca waved her hand. "No, it's not him. It's you. If I'm going to do this—" she tapped the stack of flyers in Debbie's hand "—and keep my day job, I'm going to need help. Are you interested? It's only part-time, but we could work around your schedule at the Shop-on-In."

Debbie shook her head. "You are unbelievable. You don't even know me."

"I know Eric. You're good people." Rebecca shrugged. "I need help making calls, lining up volunteers and businesses and speakers and who knows what else at this point. If I can find someone who understands the importance of what I'm doing, so much the better."

"We'll talk," Debbie muttered, and then caught the first group of parents before they could make it past the human chain.

Rebecca quickly untangled her arm and ran down the line. They had effectively blocked off all the doors. "Listen, kids—" she held out both hands "—if Principal Sepulveda calls the police, you need to drop the signs and head inside. Do you hear me? I don't want any of you having to answer questions or face any repercussions."

"We want to help," Eric said after a long pause. "Me, for one, I can't ever pay you back for all you've done. This is nothing."

Rebecca squeezed his shoulder and then did the same for every kid in the line. "Unless you agree to ditch me at the first sign of the cops, I'll have to call the whole thing off."

More than one set of eyes rolled, but they all nodded. Satisfied that she'd done what she could to protect them without scrapping their right to speak, Rebecca trotted back to the end of the line, wrapped her arm through Jen's and picked up her sign.

"Volunteers, yes. Closed minds, no," Rebecca said loudly. When she repeated it, Sarah and Jen picked it up. Eventually, the whole line was chanting. Parents were arriving and having to maneuver around the line to get inside the auditorium. Debbie made good use of the delays and managed to talk to every parent before they escaped inside.

It was working. Rebecca realized that protests were more her thing than she'd imagined. She was almost having fun.

Then EW's truck rolled to a stop in front of the school auditorium and Cole slipped out of the passenger side. Panic tightened her muscles, made it hard to breathe. For his own good, he shouldn't be here.

And she wasn't sure how she'd manage if his disapproval matched the same level it had the last time they'd met in Sarah's office.

His face was hard to read as he studied the line of protestors, but he eventually walked over to stand in front of her. "Have you lost your mind?" he asked in a low voice. "You'll be arrested."

Disappointment made it hard to stand tall, but she had a plan for that eventuality. If it happened, she would be okay. "It'll be fine. I have bail money."

He ran a hand down his face as if he was too fatigued to deal with her or the situation. Debbie shoved a flyer in his hand and then headed out to accost stragglers in the parking lot.

"Are you here to speak at the meeting?" Rebecca asked, the chanting dying down as everyone turned to listen.

"No, I'm here because someone told me that I wouldn't want to miss this." He stared at Sarah before shaking his head. "What I don't understand is why she didn't talk you out of it."

Rebecca stepped in front of Sarah. "Listen, a wise man once told me good people don't walk away from things that matter, not without regretting it. I won't regret this."

"If you lose your job? What then?" he asked as he wrapped his hands around her arms. "Don't do that for me. I'll find something else."

She snorted. "Right. I'm not doing it for you. This is for me. I want my program on my terms, and these people will give it to me or…"

Cole raised an eyebrow.

"Read the flyer. I'm expanding." She tapped her chest, the freedom of having complete say over her own future bubbling up there. At every step, she'd worried about what would happen if she lost control of the program she loved, but now, with him in front of her and her friends behind her, this was so right.

She was a different kind of Lincoln than the rest of her family. First, she was rich. And second, she'd built her own program from scratch. This new program would be what she wanted, anything she could dream up.

Cole scanned the sheet of paper quickly then he laughed at the way Sarah sang, "I told you so. Don't you underestimate any of us."

Rebecca stared at Sarah and then turned back to Cole. "Kids who don't dream? They need me, Cole. That's it. That's the key. If I concentrate on what I really believe in, the possibilities are endless and exciting and worth fighting for. This school board meeting? Who cares? They can close the school program down or give me rules or decide to run it themselves. No matter what they come up with, I'm going bigger."

She squeezed his hands. "And no one can stop me."

Cole laughed. "I thought you'd waved the white flag. You were just gathering ammunition."

"All I need are people." She motioned with her head down the line. "The ones who love me and the ones who need me. I don't need the school for that."

"Just my luck. I make a promise to keep my nose out of trouble, and I fall for a woman who will deliberately stir up trouble to do the right thing."

Rebecca jerked around to see if Sarah had heard his confession. When she nodded, Rebecca whipped back to look at Cole. "Falling for me? I was going to make this grandiose stand about you having to choose to be in or out, but you just—" She waved her hand.

Cole pinched the bridge of his nose. "We're at a protest. The police are on their way. Not exactly the time to be talking relationship goals."

"Did you ever think you'd be the voice of reason, the only hope for containing my impulses?" She shook her head. "You were so disappointed in me. First, with the break-in and then this mess. That hurt, but I needed you. I stumbled, but I'm back on my feet now. I've made my decision, Cole. I'm in. With you."

"And closer to the criminal line every day," Cole said, the corner of his mouth turned up.

"Anyone who can rile up a town and call on every single good person I know to back her up is somebody special."

They both turned to watch the cop car park. Adams and Hollister got out and stepped up on the curb.

"But what about your promise to stay out of trouble?" she asked. "This looks like trouble."

"There's more to the promise than I thought. Maybe it's not about avoiding trouble, but knowing I won't face it alone."

"Okay, but this time here's what I want you to do," Rebecca said as she tugged his sleeve. "You follow Shelly inside with the kids. We'll stay here. If you have to, come pick me up at the police station when it's all over. I might be able to talk my way out of this."

As he shook his head, Rebecca tugged him toward the door. "Inside."

He was scowling furiously when she shoved the door closed behind him. One quick look down the line showed Eric and his followers had disappeared, too.

The relief was overwhelming.

"We hear you're causing a disruption on school property," Davy Adams said as he rocked back and forth on his toes. "Couldn't believe it when I got the call."

Unstoppable now that Cole and her kids were safely inside, Rebecca smiled at the cop who'd been a Holly Heights fixture for decades. "You won't be the only one saying that tomorrow, but for the first time in a while, I know this is right."

"Protesting is right?" Davy Adams said slowly. "No Lincoln I know has ever resorted to this."

That was what she expected most of the town would be saying. She wasn't like her parents or even Daniel, although he'd shot his mouth off for what he believed in and lost his job. The town had been shocked then, too. They'd get over this surprise eventually.

"Are you going to shut this down now?" Hollister asked as he pointed at the discarded signs. "Just pick everything up and we'll call it even."

"Any news on the break-in?" Sarah asked from behind Rebecca. "If we're chitchatting."

"Yeah, we got a tip," Hollister said. "I've got a call in to the drug task force in Austin to try to track down a kid who goes by the nickname Red for questioning. When I know more, you will, too."

Rebecca watched Davy Adams pick up

the signs and wondered if she was going to meekly scurry off into the darkness.

Then she remembered Cole's face as he'd stood in front of her and admitted to falling for her. He deserved someone bold enough to stand next to him, no matter what happened. She'd messed up more than once. This time, she was going to do it right.

"We aren't leaving. When the school board meeting is over, I want to look every one of those parents in the eye. I believe in what I'm doing. So we're going to wait." It was a sign of the strength of her friendship that Jen, Steph and Sarah wrapped their arms together and resumed their place in front of the door. The chanting was weaker this time, but no one could say that the four of them were anything less than in perfect harmony.

COLE WATCHED THROUGH the narrow window in the door as the four strongest, most stubborn women he knew resumed their chant. Then he rolled his shoulders and turned to head into the auditorium. Rebecca wasn't there to speak for herself, but someone had to do it. If she lost her job for this, the whole town would suffer.

The angry guy pacing at the end of the

aisle seemed to be in charge, but there was a line of students waiting to speak into the microphone.

Cole slipped into an empty seat next to Eric. He'd figure out what was going on, then...do something. He had to do *something*.

"What'd I miss?" Cole asked.

"School board wants to reorganize the program, set up a council of directors or something," Eric whispered. "Didn't seem popular."

Cole could understand that. The more people involved in the reorganization, the harder it was to get anything done.

"First, the guy from the hospital argued what they had is working good. Don't know who the others were, but two or three places that have volunteers working for them agreed. Now we're talking."

Cole studied Eric's face. "We? Are you the ringleader?"

Eric shifted in his seat. "I spread the word about the meeting. That's all."

And that had been enough. No one had to ask the kids Rebecca had helped to come and speak on her behalf, probably because she'd been such a big part of their lives, teaching them about caring all along.

That was what he'd come to understand. People could be trouble, but the good ones were the help every man needed when life got hard. He might not avoid trouble completely, but his life would be better and happier as long as he learned his lesson.

Cole held his fist out and Eric returned the bump. "Good job."

The last student was sitting down in front of them when Eric squeezed out in front of Cole.

"Last speaker for the evening. Then the school board will discuss what we've heard," Cece Grant said. He could remember her from high school. She might be twice as expensive and half as road-weary as he was, but she could control a meeting.

"Yeah, I'm, uh, Eric Jordan. I work at the shelter." Eric cleared his throat and everyone winced at the mic's feedback. "I didn't want to at first, but I needed community-service hours. Because I've been in trouble."

Cole frowned as whispers swept through the auditorium.

"People want to blame Ms. Lincoln or even Cole for…I don't know, misleading them or something," Eric said, "but all I can say is thank you. Everything was wrong before, but they helped me find my place. The shelter is my place. Things are going right now. For the rest of my life, I'll remember that."

Eric hustled to his seat and slumped down as if he couldn't get out of the spotlight quickly enough.

Sarah had been right. For the rest of Cole's life, he'd wonder how Eric was doing. That human connection had kicked in. He had EW and Sarah and Rebecca to thank for helping him find it. And none of them were here to speak for themselves.

Before Cece could dismiss the meeting, Cole stepped up to the microphone. The heat of embarrassment immediately swamped him and he understood how Eric felt.

"I know you said last speaker, but since I'm the eye of the storm, I wanted to say one thing." Cole rubbed his forehead. "You made a mistake, taking Rebecca out of the program, but that's not the end of the world. She's persistent when she knows what's right. For her, making a difference in Holly Heights and loving your kids is the only choice. And the thing about Rebecca Lincoln is that she won't hold your mistake against you. I've never met anyone else like her. It's best to step back and watch her work."

Since he had nothing else to say, Cole kept on walking down the aisle. He didn't notice all the kids had fallen in line behind him until he was out on the sidewalk, breathing in cool air.

Davy Adams was helping Rebecca into the back of the squad car.

Rebecca Lincoln was grinning bigger than life. He'd never seen a smile like that on her face.

She was proud of herself. When the first kid held up a phone to tape it all, he hoped she was prepared to be watching the video for the rest of her life.

He stepped up before Adams shut the door. "You sure you've got bail money?"

"You and Shelly are in control of phase two, the jailbreak." Rebecca grimaced at the officers. "That's a joke, sirs."

Cole leaned down. "I'll be waiting for you when you get out."

Rebecca's lips were twitching. "Good. I might need help finding a new job."

Cole glanced over his shoulder at the kids and parents lining the sidewalk. "Well, now that you're notorious, it won't take much to get the word out if you need to start from scratch."

"Notorious. I like it." She held up a hand to stop Adams from closing the door. At least they hadn't cuffed the wildest criminals in Holly Heights. "Think it'll go my way?"

Cole reached in to squeeze her hand. "You have good friends who've done their very best to make sure it does. All that's left is the waiting." At the cops' grumble, Cole stepped back.

"Which she will be doing with us," Adams said as he shut the door.

Rebecca waggled her eyebrows at Cole and then scooted back.

"Are you going to charge them with something?" Cole asked.

"Seems like she won't be happy until we do," Adams said with a sigh. "But probably not. Doesn't seem right. She's a Lincoln."

After the cops pulled away from the curb, Cole walked over to EW's truck. "You asleep?"

"Thought I better keep the motor running, in case I needed to drive the getaway," EW drawled. "Never know when your criminal instincts will kick in."

Cole laughed as he slid into the passenger seat.

"What'd the board decide?" EW asked as he put the truck in gear.

"No idea. Doesn't matter," Cole said as he stretched his legs. "She's a Lincoln. She'll do this, help the kids in this town, with or without the school board."

"And where does that leave you?" EW didn't hesitate at the corner but headed for the police station.

"Looking at a lifetime of trouble, no doubt." Cole propped one elbow on the door. "You know us criminals. Once we get a taste of the life, it's hard to go back. She'll be protesting on a regular basis, I would guess."

EW's rusty chuckle made Cole grin. Going to get the woman who was about to become his girlfriend out of jail was a new experience. There was no sense in not enjoying every minute.

CHAPTER TWENTY

COLE KNEW THERE were certain events that would stick with him for the rest of his life. Waving goodbye to his mother for the last time. Holding a gun on a terrified gas station clerk. Standing to receive his sentence from a judge. Seeing his cell and cell mate for the first time. Finding EW waiting for him on the day of his release.

Watching the woman he'd first distrusted—and then admired more than he should—pick up her personal belongings from the policeman manning the intake desk, her smile tired but happy, would be impossible to forget.

But when she'd seen him standing there, dropped her stuff on the counter and hurried over to wrap her arms around his neck, everything had clicked into place. It was impossible to avoid trouble, but with Rebecca at his side, they could tackle whatever came.

He hadn't slept a wink since she'd ridden off in the Paws for Love van with her gang of rabble-rousers, but the memory of her sweet smile, the smell of lemons and home and the wicked laugh the four women had shared as they high-fived in the lobby were hard to forget.

Apparently, they hadn't done much sleeping, either. Sarah had looked like roadkill when she finally made it into Paws for Love around ten. She'd muttered, "Champagne" once and seemed to be mainlining coffee like it would save her life.

Now that his shift was up, he was going to have to brave her hangover in her den. Since he hadn't been sleeping, he'd had time to make some decisions.

He wasn't putting one foot in front of the other, merely surviving, anymore.

Holly Heights was home. The trailer was his. He could afford to run the air conditioner or the heat or do some renovations or even buy a car because his job was set.

It was time to look past getting by.

Now it was time to get what he wanted.

"You got a minute?" he said in a low voice as he stuck his head into Sarah's office. None of the lights were on, but she was upright and working away on her laptop.

"You bet." She cleared her throat. "Come to ask my permission to date my best friend?"

Cole's head snapped back as he considered that. "No way. Hers is the only permission I need."

"I would have given it," Sarah said with a sniff.

Cole wiped both hands on his jeans as he registered the sound of EW's truck. "I do need some permission, though."

She braced her elbows on the desk and clasped her hands together before drawling, "Yes?"

"Freddie. I want to adopt him," Cole blurted. "I've been telling myself he'd be better off without me, but that's not true. I shouldn't get so attached, either, but he's my dog."

He wished he'd taken a chance and turned on the overhead light. He couldn't read her expression well. She yanked open one of the drawers he'd managed to repair and pulled out an adoption form. "You don't meet the criteria." She slid the paper across the desk and dropped a pen on top. "No fenced yard."

"Not yet, but I'll walk him three times a day. I work in a dog-friendly place. The boss is a pushover." Cole squinted down at the paper. "And for him, I'll work on improving my place. To do that, I'm thinking about getting more work. I'm going to put a sign out on the flower beds, once they're fixed up, with my contact info, and do the same at Jen's. I want to work on building something of my own, a landscaping business."

Sarah leaned forward quickly. "You aren't leaving me, though. You can't leave me."

After scanning the agreement, Cole signed his name with a flourish. "No way. I like it here, but it's time for me to fill up my life."

He handed her the paper and watched her collapse against her chair. "Fill up your life?"

"Yeah, no more *existing*. I want to live." As he'd stared up at the ceiling through the sleepless night, like he had almost every night he'd been inside Travis, all Cole could think was that he wanted more than what he had.

The difference this time was that he could picture it easily.

Freddie was sprawled on his ugly green couch in the trailer his grandmother had left him.

Rebecca was pushing and prodding and making him laugh and making him better with a frilly apron on.

He and EW were doing more than sitting on a shady bank. Sometimes.

And he would cheer for Eric at his high school graduation.

There would be trouble, but so much goodness, too, that it would be easy to overcome.

"And you're starting with the dog," Sarah said as she wagged her head back and forth. "That's how I did it, too. Bub and I had nothing but a paid-for car and a job here at the shelter when we first started. I needed him more than anything, too. I didn't understand that was about living instead of surviving, but I can't argue with it."

"So, will you bend the rules for me?" Cole asked, then wished he hadn't. Pointing out the rules was a bad idea.

"Wouldn't be the first time I've done it," she said with a sigh. "Am I on a crime spree, do you think?"

Her wondering tone made him smile. "Les said he'd help with Freddie's care, and I could cover the cost of any meds and vaccines he needs." He pulled a wad of cash out of his pocket. "Here's the adoption fee."

"Dude. Two words. Checking. Account." Sarah picked up the cash and counted it carefully. "You've got yourself a dog." She smiled at him. "And I couldn't be happier."

"I'll borrow a leash? I've got one at home,

but I wasn't sure you'd agree, so..." Cole stood. "I'll bring it back tomorrow."

Sarah nodded slowly. "Yes. That's fine. See if you can get him out of here without howling so loudly my head rolls off my neck, please."

Pumped at the success of the first phase of his plan, Cole trotted down the hall, twirled Shelly around as she stepped out of the cat room and said, "I'm taking my dog home."

He could hear Shelly hooting and hoped Sarah didn't have sharp-shooting pains in her temple, but Freddie let out one happy bark when he saw the leash and then pranced in place. "Do you know you're going home, Fred?" Cole opened the kennel, snapped the leash to Freddie's collar and managed to grab the bag of essentials Shelly kept on hand for every new adoption.

Then she pointed at him. "The dog is good. Next is the girl?"

Cole laughed and wrapped his arm around her shoulders to squeeze. "Yeah, next is the girl."

Shelly was giggling as she patted his back. "Two handsome gents for the price of one. That Rebecca is getting a better deal than she deserves."

Cole waved a hand at Eric and Les as he and Freddie trotted back out the door to EW's truck. He pulled open the door. "Up, Freddie." The little dog leaped up onto the floorboard and then the seat, where he grinned up at EW. For a split second, Cole wondered if he should have cleared it with EW first.

The old man sniffed and then nodded. "Yeah, that's about right. Got a house, pretty girl, time for a dog." He backed out of the parking spot and turned out on the highway. "Home?"

Cole took a deep breath of the cool air coming in through the window. "You ever think about a part-time job, EW?"

That surprised him. EW raised both eyebrows. "Well, now, whatcha got in mind?"

Cole laughed. "Landscaping. You and me."

EW pursed his lips. "Let's try it and see. What's the worst that could happen?"

Exactly. They'd already been through the worst.

They didn't have to fear it anymore.

EW paused in front of the turn to the trailer park and looked at him. "Gonna get your girl or chicken out?"

Cole ran a hand down Freddie's back. "I'm going to need to borrow your truck."

Rebecca had been listening for the putter of EW's truck all day long, even if she didn't realize it. She'd gone to work like the previous evening had never happened. Art's grim pronouncement that the school board was still deliberating but he'd recommended starting a new program, one run by the administration, didn't do a thing to darken her day.

She'd be fine no matter how things worked out.

The fact that he'd spun on one heel and stalked away without mentioning her job seemed to indicate she'd continue as Holly Heights High's most dedicated guidance counselor anyway.

To celebrate, she was testing recipes for chocolate soufflé and rack of lamb and wondering how she could invite Cole over to be her taste tester. Her parents would be landing early in the morning, so the dinner party was looming.

Then she heard the truck. Before she'd decided whether to check her hair or whip off the apron, the doorbell rang. A quiet woof accompanied it.

Unless Cole had been studying Bark-ese, he had a sidekick.

Her lips were twitching as she pulled the

door open. One quick glance down showed a happy beagle in a strained but recognizable sit.

"Everyone else in this town will just walk in, Cole," Rebecca said as she bent to greet Freddie. "That's what family does. You come on in." She held her hand out, saw the oven mitt on her right hand and dropped it. "From now on, you come in."

"So I'm family," Cole murmured as he closed the door. "Not exactly what I had in mind."

Rebecca pressed her dachshund-covered hand over her heart to try to contain the hard thump. She wasn't going to remind him that he'd said "falling for." Apparently, she didn't have to.

"I owe you this grand, sweeping apology because what you said to me in Sarah's office was dead on," Rebecca said as she stacked all the cookbooks on the island. "I messed up. Thank you for not letting me back down. I needed that. You'll have to do it again and again. You and I should acknowledge here that our relationship is going to be made up of me messing up and apologizing. You will have to learn to be more gracious than you've been in the past." She pressed her oven mitt on his shoulder. "That's the only way we work."

"Why didn't you come into the shelter this afternoon?" Cole asked as he studied the goofy oven mitt next to his face. "Regretting last night?"

"Are you kidding me? I don't regret a single thing from last night." Rebecca yanked off the oven mitt and steered him over to a stool next to the counter. He sat with a grunt when she pushed hard enough. "Except I should have kissed you." She ran a finger along the edge of the counter. "I hesitated, missed my chance."

Watching him evaluate everything she said was amusing. It would never get old, surprising him. His confused expression was sweet. Eventually, he'd learn to go with whatever she said. Probably.

Cole wrapped his arms slowly around her waist. "Yeah. I know what you mean about grabbing what you want with both arms." He tugged her closer. "I'm going to start doing that, too."

"Like Freddie?" Rebecca glanced down at the beagle, who was staring hard at the double ovens. He knew where the good stuff came from. "I hope he's your dog now."

"We're a package deal," Cole said with a

sigh as he ran his hand over her back. "I hope you can live with that. He's got some issues."

Rebecca grinned. "He's not the only one, is he?"

Cole's rough laugh settled in her stomach and chased the butterflies away. "Nope, but the two of us, we can straighten out whatever issues we've got."

"Yeah," Rebecca said as she stared into his warm brown eyes. "How do you feel about rack of lamb for dinner? I'm testing recipes."

Cole pretended to think. "Guess my peanut butter sandwich will keep. Never had rack of lamb. Seems fancy, but I'm broadening my horizons."

Fancy. That was the word her mother had used to make Rebecca feel the guilt of starving children. The difference when Cole said it was that he didn't question her right to have something nice. He knew enjoying special things was important from time to time.

"And tomorrow night, we'll leave fancy behind and have chicken or my mother will never let me hear the end of it. If you tell her about this fancy food, I will make sure you regret it." Rebecca nodded to make certain he understood her.

"Meet your parents? That's too…much."

Cole ran a hand down his nape, his unease very clear. "Don't ruin their visit home by thrusting your broke, ex-convict…guy on them."

"My guy." Rebecca closed her eyes. Two steps forward and half a step back. Like a slow dance. She could work with this. "I need you to be there. You're already on their radar, Mr. Front-Page News. Just sit in the corner, keep your lips zipped about the fancy food and let me do the talking." Rebecca leaned forward. "Then, at the first sign of trouble, you have my back. We'll be a team. I need you to be my team."

Cole raised an eyebrow. "You make it sound like a bar fight."

"When my mother starts to lecture me about wasting money on this kitchen, there might be chairs thrown. I don't know. That's what I'm saying. You and me, against the world. Once they get a look at you, nobody will mess with me for long." Rebecca grinned up at him. "I think I'm good at trouble."

Cole sighed. "Too good."

"And as far as 'broke' goes…" Rebecca reached over to grab a business card off her beloved stainless steel refrigerator. "That won't last. This is Will's card. He can help you build a business plan. Then you present it to these investors I know and you're a business owner."

"It bothers you, how little I have," Cole said slowly, as if he'd suspected it all along.

Rebecca rolled her eyes. "No, it bothers you. I won the lottery. Anyone could do that. Don't give me any grief about charity or spending my own money. Will makes the decisions, but if you get this landscaping business going, I will have one or two or ten kids who'll need summer jobs." She shrugged.

Cole tipped his head back and studied the ceiling. "Fine. One question. If I'm going to do all this, meet the parents, build a landscaping conglomerate with crews of high school kids and watch your back with your mother, the cops, the town of Holly Heights…" He shook his head. "Do I at least get dessert? Something sweet, too? It's the sweet things that make life worth living." One corner of his mouth curled up.

"Can't argue with that," she said as she wagged her head. "Chocolate soufflé. If you don't like it, I'll try something else. Something with lemons." She giggled as he bent forward and pressed his nose in the bend of her neck and took a deep breath.

"Something sweet and lemony, I could get

used to that." Cole slowly traced one finger over her lips. "You know when you were talking about the guilt of winning all that money and I thought you'd lost your mind? Yeah, I'm beginning to understand being so happy you feel like it's too much."

Rebecca squeezed her eyes shut against the sting of tears. "Stick with me. For the rest of your life, you'll earn every bit of happiness."

Cole chuckled and took her hand in his. "You think there's going to be a rest of our lives?"

"Just promise to kiss me every chance you get." Rebecca pressed closer to him.

Cole bent his head down to hers and whispered, "I promise."

* * * * *

*Don't miss the next book in
Cheryl Harper's
LUCKY NUMBERS miniseries,
available February 2017!*

LARGER-PRINT BOOKS!

GET 2 FREE LARGER-PRINT NOVELS PLUS 2 FREE MYSTERY GIFTS

Love Inspired®

Larger-print novels are now available...

LARGER-PRINT BOOKS!

GET 2 FREE
LARGER-PRINT NOVELS
PLUS 2 FREE
MYSTERY GIFTS

Love Inspired

SUSPENSE

RIVETING INSPIRATIONAL ROMANCE

Larger-print novels are now available...

YES! Please send me 2 FREE LARGER-PRINT Love Inspired® Suspense novels and my 2 FREE mystery gifts (gifts are worth about $10). After receiving them, if I don't wish to receive any more books, I can return the shipping statement marked "cancel." If I don't cancel, I will receive 4 brand-new novels every month and be billed just $5.49 per book in the U.S. or $5.99 per book in Canada. That's a savings of at least 19% off the cover price. It's quite a bargain! Shipping and handling is just 50¢ per book in the U.S. and 75¢ per book in Canada.* I understand that accepting the 2 free books and gifts places me under no obligation to buy anything. I can always return a shipment and cancel at any time. Even if I never buy another book, the two free books and gifts are mine to keep forever.

110/310 IDN GH6P

Name _____ (PLEASE PRINT) _____

Address _____ Apt. # _____

City _____ State/Prov. _____ Zip/Postal Code _____

Signature (if under 18, a parent or guardian must sign) _____

Mail to the **Reader Service:**
IN U.S.A.: P.O. Box 1867, Buffalo, NY 14240-1867
IN CANADA: P.O. Box 609, Fort Erie, Ontario L2A 5X3

**Are you a current subscriber to Love Inspired® Suspense books
and want to receive the larger-print edition?
Call 1-800-873-8635 or visit www.ReaderService.com.**

* Terms and prices subject to change without notice. Prices do not include applicable taxes. Sales tax applicable in N.Y. Canadian residents will be charged applicable taxes. Offer not valid in Quebec. This offer is limited to one order per household. Not valid for current subscribers to Love Inspired Suspense larger-print books. All orders subject to credit approval. Credit or debit balances in a customer's account(s) may be offset by any other outstanding balance owed by or to the customer. Please allow 4 to 6 weeks for delivery. Offer available while quantities last.

Your Privacy—The Reader Service is committed to protecting your privacy. Our Privacy Policy is available online at www.ReaderService.com or upon request from the Reader Service.

We make a portion of our mailing list available to reputable third parties that offer products we believe may interest you. If you prefer that we not exchange your name with third parties, or if you wish to clarify or modify your communication preferences, please visit us at www.ReaderService.com/consumerschoice or write to us at Reader Service Preference Service, P.O. Box 9062, Buffalo, NY 14240-9062. Include your complete name and address.

LISLP15

LARGER-PRINT BOOKS!
GET 2 FREE LARGER-PRINT NOVELS PLUS
2 FREE GIFTS!

HARLEQUIN

super romance

More Story...More Romance

HSRLP15

READERSERVICE.COM

Manage your account online!

- Review your order history
- Manage your payments
- Update your address

> ### We've designed the
> ### Reader Service website
> ### just for you.

Enjoy all the features!

- Discover new series available to you, and read excerpts from any series.
- Respond to mailings and special monthly offers.
- Connect with favorite authors at the blog.
- Browse the Bonus Bucks catalog and online-only exculsives.
- Share your feedback.

Visit us at:
ReaderService.com